$\mathcal{J}$ack grabbed my shoulders again, strong enough to make me wince. "Don't you dare say that. Saving you is the *only* important thing."

Slowly I brought my hands up and placed them on either side of his face. "But I can't live with blood on my hands. I can't live knowing I'm the reason that girls like Tara and Ariel will become targets of the immortals. I can't. Saving me will mean nothing if more people die. The only way to save me . . . really save me . . . is to destroy the Everneath."

He closed his eyes and then hesitantly released his grip on my arms. "Okay. Then we destroy the Everneath."

TRUE

An EVERNEATH Novel

BRODI ASHTON

BALZER + BRAY
An Imprint of HarperCollins*Publishers*

For my mom and Erin . . .
You are my girls. My people. My home.

Balzer + Bray is an imprint of HarperCollins Publishers.

Evertrue

www.epicreads.com

Library of Congress Cataloging-in-Publication Data
Ashton, Brodi.
Evertrue : an Everneath novel / Brodi Ashton. — First edition.
        pages   cm
Summary: "Nikki and Jack take on the underworld to free themselves
of the Everneath's power"— Provided by publisher.
ISBN 978-0-06-207120-0 (pbk.)
[1. Supernatural—Fiction. 2. Future life—Fiction. 3. Love—
Fiction. 4. Hell—Fiction.] I. Title.
PZ7.A8276Ew   2014   2013014513
[Fic]—dc23   CIP
                                                              AC

Typography by Ray Shappell
14 15 16 17 18 LP/RRDH 10 9 8 7 6 5 4 3 2 1
❖
First paperback edition, 2015

"Some of us think holding on makes us strong; but sometimes it is letting go."
—Hermann Hesse

THE EVERLIVING

Mythology enthusiasts call them Akh ghosts, Akh referring to life after death.

Others call them the souls of the dead, the inhabitants of the Underworld.

But I know they are really the Everliving. They live in an Underworld known as the Everneath, and every hundred years they must feed on—steal emotional energy from—a human sacrifice, called a Forfeit.

I was once a Forfeit.

Now I am an Everliving.

But I will destroy the Everneath before I feed on another human being. And I will destroy anything, or anyone, that stands in my way.

PROLOGUE

TWO WEEKS AGO
The Surface. My bedroom.

*J*ack rubbed his eyes and sat up in my bed. "Wait. What did you just say?"

"The Everneath," I replied. "I said I want to take the whole thing down. Let's blow it up. Nuke it or something." My hands started to shake.

Jack glanced at the clock, then reached out toward me. "Come back to bed. Everything is fine. The Tunnels aren't coming for either of us. It's over."

Over. It would never be over. Not anymore. I glanced at the open window, the one Cole had just jumped through after he'd stolen my heart. Jack followed my gaze, saw that the window was open, and looked at me with furrowed brows as if finally sensing that something was very wrong.

"What just happened, Becks?"

"Cole was here." My voice sounded shaky. "He said that I fed off him three times in the Everneath. He said I've lost my heart now. He saw a compass on my desk, and he took it, and . . . and . . ." I gasped.

Jack was by my side in a flash, his thick arms around me. "Shhh. It's okay. Slow down. You're saying Cole stole a compass?"

I squeezed my eyes shut. "It was lying there on my desk. He said it was my heart."

Jack held his breath for a moment. "Your heart?"

I nodded and took a deep breath, then did the one thing I'd been scared to do. I grabbed Jack's hand and placed it over my chest where my heart should've been, just as Cole had taken my hand and done the same thing only minutes before.

There was nothing. No heartbeat.

My breathing became frantic. Jack pressed his hand harder onto my skin, held it there for a long moment. His face turned pale. "How . . . ? Why . . . ?"

His voice drifted off as if he weren't sure what question he wanted to ask.

I flashed back over the past week, to the journey Cole and I had taken through the labyrinth to the center of the Everneath to rescue Jack. The next words spilled out. "When we went through the maze to find you, there were times I had to feed on Cole to keep going." I shook my head. "He said that since I fed on him three times, I'm going to become an Everliving. Then he said there were certain perks for the Everliving who held my heart. Then . . . he took off with the compass." I stared at Jack. "My heart."

Jack looked at the open window. "Why didn't you wake me?"

"You were so tired. And I didn't think there was anything to be afraid of. It was Cole. He . . . he helped me rescue you. He was . . ." *My friend.* I squeezed my eyes shut and chastised myself. My friend. How could I have been so stupid? So blind? "He tricked me. He only came to the Everneath to get me to feed on him. He never meant to save you. He was even surprised you were here. I should've seen it coming."

I felt my knees buckle, but before I sank too low, Jack held me tighter. "Shhh. It will be okay, Becks."

"We have to destroy it," I said. "The Everneath. We have to take the whole thing down." How could my blood be pulsing so fast without a heart?

Jack nodded and pulled me over to the bed, where we both sat down. "Let's think this through. The first thing we have to do is get your heart back." At my manic expression, he held his hand out, palm down. "First, your heart," he repeated. "Then, after we get it back, we'll talk about blowing stuff up. I promise."

"Why?" I sniffed. "What will getting my heart back do?"

"Cole obviously wants it for some advantage. Maybe so he can always have the threat of breaking it."

I shook my head. "That's the thing. We were wrong about his heart. His guitar pick. It wouldn't have killed him if we had broken it that night." I blew out a breath of air. "He told me every Everliving has two hearts. A Surface heart and an

5

Everneath heart. Break them both, and you become mortal again. That's how the woman who turned him into an Everliving regained her mortality. But breaking just the Surface one?" I racked my brain, trying to remember what it would mean. All I knew for sure was that it wouldn't kill him.

"Then that's why he wants it. Breaking that heart is the first step to making you mortal again. You can't become human if he has your Surface heart." He grimaced. "I still can't believe we're talking like this. How did he . . ." His voice trailed off as he shook his head. "That bastard."

"It's my own fault."

He gave me a stern look. "Don't say that, Becks."

"It's true. I trusted him. I begged him to come with me. I gift wrapped myself for him, with a giant red bow."

He pressed his lips to my head. "My life was on the line. I would've done the same thing."

I looked up at him. He dipped his head and kissed me, and in that moment the calmness of his soul washed over me like a warm blanket, quieting my fears. It wasn't long ago that we couldn't kiss without me stealing energy from him, but this was just a regular kiss.

Wait. It was *just a regular kiss.*

If I were a true Everliving, wouldn't there be a transfer of energy? There was always a whoosh of emotions shifting from one person to the other whenever Cole's lips had gotten near mine. Wouldn't it be the same for me now?

I pulled back.

"What is it?" Jack asked.

"I didn't feel anything. Nothing. I didn't take anything from you. If I were an Everliving, I would've stolen energy from you."

Jack breathed out through his nose. "See? You can't be an Everliving yet. It can't be too late. It's not. We'll find your heart; we'll break it. It's not too late."

I nodded and then leaned into him and buried my head in his chest. Maybe Jack was right. I didn't feel any different, except for the fact that I didn't have a heart; but even without it, I had a pulse. I'd kissed Jack without stealing any energy from him. Relieved, I lifted my face toward his again. Maybe it wasn't too late.

ONE

The Surface. The library.
Ninety-nine years until the next Feed.

My bitterness toward Cole had reached extreme levels. There had to be a special word for how I felt about him, but I couldn't figure it out. Hate wasn't enough. It didn't convey the eternal aspect of my feelings. It didn't explain the exponential enormity of its growth every day.

Cole had once told me how some punishments were perpetual: Sisyphus rolling the rock up the mountain only to have it roll back down again; Prometheus getting his liver eaten every day by an eagle only to have it grow back the next day and be eaten again. My hate for him was just as timeless. Just as undying.

I heard Jack shift in his chair.

"You're doing that spiral-of-hate thing again, right?" Jack said.

I opened my eyes and caught a glimpse of him looking at me from under the lampshade on the desk in the corner of the library. He set down a yellowed piece of paper on a large stack of similar pages, all part of the documents I'd taken from Mrs. Jenkins's house after she'd been killed.

I shook my head, trying to erase the memory of finding Mrs. Jenkins's body on her couch, the life drained out of her. Cole had told me Max and the other Dead Elvises had killed her. She'd known too much about me, and Cole didn't want word getting back to the queen that a Forfeit had survived the Feed. I didn't know how Cole planned to take over the throne, but I knew he was counting on the element of surprise.

The documents in front of Jack were the only thing left of Mrs. Jenkins. And since Cole had taken my heart two weeks ago and then left town—like he always seemed to do when we needed him—these documents were all we had to focus on.

"How did you know I was doing the spiral-of-hate thing?" I said.

Jack frowned. "Because your eyes were squinty. And your hand was over your heart. And you have that look that says you want someone's head on a stick."

I reached across the table and brushed a clump of brown hair from his cheek. "You hate him too."

He shrugged. "That's an absolute. But I'm trying to focus my hate on finding a cure for your . . . condition."

"Is that what we're calling it? A condition? I'm missing a vital organ. I'm not sure if *condition* covers it."

"We still don't know if you're an Everliving. You haven't

been able to feed on me."

Jack was right. Since that first night, I'd tried to feed off him, but nothing had happened. Could it be possible that Cole had stolen my heart yet I was still human?

If Cole were here I'd ask him, but he'd taken off with the band. And most likely with my heart. Jack and I had camped out at his condo for three days before we started seeing internet chatter about a Dead Elvises concert in Milwaukee. He'd been gone ever since.

"Can I be truthful?" I asked.

"You mean, can you be pessimistic," Jack said.

"Truth. Pessimism. They're sort of one and the same lately."

Jack sighed. "Go ahead."

"We've been through the documents. A thousand times. We've found nothing."

Jack pointed to one of the papers he'd been looking through. "Actually, this one has instructions on becoming a Shade. Apparently if you've been an Everliving long enough and then you miss a Feed, you become a Shade."

Miss a Feed. I'd known only one Everliving who'd missed a Feed. I thought back to my trip through the labyrinth. "Cole's friend Ashe missed a Feed. He looked like he was made of smoke. Maybe he was becoming a Shade." I shook my head. "It doesn't matter. Instructions on how to become a Shade don't help me."

"You never know what will help. We'll keep looking." He

leafed through a few more pages, then held up one. "Here's something about a glowing rock. Maybe that will mean something. Something we could take to Professor Spears."

I rolled my eyes and glanced out the window. We'd done that already too. We'd gone to Professor Spears. He was able to help us once before, when he'd deciphered an ancient bracelet and told us that Cole's heart was an object.

Last week we'd sat in his office and told him the truth about Cole, and me, and my missing heart, and the fact that I was an Everliving now. He'd accused us of playing an elaborate prank on him. Stopped just short of running us out of the building. We'd had Meredith's bracelet with us, but that wasn't necessarily proof of anything; and I didn't think documents about a glowing rock would make any difference. It was frustrating that I couldn't make him understand.

"Professor Spears can't be the only person who knows about this stuff," Jack said.

"He's not, but the people who do know about it—the Daughters of Persephone, or the Everlivings themselves—don't exactly have loose lips." From the window, I could see across the street to the city park. A mother and father taking turns pushing their toddler on the swing, a man throwing a Frisbee to his golden retriever, a bunch of girls playing some sort of game that involved tagging and freezing, out enjoying the blue sky of the coming summer. But my focus was on the mother and father. Would Jack and I ever grow old together?

Would I ever grow old at all?

"Look at me, Becks," Jack said.

I turned away from the window toward Jack.

"We'll find a way to save you."

I smiled. "Look at *me*. I don't need saving. I'm just not going to ever grow old. And then when the next Feed happens, in ninety-nine years, I'll skip it and die. I'm not ancient, so skipping a Feed won't make me a Shade. So we have ninety-nine years."

There was one part of my diagnosis that I hadn't told him about yet, though. The day after Cole had stolen my heart, I'd started to feel weak. The feeling had only gotten progressively worse since then. But I didn't want to scare Jack.

Jack reached across the wide desk and put his hand on my cheek. I was surprised he could reach so far, but then again, he'd come out of the Tunnels so much bigger and taller than he had been before. It affected his wingspan.

"Maybe you're the one who needs saving," I said.

Jack raised an eyebrow. "Why is that?"

"Because you came out of the Tunnels bigger. And taller. And who gets taller at eighteen years old?"

Jack pressed his lips together and dropped his hand. "Nobody dies from getting taller. And bigger."

"Yes, but there was that one boy in Indiana who died from too many abs."

Jack's lips quirked up in a grin. "Now you're just making stuff up."

"Nothing is as it seems in the Everneath. The fact that it made you bigger . . ."

"We're not going to worry about maybes right now either. I don't know why I came back bigger, but at least I have all my vital organs." He reached his hand across the table again, only this time he placed it directly beneath my collarbone. "Call me selfish—and really, I'm completely selfish when it comes to you—but I want you. All of you. Your heart included."

"You have my heart."

"Only metaphorically."

"If you want to drop the metaphors, you can have my hands," I said.

Jack smiled, and then he wrapped his fingers around my wrists and brought my hands to his lips. He kissed each fingertip. "What else can I have?" he asked.

"Hmmmm," I said, still focusing on the way his lips moved softly against my skin. "My elbows. I can throw those in for good measure."

He released his grip on my wrists and grabbed my elbows. "If I have the elbows, I might need the rest of your arms."

"I think we can negotiate those," I said.

With a grin, he stood up and pulled me to a nearby corner behind a wall of books. He guided me gently until my back was up against the wall. His hands moved up and over my elbows to my neck. I looked past him to make sure no one could see us; but when he pushed the collar of my shirt aside and put his lips on my shoulder, I stopped caring if we were in anyone's view. I shivered.

"Um, we never discussed the shoulders," I said, my voice ridiculously breathless.

"Sorry," he said. "I get carried away talking about elbows and things."

My head tilted so his lips could get better access to the base of my neck. "Just wait until I tell you about my kneecaps."

He put his lips on mine, and it was a long time before I thought about kneecaps again.

A buzzing sound made us pull apart and catch our breaths. Jack pulled out his phone and checked the screen.

"Jules just texted. She and Tara Bolton want to know if we're up for a concert. Apparently the Deads are doing a surprise gig in Salt Lake."

My eyes went wide. "Cole's back in town. That means . . ."

"That means we have plans tonight." He grabbed my arms and looked into my eyes. "Cole would never leave your heart in another city. He wouldn't risk it being so far from him. And I don't think he'd chance taking it with him to a concert. I bet it's at the condo now. Which means tonight we're going to find your heart."

TWO

NOW

The Surface. Home.

I raced through a dinner of pizza and wilted salad with my dad and Tommy. It reminded me that if my life ever got back to normal, I was going to make some changes of the nutritional variety around here.

I shoved the last pepperoni into my mouth and put my napkin down on my plate.

My dad froze with his full piece of pizza halfway to his mouth. "Is there some speed-eating award you're going for tonight?"

Tommy giggled.

"No. I'm just getting ready to go out with Jack," I said, pushing myself back from the table. "May I be excused?"

"That's fine. But don't be too late. Summer school starts tomorrow, right?"

I sighed. As if he didn't know. As if he didn't make special arrangements with Mrs. Stone to allow me into the class even though my grades weren't exactly stellar.

My dad still had hope for my academic excellence.

"I'll be there." *Right after I break into the Dead Elvises'*
condo and retrieve my missing heart.

I stood up and ruffled Tommy's hair as I walked out of the
kitchen. Jack would be waiting for me in my room to make
our plans. My stomach erupted in butterflies. Breaking and
entering.

This was a first for me.

Midnight. The parking lot of Cole's condo.

There were no lights on inside Cole's place.

At least I guessed there were no lights on. I couldn't see
every angle from where I sat in the passenger seat of Jack's car.

Jack opened the brown paper bag at his feet and took out
one of the black ski masks. He tossed it onto my lap, and my
feet literally went ice-cold.

"What if it's a trick?" I said.

Jack froze, one side of his lips raised in a half smile. "You
mean like an ambush?"

I nodded.

Jack turned fully toward me, resting one elbow on the
steering wheel and flashing me a reassuring smile. "So you're
saying the Dead Elvises faked a concert tonight in the city,
and fake sold tickets, and fake booked the venue, all so they

could turn out the lights in their condo and wait, real quiet like, crouched behind the furniture, on the off chance we were planning to break in?"

I nodded again. "Exactly. That sounds reasonable. We should just go home."

He shook his head. "We wouldn't be doing this if we didn't have to. If it didn't mean the best chance to cure you."

"I know," I said. "But I can't help wondering if it's a trap."

"Cole needs you alive. That's why we *can* feel safe doing this." At my concerned expression, he added, "Look, Jules is at the concert. I'll text her to see if the band's really there or if they're just holograms."

He pulled out his phone and tapped on the screen. I stared at the darkened condo again and bit my lip.

"Have we thought through everything?" I said.

Jack continued to type while talking. "We know they don't have an alarm system."

"Not as of a couple weeks ago," I said, remembering the last time I was in Cole's apartment. Before we'd gone to the Everneath to save Jack. Before Cole had betrayed me. It was a lifetime ago.

"You know the code to his door," Jack said.

"One-four-oh-seven," I said. I'd seen him open the door enough times to remember.

"And we know Cole has a safe in his wall," Jack said.

I nodded. I remembered seeing it.

"We know the one thing we're looking for," Jack said.

I nodded and frowned. "A compass. My heart."

If we could find it and break it, maybe that would cure me. If not, it was still a big step toward making me human again.

Jack reached over and squeezed my hand. "It's in the safe. Has to be. And once we get into the safe, you'll know this was worth it."

He took the cordless drill out of the bag next and held it pointed outward, like a cornered cowboy would wield a gun.

I stared at it. "Explain the drill again?"

"Safecrackers always use drills," Jack said, exasperated, as if he'd told me this a hundred times.

"Safecrackers *in the movies*," I clarified.

"Yes, and all movies are rooted in some truth."

"Like *Xanadu*? With the roller-skating Greek muses?" *Xanadu* had been one of my mom's favorite obscure movies.

"Yes," Jack said, forcing a straight face. "Everyone has a roller-skating Greek muse. And you, Becks, are stalling."

I nodded. "I'm about to commit a felony. Of course I'm stalling."

"It's not a felony. It's self-defense."

I took a deep breath and then pulled the ski mask over my head. "Let's do this."

Jack's phone vibrated with a text and he checked the screen. "Jules says she's loving the concert." He put the phone in his pocket. "It's not a trap. We're a go."

We left the car and crept up the stairs to the balcony where the front door was located. There was movement in the front window of the condo adjacent to Cole's, and I started to rethink the ski masks.

"You know, if someone did see us, the masks would probably draw *more* attention to us, not less."

"Too late," Jack said.

We reached the door, and I entered the code into the keypad. The light above it turned red and flashed several times before going dark again.

I tried the handle, but it didn't budge.

"Do it again," Jack said.

I reentered the code, paying special attention to the numbers, but again it flashed red.

"Crap," I said.

A motion-sensor light turned on at the end of the balcony. I ripped off my mask. "Let's go."

Jack shook his head. "We're already here. We're not wasting this opportunity. There's only one thing to do."

"Jump off the balcony?" I suggested hopefully.

Jack smiled. He took a step backward, raised his foot, and lurched at the door. It cracked open, shattering the part where the lock had once been. A dog barked in the distance.

"Seriously?" I whisper-yelled. "That was the 'only one thing to do'?"

"We're in, aren't we? Besides, if we steal back your heart, Cole will definitely know we've been in here, so it won't matter that the door is broken."

We went inside and shut the door behind us. Jack turned

on a flashlight and tossed it gently to me, then grasped the drill he was carrying in both hands and held it in front of him.

I wasn't sure he'd even need the drill. I wouldn't have been surprised if he could simply grab the safe in his hands and rip it clean in two.

We made our way quickly to Cole's bedroom. I shone the light until it landed on the metal box in the wall.

"There it is," I said.

We ran forward. Jack tossed the drill onto Cole's bed. From here I could see that the drywall around the safe looked to be covered in fresh paint, as if it had just been installed. I didn't get a chance to comment on it because Jack reached an arm back and punched a hole in the wall to the right of the safe.

"Jack!" I said.

"I'm fine." He reached his arm into the hole he'd just made, past his elbow, grabbed hold of the back of the safe, and ripped the entire thing out of the wall.

My mouth hung open for a long moment. Moves like that only happened in superhero movies. I didn't know he was *that* strong.

He brought the safe over to a desk in the corner of the room, then picked up the drill again. But before he turned it on, I caught a glimpse of something scratched into the metal surface of the front of the safe. We didn't see it earlier because of the dark.

"Stop," I said. I pointed to the note.

Turn me, it said.

Underneath the words was a large arrow pointing to the

side of the box, where a small crank was sticking out of a hole in the metal.

"Why does it have a crank?"

"More important," Jack said, "why does it have a note?" After a moment's hesitation he reached out and pinched the end of the crank.

"Wait!" I said.

He froze.

"What if it's booby-trapped?" I said. "Like with a bomb?"

He looked at me. "That makes no sense."

"Well, what if there's something horrible inside?"

"Like what?"

I shrugged.

Jack started to turn the crank.

"Like a head!" I blurted out. "A severed head." I put my hands on the safe, measuring the length, height, and width. "That's about head size."

I could tell Jack was raising an eyebrow even under his ski mask. I reached up and pulled off the mask. Yep, he was raising an eyebrow.

He tilted his head. "So Cole decapitates some random person, puts his head in this safe, adds a crank, and leaves a note so that anyone who breaks in would be . . . grossed out enough to leave without taking anything?"

I nodded again.

He turned the crank one full rotation. Nothing happened. He turned it again, and again, and a slow tune began to play.

Jack looked up at me. "Is that . . . ?"

"'Pop Goes the Weasel.'" I nodded, my metaphorical heart already sinking. Nothing good could come out of "Pop Goes the Weasel."

Jack turned the crank faster and faster; and when he reached the "pop" part of the melody, the top of the safe burst open, and a clown's head exploded out. I jumped at least a foot off the ground, even though I could see it was a harmless piece of plastic on a coiled spring.

On the clown's bow tie hung another note.

Jack leaned forward to read it.

"It says, 'Bet you were expecting a heart, shaped like a compass. . . .'" Jack paused and pulled the note off the bow tie. ". . . And then he drew a frowny face."

I snatched the note from his hand, looked at it briefly, crumpled it up, and threw it into the corner of the room. At the same time, it felt as if I'd crumpled up any lingering hope and thrown it away.

"I hate Cole," I said. I looked at Jack, the full weight of my immortal future pressing heavy on my shoulders. "Tell me it's going to be okay. Tell me I'll be human again."

Jack nodded and put his arm around me. "It's going to be okay. You're going to be human again."

Jack held me for a few moments until his phone vibrated. He pulled it out of his pocket.

He read the screen and frowned.

"Who's it from?" I asked.

"Cole. It says, 'No, she won't. She's going to be a queen.'"

My eyes darted around the room, searching for whatever microphone was relaying our words back to Cole, but I couldn't see anything out of the ordinary. I closed my eyes.

"I'd rather die than be your queen," I said.

Moments later another text buzzed through, and Jack read it aloud. "It says, 'Let's see what the Hulk has to say about that.' I can only assume by 'Hulk' he's referring to me."

"It's not his choice whether I live or die," I said loudly toward the ceiling. Then I turned toward Jack and whispered, "It's not your choice."

"I know," Jack whispered back. "I know, Becks."

I put my hand over my mouth, annoyed at myself for giving voice to the one wedge between me and Jack, the one thing that we would always disagree on. I would rather die than rule the Everneath. Jack would rather I live, no matter the cost. It was true, but it gave Cole too much information. When it came to me, he had a track record of exploiting any and all weaknesses he could find.

And now he was listening to every word we were saying. Max and Gavin probably started their guitar-and-drum duet when Cole discovered we were in his place.

Jack mouthed the words *Let's go.*

I nodded. I didn't want to let Cole overhear anything else. Jack took my hand, and I followed him to the front door and through it to the balcony. He shoved the door closed despite the shattered lock, and we had just started down the balcony when I noticed a dark figure blocking the staircase. Jack saw him too and jerked to a stop.

I couldn't see his face, because he was backlit from the light on the stairs, but his silhouette showed he was wearing a hat with a wide brim—maybe a cowboy hat?—and a long coat, like a trench coat.

Whoever it was, he just stood there. I couldn't actually see if he was looking at us or not, but for some reason I *felt* his eyes on me.

"Try to act normal," Jack said. It was a little late for "normal," considering we'd just come stumbling out of the condo, shoved the broken door shut, and then frozen at the sight of the man.

Nevertheless, we started walking toward him.

He made no move to stand aside. Jack flipped on the flashlight and shone it momentarily in the guy's face, and at first I didn't notice anything strange until I got a look at his eyes. They were pitch-black. A chill went down my back as the man smiled, revealing two rows of black teeth.

We stopped again.

"Um, let's go down the back way," I said, my voice cracking.

"What back way?" Jack whispered.

I pulled on his arm. "I don't know, but there's got to be a back way. If not, we'll make one."

Jack nodded. "I think that's a good idea."

We ran in the opposite direction, following the balcony past several other condos, until we saw an emergency exit sign.

Jack barreled through the doorway, and we ran to the car.

When we got there, I lunged toward the passenger's side. I was about to rip the door open when my knees buckled beneath me. I caught the side of the door just before I fell to the ground.

"Becks? You okay?"

"Yes," I called out, trying to mask how out of breath I was. I still didn't know what this new weakness meant, and until I did, I didn't want Jack to worry.

Part of me, the naive part maybe, hoped the weakness would go away before anybody else noticed. Part of me hoped the weakness had nothing to do with my missing heart.

But another part of me knew it had everything to do with it.

THREE

NOW

The Surface. In the mountains.

"Who was that guy?" Jack said, driving way too fast down the mountain switchbacks. "Or maybe I should ask, *what* was that guy?"

I shrugged. "I don't know. I've never seen anything like it. Maybe we didn't get a good enough look at him. We only had a glimpse. Maybe he was dressed up for some . . . costume party."

"Right. Costume party. In June. On a balcony. By himself."

I glanced in the side-view mirror several times over the next few minutes, even though I couldn't think of a reason the man in the trench coat would've been following us.

When I was sure we were in the clear, I said, "The bigger problem is, Cole anticipated us."

Jack sighed and flipped on the signal to turn into my subdivision. "So what do we do now?"

"Move to Tahiti," I said. I stared out the window as Jack pulled up in front of my house.

"That would look suspiciously like running away from our problems." Jack grabbed my hand and brought it to his lips. "Meet you in five?" he said.

I nodded. "I'll leave the window unlocked."

I ran inside, straight past my dad's study. As I walked by, he looked up from his laptop.

"It's a little late. How was your date?" he asked.

"Fine." *We broke into an immortal's condo, looking to steal my heart, which is now a compass. But we came up empty-handed.* "Um . . . the usual boring stuff. Good night," I called out over my shoulder.

"Next time, you're home by midnight," my dad said back.

As I got ready for bed, I could no longer keep my disappointment at bay. We didn't have my heart, so we were no closer to turning me back into a human. Not only that, but tonight showed that Cole had anticipated we would search his apartment. He wasn't just one step ahead of us; he was several.

He'd predicted we'd go for the safe.

I shook my head as I put toothpaste on my toothbrush. Cole had always known me too well. It was how he'd convinced me to go to the Feed with him in the first place. It was how he'd been able to trick me into feeding on him three times in the Everneath.

I washed my face and then looked at myself in the mirror and yawned. There were dark circles under my eyes, the kind that had only ever appeared when I'd been out all night, and my face was paler than usual.

Maybe I wasn't sleeping very well.

I went to my room and opened the window for Jack.

"Are you okay?" he asked.

My hand flew up to my face. It must've been more noticeable than I thought. "Yes. I just suddenly felt really exhausted."

Jack frowned. "Are you sick?"

I shook my head. "No. I'm sure I'm just tired from breaking and entering. Nothing more."

Jack pressed his lips together as if he were reluctant to give up on the subject, but I pulled him toward my bed and wrapped my arms around him.

"We're never going to find my heart if Cole doesn't want us to," I said, my eyelids drooping. "Now that he's back in town, I say that tomorrow we confront him."

Jack smiled. "Tomorrow you have summer school."

"Ugh," I said. "Okay, after summer school." I could hear the exhaustion in my voice.

"Just sleep for now, Becks. We'll figure it out."

When I could no longer keep my eyes open, I fell asleep entangled in Jack's arms. There was nowhere else I'd rather be. I just had to find a way to stay there.

At night. My bedroom.

I'm running down a series of hallways. Something, or someone, is after me. The walls of the hallways begin to close in. Hands reach out from deep within the walls, grabbing at my hair, my arms, my legs.

I turn a sharp corner and run into a tall, regal woman with fiery red hair.

The queen of the Everneath. Adonia. My heartbeat speeds up at the sight of her.

"I see you," she says.

"No," I try to say, but no sound comes from my mouth. I scramble backward and trip over something at my feet.

It's a body. Lying on its stomach. I grab the shoulder and turn the body over, and there is my own face, staring back at me. Lifeless. I try to scream, still unable to make a sound.

The queen crouches down beside me. "I see you. You will try. You will lose. You will die."

"I don't want the throne!" I try to scream, but it comes out in a whisper. "I don't want it!"

I woke with a start, my hand pressed against my chest. I knew it was a dream. Only a dream. But dreams had a funny way of being connected with the Everneath. I was scared the queen really could see me: the girl who threatened the throne. What was worse, I was scared the queen would *find* me.

It took me several long blinks to wipe the cobwebs from my eyes, and even then the world seemed smoggy, as if I'd taken a sleeping pill last night.

Jack wasn't in bed, so I hoisted myself up and went to the kitchen looking for him. Movement from the window caught my eye. There he was, standing in front of the chestnut tree, his feet apart in an athletic stance, his shoulders hunched, his fists in front of his chest, ready to throw a block. He cocked his arm back and then punched the trunk of the tree over and over, his knuckles becoming bloody and torn. Shards of wood exploded from the tree each time his fist made contact.

I grabbed the windowsill for support. I'd never seen anything like it. Yes, he'd punched through the wall last night, but this tree was a solid oak.

He wouldn't let us focus on the mystery of why he'd come back the way he had, because he said we had more pressing matters, such as my immortality. But watching him right now, I wondered if we were focusing on the wrong thing.

I leaned closer to the window. "Jack!"

He didn't turn around for a moment. His shoulders relaxed and lost most of their rigidity from just seconds before. But no matter how he tried to compose himself, I knew he was upset about our failed attempt to retrieve my heart. Even more upset, probably, that I had told Cole I'd rather die than become queen of the Everneath. After everything we'd been through, I knew that Jack would prefer I stay alive no matter the cost. It was the one point we'd never agree on. I would never become an Everliving if it meant feeding on other people. At the same time, he would rather become my Forfeit than see me die.

I'd given up hope that we'd ever agree. Now I could only hope it would never come to that.

He finally turned around and flashed me a dazzling smile.

"Hey, Becks," he said. "I didn't know you were awake."

"I didn't know you hated trees so much." I frowned. "What are you doing?"

He looked down at his hands, his bloody knuckles. He stretched his fingers wide and clenched them again. "I don't know. I was trying to see just how much pain I could withstand."

I let out a breath I didn't realize I was holding. "A lot, apparently. Do you feel better now, knowing?"

He nodded, about as out of breath as if he'd just jogged for a block. I'd exerted more effort climbing out of bed. There was no wincing or tightness in his eyes. No sign that he'd felt any pain at all, even as a small drop of blood ran down his hand and off his finger. He wiped it on his jeans.

A folded piece of paper at his feet caught my eye. "Did you drop something?"

Jack looked down and quickly scooped up the paper, putting it in his pocket.

"What was it?" I asked.

"Your note."

He didn't have to specify which note. I knew the one. Last year, after the Christmas dance, he had left a note in my pocket with two words written on it.

Ever Yours

When I'd gone to the Everneath to save him from the Tunnels, I had brought the note and left it in his hand. He'd literally used it to find his way back to me. Now he never let it out of his possession.

"Come inside," I said. "I'll make us some coffee before school."

He nodded again and walked away in the direction of my front door, using the sleeve of his hoodie to wipe the sweat from his brow. Beating up trees must've been quite a workout.

Jack came in, and I started the coffeemaker. He sat down and absentmindedly reached for the watercolor painting on the kitchen table, a summer art project by Tommy.

When he finally looked up at me, his mouth dropped open a little. "Becks, you look worse now than you did last night."

I put my hand up to my cheek. I hadn't had a chance to look in a mirror. "I don't think I slept very well. Bad dream."

He came over and put his arms around me, pulling me close. "What about?"

"The queen. She had me trapped in a hallway with thousands of hands sticking out. She kept saying that she sees me. I couldn't hide." I left out the part about the dead body at my feet. I didn't want Jack to worry about my state of mind. "Doesn't mean anything."

"You're right," Jack said. "It doesn't. She doesn't know you exist, and the good thing about Cole is that he will guard that knowledge to the grave. But the sooner we confront him, the better."

"It'll have to wait until after school."

Jack's phone buzzed with an incoming call. As he pulled it out of his pocket, I glimpsed the caller ID.

"Does your mom know where you spend your nights?" I asked.

"Everyone knows where I spend my nights," he said, pressing the ignore button and putting the phone back in his pocket.

"Then why doesn't she do anything about it?"

"She's not about to do anything that might push me to 'run away' again. So I guess my time in the Tunnels turned out to be a good thing." I sat down, and his hand trailed down my shoulder and my back. I shivered into him. "Why?" he said. "What does your dad think?"

"That I'll always be twelve years old. Going on eleven. He doesn't know."

"He knows," Jack said, always reading my mind. "He just refuses to see."

I shrugged. "He'd kill you if he knew."

"He knows, Becks. He's just trying not to lose you again."

We drained our cups, and I rinsed out the first one and put it in the sink; but as I was cleaning the second one, I accidentally dropped it and it shattered in the sink. Jack came up behind me and put his arms around me.

"Don't be nervous," he said.

I shook my head, confused. I wasn't normally a klutz. The coffee cup hadn't even been slippery. "About summer school? I'm not. It must've . . . slipped or something."

He dipped his head toward my neck; but before his lips could make contact, the door connecting the kitchen to the garage swung open, and my dad rushed in. Another one of his "surprise" visits that worked almost as well as a chastity belt.

Jack sprang away from me as if I'd given him an electric shock.

"I forgot my travel mug," my dad said. "I trust I'm not interrupting anything."

"No, Mr. . . . Mayor," Jack said, his voice shaky.

Mr. Mayor? I rolled my eyes. Could he be any more formal? "Actually, Dad, we were just about to leave for school," I said.

My dad raised an eyebrow. "Great. We can all walk out together." My dad looked at his watch. "I have to get to the office."

I nodded and pulled out my own phone to check the time.

My dad stared at the hand that held the phone. "What's on your wrist?" he said. "Did you hurt it?"

Confused, I looked down. Right along the wrist line there was the faint shadow of a dark band. It wrapped around the entire circumference of my wrist, as if a watch band had rubbed some of its color off on my skin.

But at first glance it looked like a light bruise.

I pulled down my sleeve, glimpsing Jack's suddenly wide eyes. "It's nothing. I think my bracelet just left a mark."

I smiled and kissed Dad's cheek, grateful once again that

my dad wouldn't have noticed that I didn't wear jewelry.

I grabbed my bag, and Jack followed me out the door, staring intently at his phone as he walked. Once we were in the car, I jabbed my elbow into his ribs.

"You seemed enthralled with the blank screen of your phone back there," I said.

"What's on your wrist?" he said. The effort he used to force his voice to sound calm had the opposite effect. He sounded devastated. "Did I do that? Did I grab your wrist the other night?" He sucked in a deep breath. "Did I hurt you?"

"No," I said. "No. I don't know what it is, but it doesn't hurt." I held out my hand in front of his face, twisting my wrist back and forth. "It's not anything."

Jack closed his eyes and nodded. "Okay." The second he turned on the ignition, my phone buzzed with a text.

I checked the screen. "From Cole," I said.

"What did he say?"

I took a deep breath as I reread the message on the screen. I involuntarily looked at the mark on my wrist before I read the text out loud. "He's asking if my shackle has appeared yet."

Jack pressed his lips together, and his nostrils flared. "Is he talking about your wrist?"

I shrugged.

"How would he have known?"

"It's probably a coincidence," I said, but the way it came out didn't sound very convincing.

"Text him back. Tell him we need to see him. Now."

I texted and got an immediate response. "He says he'll see me at school."

Jack sighed. He gunned the gas and then let up off the pedal as if he couldn't decide whether he wanted to get me to school faster or never take me there at all.

FOUR

NOW

The Surface. On the way to summer school.

*J*ack took the corners tight. Fast. As if he'd decided on speed over turning in slow circles.

I was happy he was paying so much attention to driving that he didn't see my face, because my reaction to Cole's text was a little more baffling.

It was exhaustion. I fought to keep my eyelids up. My head kept tilting to the side as I started to drift off. I thought maybe some fresh air would help, but when I went to raise my hand to open the window, nothing happened. My hand didn't move from its position on my thigh.

I stared hard at the hand, willing it to go up, but Jack pulled in front of the school before the hand actually moved.

It was as if I were on a ten-second delay.

Jack threw the car into park and then turned to say something to me, but whatever it was he wanted to say got caught in his mouth once he saw my face. His eyes grew wide.

"What?" I said.

"You're so pale. And the circles under your eyes are even darker than they were. You look . . ." His voice faded away as he seemed to catch himself from saying something else.

"I look what? Say it."

He frowned. "You look worse than when you first came back from the Everneath."

Without hesitating, Jack leaned forward and kissed me. Still, there was . . . nothing. No exchange of energy. Our kiss was just a kiss.

He pulled back. "It's still not working. I didn't feel any energy leave me."

"Me neither." I sighed. "So maybe this weakness is a human thing, not an Everneath thing."

Jack frowned again and looked as if he didn't believe me. "Maybe we should go to a doctor."

"Hah!" The exclamation was involuntary, as if I didn't have the energy to control my immediate reactions. For a moment I felt a burst of energy, and it showed itself through words pouring out of my mouth. "Sorry. I just . . . suddenly I thought about how that visit would go. The doctor pulls out a stethoscope, holds it to my chest, and asks me to breathe deep. Then he gets a really confused look on his face. He puts the little listener thingy on another spot. Then another. He'll be speechless. And then we'd have to act all surprised and be all 'What? No heartbeat? Huh. Funny. Moving on, the bigger problem is why do I have circles under my eyes?'

"And he'd say, 'Wait a second. Did you hear me? No heart!' And we'd be all 'Yes, yes, we heard you. But other than missing a major organ, what's wrong with me?' And then he'd go on and on about the whole no-heart thing, and then I would try to distract him by doing that dance I do—you know, the one that looks like the running man. . . . But before I finish my entire routine, the doctor would be texting the CIA to tell them about my lack of heart, and the rounds of involuntary government testing would begin. And then—"

Jack leaned forward and cut off my next word by covering my lips with his. It was a few minutes before we stopped, and by then I'd forgotten everything except the feel of Jack's lips pressed hard against mine.

When he stopped to breathe, he said, "It's not the CIA."

"What?" I said breathlessly.

"It's not the CIA who would conduct the government tests. That's just silly."

I squinted one eye. "*That* was the silliest part of my whole Nikki-at-the-doctor scenario?"

"Well, the dancing was kind of silly." Jack's smile faded slowly into a frown as he touched the circles under my eyes. "I just hope you're right. I hope it's a human thing."

"It is," I said, the exhaustion settling back in.

Jack got out of the car and opened my door. I stepped out and stood up straight, and that's when everything went black.

I came to a few moments later, on the ground looking up at the sky. And Jack's face.

"Becks! Are you okay?"

I nodded and sat up.

"Take it easy," Jack said.

"I think . . . I just stood up too fast."

Jack's brow furrowed.

"I'm okay," I said, struggling to speak. "Really. That's all it was. I didn't eat very much this morning; all I had was coffee. I'm fine."

I grabbed his hand, and he helped me up. He didn't let go of my fingers.

"I'm fine," I insisted. "I'm going to go to class. I'll see you in a couple of hours."

"You sure?"

"Yes. I'm sure. I've got a granola bar. I'll eat it on my way in."

He pressed his lips together and sighed. "Okay. I'll be here."

I left him standing there. I tried to walk with purposeful, steady steps; but the entire time, I knew that this was a symptom of my missing heart, and that nothing on the Surface would fix it.

I entered through the glass doors, a completely different person than I'd been one year ago, although you wouldn't think it to look at me.

And that's what the few people in the halls were doing right now. Looking at me.

I could understand why, after Jack's disappearance last spring and my rumored involvement. I think the story went something like this: I had drawn Jack into my web of crazy, and then just when I'd had him in my trap, I'd chased him out of town.

I didn't care as much about the rumors this time, though.

I was still skinny. Skinnier than I'd been when I'd returned to school last year. But back then my soul was weak. Now it was strong. I didn't look it, but I knew what I was capable of. I'd traipsed through the three elemental rings of the labyrinth to reach the heart of the Everneath and save Jack. The trip had nearly killed me.

Rumors were nothing in comparison.

But I lowered my head as I remembered what the trip had cost me. Cole had tricked me into feeding on him three times in the Everneath. So in a way, maybe the trip did kill me.

I shoved my backpack farther up on my shoulder and wound my way through the halls to Mrs. Stone's summer Creative Writing class. I turned a corner and nearly ran headfirst into Jules.

"Becks," she said in that breathless voice she used when she was unsure about something. She was probably unsure about a lot of things when she saw me, starting with the fact that both of us knew I was keeping secrets from her. Secrets such as where I'd been when I'd disappeared last year. Where Jack had been when he had disappeared in the spring.

I had so many relationships to mend, and Jules was at the top of my list.

"Hey, Jules," I said. "You look great."

She instantly smiled, and I remembered how easily Jules could forgive, if she felt as if someone was willing to meet her halfway.

"Thanks. You look . . ." Her voice trailed off as she got a look at my face. "Are you okay?"

I nodded and turned to look down the hall, partly so I could check for Cole and partly so she couldn't get a clear look at my face.

"Didn't get much sleep. Are you doing Creative Writing?" I said.

She nodded.

"Do you want to sit together?" I asked.

"Great!" she said. I couldn't tell if her enthusiasm was forced or genuine.

We walked together in silence the rest of the way. Things were nowhere near normal, but it was a start.

In Mrs. Stone's classroom, I went down the second row, she went down the first, and we took two desks next to each other. Tara Bolton walked in moments later, and Jules waved to her, motioning to the seat in front of her. When Tara sat down, she smiled hesitantly toward me, then turned around to talk to Jules.

I caught maybe every third word she said, but I smiled as if

I knew what was going on. Where was Cole?

The rest of the class settled in. My suspicions had been right: the students there were all the main competitors for valedictorian.

There were no bells since it was a summer class, but the moment the clock above her desk read ten o'clock, Mrs. Stone turned to the blackboard and wrote the words *The Twelve Labors of Hercules.*

"Welcome to summer school," she said in that voice that sounded as if she were in a Shakespearean play. As a side job, she gave private voice lessons for aspiring actors at night, so she always enunciated her words clearly. "This is Creative Writing, and just because it's a summer class, that doesn't mean you won't have homework tonight. So if you are not in the mood to work—"

She didn't get to the threat part, because right then the door swung open.

If I had had a heart, at that moment it would have exploded in my chest. Cole had just walked in the doorway, only it didn't look like him. Instead he was taller, darker haired. His alter ego, Neal. It was a disguise he used only when he needed to pass as a high school student. It took a lot of energy for him to change his appearance, so he used the disguise only when he really needed to.

But why would he need to today? I hadn't seen Neal since before the Tunnels came for me, when Cole had enrolled as a student at Park City High just to get closer to me.

I wasn't surprised he was appearing as Neal. It was my reaction to seeing him that shocked me. That spiral of hate that I'd been nurturing suddenly burst in my chest, running through my veins and reaching my fingers and toes. It was all I could do not to run at him, head and shoulder first, as if I were a linebacker or something, despite the fact that I knew that if I tried, I'd collapse in an exhausted heap on the floor before I even reached him.

What was my problem?

I'd known he would be here. I thought I'd been prepared. But now that he was in front of me, I wasn't thinking about lost hearts or mysterious wrist shackles or the fact that I'd just fainted minutes before.

All I could focus on was the hate.

FIVE

The Surface. Mrs. Stone's classroom.

My hand froze with my pencil midair, as if I were posing with a dart, about to throw it at a target. The tip of the pencil pointed toward Cole.

He caught my eye and smirked, then turned to Mrs. Stone. "Sorry I'm late. Traffic."

Mrs. Stone narrowed her eyes. "Not a great precedent to set on the first day of class, Mr. . . . ?"

"Black. Neal Black."

I couldn't move. Mrs. Stone nodded toward me, and for a moment I was terrified she would say something like *You know Nikki, I'm sure.*

But then I realized she wasn't looking at me; she was looking at the seat next to me, on the opposite side from Jules. With dread I noticed it was the only empty seat in the room. And considering my uncontrollable reaction to Cole, I wasn't sure I would survive sitting by him for the entire class.

I grabbed the sides of my desk, as if I were about to pick it up and move it. Like a crazy person.

Cole walked over and noticed how I was grabbing my desk. He raised an eyebrow. "I think when Mrs. Stone said to take our seats, she didn't mean literally *take our seats.*"

I released the desk.

He plopped down in the chair and whispered, "What's wrong? You knew I was coming."

I took a few deep breaths in and out. "I know. But I hate you."

He smiled. "Did you just figure that out?"

I closed my eyes and leaned over my desk. "It's, like, painful." I made an O shape with my mouth and blew out some breaths, just like I'd seen women in labor do on television.

Cole put his hand on my back. "Breathe. Just breathe. Try not to die of hate."

Mrs. Stone struck her ruler on the end of her table. "If I may continue?"

Cole sat up straight and nodded as if to say *You may proceed.*

"As I was saying, we are first going to cover the structure of haiku, and just to make it interesting, we're going to add a taste of mythology. Specifically, Hercules. Yes, the strong man often is perceived as an oaf. Light on the brain cells, heavy on the biceps."

Cole leaned over and said under his breath, "We all know someone like that, don't we?"

I didn't take my eyes off Mrs. Stone.

"But he was victim to one of the worst curses in mythology: the inability to know good from evil. Because of this, he committed many acts of violence. Even murder. Later in his life the curse was lifted." She paused dramatically. "Can you imagine the pain? Having to face the things you had done in your life at a time when you had no morals? A time when you didn't know right from wrong? In this way, lifting the curse placed a whole new curse on Hercules. The curse of remorse." She pointed to what she had written on the board, about the twelve labors. "We will divide up into teams of two, and each team will be assigned one of Hercules's twelve labors. Throughout the course, as we learn about the different writing styles, you will write about that particular labor in that particular style. Now, choose your teammate."

Crap. I turned to Jules, but Tara Bolton whipped around in her seat as if she'd heard a gunshot or something. Jules looked from Tara to me and gave me an apologetic shrug.

I turned behind me, but Lisa Papadakis was leaning to her right, making plans with Shalese Glenn. I desperately looked to the front of the room just as Cole pushed his desk next to mine with a loud squeak against the tile floor.

I threw my hand against his desk, but I couldn't do anything more than slow it down. I didn't want him anywhere near me.

"It's not necessary to push our desks together," I said, but he ignored me.

"Everyone paired up?" Mrs. Stone said. "Good. I'll assign each team a number, and you will get the task of the corresponding number."

Cole and I were assigned number five. The task of cleaning the Augean stables in a single day.

"As I said, your first writing style is the haiku." She spent the next twenty minutes reviewing the form and the history behind it, and then gave us the rest of the class time to start our own haiku.

The background hum of the rest of the class gave me the chance to speak without whispering. And as long as we were together now . . .

"I want my heart," I said, my voice shaking.

Again he ignored me. "Cleaning stables in haiku form," he said, leaning closer to me than necessary. "I love high school."

"I want my heart."

"Do you want to write or shall I?" Cole said loudly, ignoring me.

Mrs. Stone glanced at us, so I pulled out a notebook and started writing in it as if we were working.

"I want my heart. I'll trade you for it. I'll give you anything. Almost anything."

He tilted his head forward in a challenging way. "Give me you."

"Anything else."

Cole raised an eyebrow. "You think I care about anything else?"

I looked down at the floor. "Where is my heart?" I said.

"You're always asking the wrong question."

I raised my head. "What's the right question?"

He paused dramatically. "Why are you going to summer school when you're dying?"

I froze with my pencil hovering above the paper. "I am not dying. You made me immortal."

Quick as a flash, he grabbed my wrist and pushed up my sleeve. He studied my wrist for a moment before I yanked my hand away. "The shackle," he said. "It's there."

"So?" I pulled my sleeve back down.

He frowned, and when he spoke again his voice was soft. "You're getting weak, aren't you?" It wasn't a question. It was a statement. "Quickly, too."

"No," I said. The word came out shaky.

Cole ran his hand through his messy hair. "Yes, you are. And that means you're beginning the transition. Your body doesn't know how to metabolize outside energy sources yet."

I leaned closer. "That's ridiculous. I fed off Jack twice last year." I tried not to think about all the times I'd tried to feed on him in the past two weeks only to fail.

"But you were human then."

"I still am human."

"No, you're not. Now your energy isn't simply energy. It's

life. It's your survival. And until you make the full transition, until you feed on a human for a century, you will be in this limbo state, where there's only one source of nutrition."

I froze. *One source of nutrition?*

Mrs. Stone rapped her ruler on her desk. "Time's up. Do I have any volunteers to read their haikus?"

The class collectively sank a little lower in their seats. I couldn't take my eyes off Cole.

"Mr. Black. You and Miss Beckett seemed intent on the assignment," she said with a suspicious gaze. "Care to share?"

I opened my mouth to explain we hadn't come up with anything yet, but Cole spoke first.

> *"For the fifth labor*
> *what better treat than to sling*
> *giant chunks of dung."*

There were a few snickers throughout the room. Tara sat there with her mouth open. Stephanie Jarmon looked at Cole as if he had just written the Declaration of Independence in thirty seconds.

Mrs. Stone gave one more rap of her ruler. "Well, Neal. You certainly have the haiku format down, although your word choice could use a little . . . finesse."

"We *are* talking about cleaning stables," Cole said, a cheeky grin on his lips.

She couldn't help a smile, then checked her watch. "We'll

take a five-minute break. Go do what you need to do. Be back here by eleven."

The classroom broke out into a loud murmur. I heard bits and pieces. Mostly about how "Neal" spontaneously haikued.

All I could think about was what my one source of nutrition would be.

I left my books on my desk and followed Cole out of the room. I grabbed his arm and started to pull him toward the courtyard. Nobody would be there. We could talk without everyone staring.

Cole let me pull him, saying loudly, "Lead on. I like a woman who—"

"Shut up."

We got to the courtyard and I looked around to make sure we were alone, then closed the door behind us and went over to one of the tables.

"Talk," I commanded.

"About what?"

As if he didn't know. "What's happening to me?"

"Ah, that." He leaned back and lifted his feet to rest them on another chair. "Nik, you're going through the change, from human to Everliving." The way he said "the change" made me think of parents giving their child "the talk." He sighed. "The shackle means you've started the transition. Like I said. That means you can no longer make your own energy. You have to get it from somewhere else."

"Why can't I feed off Jack?"

He frowned at the mention of Jack. "Because your body doesn't know how to convert other people's energy into your own immortality yet. You're like a newborn bird. You don't have the skills yet to feed yourself, so you have to depend on your mother bird for sustenance until you make the full transition."

"What if I don't want to make the full transition?"

He took in a deep breath, looking pained for only a moment before he spoke. "Silly Nik. Always looking for ways to die. Here's the deal. Until your first Century Feed, you survive only by eating the food the mother bird brings for you. But the food from the mother bird will sustain you for only so long, just as a baby can only survive for so long on formula. When it's time for you to Century Feed, a second shackle will appear on your other wrist. The process takes different lengths of time for everyone."

"I thought I wouldn't have to . . . Century Feed for another ninety-nine years, with all the other Everlivings."

He pursed his lips. "That's not how it works with new baby Everlivings. As soon as the nutrition from the mother bird stops working, usually a few weeks after you lose your heart, you have to bring a Forfeit for a Century Feed."

Everything around us seemed to go blurry. *A few weeks?* I'd thought I had ninety-nine years. He had to be wrong.

I narrowed my eyes, bringing my vision into focus again. "Who, exactly, is this mother bird?"

He clapped his hands together and rubbed them. "That's the best part. The mother bird is the Everliving who holds your heart."

The Everliving who holds my heart. Cole stole my heart from my bedroom two weeks ago. He'd said there were special perks for the Everliving who held it. Cole was the mother bird? I closed my eyes.

"What does that mean?"

"It means I am your only source of survival." His face broke out into a wide grin. "I wish Gavin were here. I'd have him give me a drum roll."

"Stop playing games. Tell me."

He raised an eyebrow, gave me a devilish wink, then grabbed me and kissed me.

SIX

NOW

The Surface. The school courtyard.

I tried to pull away, but then I felt the unmistakable surge of power from Cole's lips to mine; and with that first morsel of energy, my limbs, which had previously felt like noodles, suddenly filled with vitality.

I didn't realize how weak I'd become until I felt how much life was being restored.

And it wasn't just energy that transferred to me. Images began to flood my mind. A flash of a blond boy, working the fields, on a farm, maybe, in a place where the sky was insanely blue and the mountains encroached on the little valley. That blond boy had to be Cole, somewhere in Norway from a time before he was immortal. Whatever the memory was, it became embedded in my brain.

I remembered getting bits and pieces of his memories when he'd fed me in the Everneath. But I didn't want to focus on his memory now. All I cared about was the strength I was getting.

I felt it rush through me, reaching my fingertips, my toes, and finally lifting to my face.

When he pulled away, I was the one who leaned in for more.

"Now do you understand?" he said, his voice breathless. He closed his eyes and whispered, "Nik, we are each other's lifeblood. We always will be."

I couldn't speak. The drinking fountain in the corner of the courtyard shuddered to life, and I caught a glimpse of my reflection in the stainless steel. Even in that distorted vision, I could see that my cheeks had color in them and that the circles underneath my eyes had disappeared.

And the change wasn't just on the outside. I could feel it under my skin. It took me maybe ten seconds to understand the implications of what had just happened. I'd been getting weak, and Cole had made me strong.

I stared at him. "So am I going to be okay now?"

He nodded. "As long as you feed on me every night."

"Every night?"

"Yes. You can't miss a night if you want to, you know, stay alive." He smirked. "Which I understand never seems to be your priority."

He was saying he was life. And at his discretion, he could give me life or he could take it away. He had the ultimate power over me. And I had let it happen. I'd asked for it to happen, first when I'd begged him to take me to the Feed and then when I'd voluntarily fed on him three times in the Everneath. The first time was just a kiss to show him I was the real me and not the Siren about to lure him into a trap. I hadn't known I was feeding on him. The second two times, I'd known I needed the energy, but I'd been so close to saving Jack that I wasn't willing to go back to the Surface. I was impatient. I'd fed on Cole to stay in the Everneath.

He knew I would. He always had the power.

I clenched my fists and punched his chest. I'm sure it felt like a feather duster pounding on a brick wall, but I couldn't help it. I hit him as hard as I could, trying to pulverize the past away. Crush the decisions I'd made, such as trusting Cole in the first place. Beat on the weak girl who had gone with Cole to the Everneath.

Stupid girl. Foolish girl.

Cole let me hit him. And why not? Sure, he had just given me a dose of energy, but I still felt as powerful as a sponge.

The fact that I wasn't hurting him made me hit him even harder. Cole glanced down at my futile attempts to inflict pain, and then in a swift move, he pulled me to him and held me against him so that my arms were pinned against his chest.

"I know," he said. "I know it's a choice you'd never allow yourself to make. You'd never give in to the life of an Everliving. So I chose the life for you, because I know something you refuse to recognize."

"What's that?" I said, my voice muffled against him.

He held me back just enough so I could see his face, and his determined frown. "You were meant for this life. With me."

I tensed against him. Did Cole really believe that, deep

down, I wanted this? My eyes stung, a sure sign tears were on their way.

"Hear me out, Nik. Remember the moment we met? At the concert at Harry O's? Everything in your life—your decisions, your joy, your pain at losing your mom—all of it was the universe guiding you to cross paths with me. And everything in my life, up until that point, directed me toward you. I knew it, but I didn't believe it until you survived the Feed."

I pushed against him, but he held me tight. "You're delusional," I said.

"I'm the delusional guy who's going to keep you alive." There was a fire behind his eyes.

I set my jaw. "You're the delusional guy who killed me in the first place."

I turned around and ran out of the courtyard with a renewed energy in my veins. A fire that Cole fed me, from his lips to mine. In order to survive, I was dependent on the person I hated the most. A person who just over two weeks ago had had a place in my heart. I had been sure during our trip to the Everneath that Cole was my friend. He could've been the good guy. He could've been my hero.

Instead, he'd tricked me.

Pausing in front of the door to the hallway, I realized that there was no way I could sit through the rest of the class. I wandered to the front of the school and noticed a black sedan parked down the street. Jack's car. I sighed as the bands of strain around my chest loosened. I didn't even realize how much tension I was feeling at that moment until the sight of Jack's car released it. I ran toward him. The driver's-side door opened, and Jack, taking in my manic state, started jogging toward me, eyes wide with concern. We collided, and he gathered me in his strong arms.

"Shh. It's okay," he whispered with his lips next to my ears. "Everything's going to be okay."

My breathing slowed as he held me tight. His calm heartbeat tempered my own racing pulse.

"You're shaking," he said.

He studied my face. Eyes, lips, nose. My pink cheeks. I saw the subtle change in his expression.

A small smile crept onto his lips. "You're feeling better." He pulled me toward him again, but this time he pressed his lips against mine and kissed me as if I were water in a desert.

I put my fingers in his hair, knotting them, pulling him closer.

He broke away. His eyes were wild. "Sorry, I—"

"Don't you dare apologize," I growled.

He squeezed his eyes shut, as if he were trying to restrain himself.

"No," I said, knowing that the kiss was over but refusing to accept it. "Stop stopping kissing me."

I bit my lip as I realized how ridiculous my words sounded. Jack's lips twitched, and he opened his eyes. He shook his head almost imperceptibly. "How did you do it?" he asked, effectively changing the subject from our kiss to the new pinkness in my cheeks. "Did you . . . eat something?"

I glanced back at his car. "I think you should sit down."

His face went blank, and then his eyes narrowed. "What happened?"

"Let's get in your car for a minute." I turned him around and gently guided him to the car. He let me.

When we were seated inside, I could see that his face had drained of color.

"It's okay," I said. "Everything's okay." I realized how often we said these words to each other. I wondered if they'd lost their meaning yet.

"Just tell me, Becks. The anticipation is worse than knowing. Was Cole there? Did he do something?"

I closed my eyes. This was one of those times when the anticipation was better than knowing. "Cole was there. He wasn't interested in trading anything for my heart. He knew I was getting weak. He says I'm dying, but he can save me. By . . . feeding me."

I waited. No noise from beside me. I opened one eye.

Jack was staring straight ahead out the windshield, clenching the steering wheel. It didn't look as if he was breathing. I'd never seen him so still. I looked at his hands. The knuckles on his fingers were white.

"Jack?"

"Give me a minute," he said.

Finally, I saw the rise and fall of his chest. He closed his eyes and slowly released his grip on the steering wheel. Deep divots appeared where his fingers had been, distinct impressions in the hard plastic.

"If it's a matter of you needing energy, *I'll* feed you," he said.

I shook my head. "It doesn't work like that because I'm in 'transition,' he called it. We know he's telling the truth. We've tried it."

"So Cole holds your life in his hands?"

I nodded.

He blew out a breath, and I thought he was coming back to me until he growled, "I'm gonna kill him." He grasped the door handle and yanked hard.

"Jack, no!" I didn't know if he was serious about killing Cole or not, but his eyes were blazing. He didn't stop. He exploded out of the car and slammed the door behind him. I jumped out as fast as I could and threw myself in front of him, my hands on his chest.

"Stop!" I dug my feet into the ground and threw all my strength into stopping his forward momentum. It took every bit of energy I had, even the new stuff Cole had just given me. His eyes looked strangely vacant, so I figured the fewer words, the better. "Listen to me. You hurt him . . . you kill me."

He froze, staring at me.

I nodded slowly, trying to emphasize visually the truth of my words. With a small, twitchy shake of his head, the vacant look in his eyes slowly vanished.

"Becks." He clenched and unclenched his fingers, and I

wasn't sure we were out of the woods yet.

"Just come back to the car."

He didn't move.

"Come," I commanded, taking his large hand in mine. He allowed me to drag him back to the car. Once we were inside, he dropped his head against the steering wheel.

"Wow," he said, breathing slowly. "I don't know if I've ever felt so angry so quickly."

I stared at the deep finger impressions on the steering wheel. Angry might have been an understatement.

He looked at me. "Okay, Becks. I'm okay now. Tell me everything." He frowned. "Cole fed you?" The words seemed to have a hard time finding their way out of his mouth. His hands started shaking.

I squinted one eye. "Um . . . maybe we should go somewhere else, where things aren't so breakable—"

"I'm okay now. What happened?"

I pressed my lips together, resigned. "During Creative Writing, he confronted me about my . . . weakened state. He said that I'm like a baby bird, and as long as he held my Surface heart, he was the only one who could feed me." I thought about all the other things I'd learned, and I realized that the only way to get through it was to blurt it all out. "He said that without his nutrition every night, I'll die. Feeding off him is the only way I won't die. At least . . . until even his nutrition isn't enough."

"What happens then?" Jack said in a soft voice.

I swallowed hard. "Then I have to feed on a Forfeit for a century. Immediately. Not in ninety-nine years like we'd thought." My voice caught. "And if I don't, I die."

Jack's mouth opened and then shut again. Opened and shut. And then he grabbed my arms and hoisted me over the center console until I was sitting in his lap. He crushed me to his chest so strongly that any more force would probably have broken a rib. But I didn't protest.

It was either this or he would storm into the school and tear Cole apart. With me, he knew he had to stay in control.

"So the ninety-nine years we thought we had . . . now it's just weeks? Maybe?"

I nodded. "It might even be days." We'd gone from having ninety-nine years to this.

Jack sighed and held me tighter. I wondered about the thoughts he wasn't giving voice to, and if they were as hopeless as my own.

SEVEN

NOW

The Surface. In Jack's car.

$\mathcal{I}$ stayed in his arms for I don't know how long, with my ear against his chest, listening to the rhythmic rise and fall of his breathing. As he expelled his breath, his chest shuddered.

I wondered about his temper, his instant anger from a few minutes ago. It seemed so un-Jack-like. I glanced at the steering wheel and disentangled my right hand to run my fingers over the divots there. I closed my eyes and shook my head. One supernatural problem at a time.

"I have to go," I said. "I left my book in Mrs. Stone's classroom."

His grip around me eased slightly. "Hurry back."

"I will."

"When do you have to feed off him again?"

I cringed. "Tonight."

I left Jack sitting in his car, listening to his iPod. By now the students were streaming out of Mrs. Stone's class, so I darted inside and found a note sitting on top of my book. It had Cole's handwriting on it.

I'll be at your window tonight. Midnight. Wear something comfortable. I'm blushing just thinking about it.

I crumpled the paper and tried to keep myself from sinking to the ground.

I was so wrapped up in the note that I didn't notice Daphne Bentley sidle up next to me.

"So, Nikki, how do you know that Neal guy?"

I looked at her with what I'm sure was a blank expression. She tilted her head. "That *is* his name, isn't it? Mr. Tall, Dark, and Obvious Hip Dents?"

I shook my head in a clearing-the-cobwebs kind of way. She was talking about Cole-as-Neal.

"Yes, that was Neal. Sorry, Daphne, my brain is . . ." I made a hand gesture near my head, my best impression of a brain made of macaroni.

"No problem. I was just wondering if you knew Neal." She paused. "And more specifically, if you know whether he's seeing someone."

Seriously? Was she asking me to set her up with an immortal from the Underworld who sucked the life out of humans just for fun?

I closed my mouth, which had apparently been hanging open. "I think he is seeing someone," I said.

She frowned. "Who?"

I wasn't expecting further questions. "Um, a girl. Nancy."

Were girls named Nancy anymore? "She lives in . . . Canada."

She looked like she was trying to raise a single eyebrow, but she didn't have the ability. "Well, Canada isn't here, is it?"

She stared at me, waiting. For what, an answer? "Um, no. Canada is . . . north of here."

She gave me a curt nod and stalked away.

"Glad we established where Canada is," I muttered under my breath. I guess if you knew nothing about Cole, he could be attractive. Even in his Neal form, which wasn't as dazzling as his natural form, he was still more magnetic than any other guy at school.

I shook my head and hurried toward Jack's car. When Jack saw me coming, he leaned over and opened the door.

I slipped inside and blurted, "Cole left me a note saying he would be at my bedroom window at midnight."

Jack put his hand over his mouth and rubbed.

"Breathe," I said.

He nodded, but I couldn't hear any air being expelled. He finally lowered his hand, with enough force that I thought he would tear his lips off as well.

His gaze met mine. "No," he said.

"Um . . . no what?"

"No. No letting him in your bedroom."

I was silent for a moment. "I don't think you're grasping the necessity of the nightly feeding."

"No, I am."

"So you're just tired of me being all, you know, in and of

this world?" I said it as if being alive were overrated.

His lips twitched. "I'm not saying that. But Cole's looking for control. He always has been, and now he thinks he has it. He thinks he has access to your bedroom. Don't let him have it." At my alarmed expression, he squeezed my hand. "I'm not saying never feed on him. But don't let him in. We'll do it on our terms. At his place. He wants this chance to get intimate with you."

I blushed.

"I don't mean it that way, although I'm sure he wants to be intimate with you like that too." His voice was soft. "I mean that he wants to be the closest person to you. He needs you to be dependent on him, like he's dependent on you. Let's make sure that doesn't happen. He wants access to your bedroom, but we won't give it to him. He wants you alone. We won't let that happen. We'll go to him, and we'll make it clear that wherever you go, I go."

I eyed him, thinking about the logistics of feeding off Cole. "You know I have to get near him to feed off him."

"I can handle that," he said.

I looked pointedly at the dents in the steering wheel. "*Can* you handle it?"

He sighed. "It's either that or I have to leave him alone with you, and that's not going to happen."

I nodded, knowing exactly how he felt. "Okay. We do this by our own rules." I grabbed my phone and began typing.

We will not be meeting in my bedroom. Jack and I will meet you at your condo at midnight.

Two minutes later there was an answer.

Sounds kinky. I'll break out the whips and chains. You wear that pair of black boots I like.

I rolled my eyes, already dreading midnight. I was going to feed on Cole. There wasn't any way around it that I could see. If I didn't feed on him, I'd get weaker and weaker until I died. Would it take a day without feeding for that to happen? Two days? I didn't know. But judging by how quickly I'd lost all my energy and how quickly I'd regained it when Cole fed me at school, I knew it could happen fast.

I could do this. I would feed on Cole for . . . for how long? Days? Weeks? Until I actually took another human to the Feed, which would never happen, because I would never do that to someone.

So I would feed on Cole until I found a way to become human again, or until I died. Whichever came first.

Jack nodded, his lips forming a thin, tight line. He put the car in gear and turned in the opposite direction of home.

"Where are we going?" I said.

"Jules wanted to meet us for coffee. I told her we would. It will be good to get our minds off tonight."

I grimaced. I was pretty sure it would take more than coffee to get our minds off it.

Inside the coffee shop, Jules and I sat on one side of the booth and Jack sat on the other. Because of everything the three of us had been through, we weren't about to fall into the old conversational patterns of good friends; but after two cups of coffee, the moments of silence were slightly less awkward. Still, that was more mending than we'd done in the past six months combined.

Jules got us caught up on the latest summer gossip, but since all I could think about was feeding on Cole tonight, I didn't pay much attention until she mentioned the Dead Elvises.

"I heard that Ariel Hughes is seeing the Dead Elvises' drummer," she said.

"Gavin?" I said, surprised.

Jules nodded.

"But I thought Ariel was still with Luke Davis," I said. "They've been joined at the hip since the eighth grade. You couldn't walk down the hall without seeing them jammed up against some locker making out. They've been a couple for years."

"I know," Jules said, seeming relieved that I was finally intrigued by the speculation. "I wouldn't have believed the rumors if I hadn't seen her myself, backstage at the Deads concert last night. She made sure the audience could see her waiting in the wings."

I glanced at Jack, whose eyes were narrowed. The Dead Elvises didn't date. They only ever searched for their next Forfeits. Everything else was left to meaningless one-night stands. What did it mean that Gavin was suddenly in a relationship? With a girl who was supposed to be taken?

"Jules, what happened between Ariel and Luke?" I said.

The intensity of my voice took her by surprise. "I'm . . . I'm not sure. I heard that Ariel accused Luke of cheating, but Luke denies it."

I shook my head, instantly flashing back to when I'd thought the same thing about Jack—that he had cheated at football camp—but Cole was really to blame for the misunderstanding. He had manipulated my emotions to make me more suspicious of Jack. Could Gavin have pulled the same trick?

I faced Jules straight on. "Luke would never cheat on Ariel. Never. There has to be something more to it."

Jules gave Jack a confused look, then put her hand over mine. "It happens, Becks. People break up all the time."

I sighed. "That's not what I'm worried about." I stopped short of saying anything more.

"Then what *are* you worried about?" Jules said.

Jack leaned forward. "The Deads are dangerous, Jules. Becks would be concerned about anybody dating them."

"Why?" Jules asked.

"We can't say—" Jack started, but I interrupted.

"Cole is why I disappeared last year," I said. There were too many lies. It was time to talk about the truth, especially now that another girl might be involved. Maybe not the whole truth, but at least a version of it. "Cole's why Jack disappeared. The entire band is bad news, and anybody associated with them gets hurt. This is the truth, Jules. You saw what happened to me. You might not know all the details, but you saw how changed I was. How broken. The band has ways to influence people. Make them do dangerous things they wouldn't normally do."

Jules looked to Jack, who nodded. "It took everything we had to free Becks from their world. It nearly killed both of us."

I wasn't sure Jules would've believed just me, but having Jack corroborate the story was enough for her.

Then the color drained from her face. "Oh no," she said.

"What?" I said.

"Tara."

"Tara Bolton?" I said. "What about her?"

"This morning she was going on and on about how she had a date tonight. With Maxwell Bones."

Maxwell Bones. Second guitar for the Dead Elvises. Another Dead Elvis on another "date." What was going on?

Worry lines showed in Jack's forehead. He took Jules's hand. "We need a favor."

"What?" Jules said.

"We need you to text Tara and find out where she is right now."

He said the words running through my mind. He obviously felt the same urgency I did. Jules nodded and pulled out her phone. She typed in a message to Tara, and then we all waited.

Nobody spoke for a few moments. I took Jules's hand and squeezed. "I'm sorry to lay all this on you."

She shook her head. "Do you know how long I've waited

to hear something from either of you? Something that's not a lie?"

I glanced at Jack, who looked at me with a faint smile. "So you believe us?" I said.

She nodded. "I know it's not the whole story, but I knew what happened to you had to be something really bad."

Really bad. To say the least.

Jules's phone rang with a new text.

"Tara says she's at Grounds&Ink," Jules said.

Jack and I both stood up, and Jules slapped a ten down on the counter.

"I'm coming with you," she said.

Jack shrugged at me.

"Okay," I said.

Jack drove fast to Grounds&Ink, a café in town that was part pool hall, part coffee shop. When we got inside, we scanned the crowd.

"There," I said, pointing to a booth in the farthest corner.

Max and Tara both sat on the same side of the booth. Max had his arm draped on the backrest behind her. The scene was cozy. Intimate. I'd only ever seen him that way with one other person.

Meredith Jenkins. His last Forfeit.

I stalked over to the table.

Max glanced up at me and back at Tara; and then when recognition hit him, he looked back at me, eyebrows raised.

"Nik?" He took in the two faces behind me: Jack's and Jules's. "Cole's not here," he said.

"I don't care about Cole," I said. "What are you doing here with Tara?"

"Hey!" Tara said, frowning. "That's none of your business."

Max just smiled. "What's it look like I'm doing? I'm getting to know her a little better."

"Why?" I said. "She's not a Daughter. It hasn't been ninety-nine years."

Tara slammed down her cup. "What do you mean I'm not a daughter? Of course I am."

I rolled my eyes. I wasn't going to get anywhere with Tara listening to every word.

"Can you please come outside and talk to me?" I said to Max.

Max shook his head.

Jack and his biceps took a step closer to Max. "Pretty please," he said in a deep, gruff voice that infused more threat into those two words than they'd ever had before.

"Fine," Max said. "So happy we were able to save you from the Tunnels."

Max stood and started to follow us out.

Tara raised her hands. "What the hell, Nikki?"

Jules sat down in the seat Max was formerly occupying, put her arm around Tara, and waved us away.

Thank you, I mouthed to her.

I led us out of Grounds&Ink, followed closely by Max and

then Jack behind him. When we got outside, Max threw up his hands.

"Okay, you got me alone. What's the problem?"

Jack stood there, folded his arms across his chest, and nodded at me.

"The problem is, Dead Elvises don't casually date," I said. "So what are you doing with Tara Bolton? And why is Gavin messing around with Ariel?"

Max smirked and shrugged. "Maybe we changed our ways."

"Cole made it clear Everlivings never change," I said. "*I* may only have weeks until I have to feed, but for *you* the next Feed isn't for another ninety-nine years. And even then, you should have plenty of Daughters of Persephone lined up for the privilege of becoming your Forfeit. So why are you getting mixed up in 'relationships'?"

Max lost his smirk, glanced at Jack and then me. "I don't have to answer you."

He turned away, but I put my hand on his chest and stepped in front of him. "Yes, you do."

A couple who had just come out of Grounds&Ink stared at us, but they didn't stop. Max smiled. "Look at you. You're going to make a great queen."

"I'm not going to be queen," I said, a fierce growl in my voice.

"Not without our help," Max said. "You're why we're doing this. You're why we're looking for Forfeits."

"Why?"

He stepped toward me, towering over me, his face grim. "Because if we're going to take down the throne, we're going to need all the energy we can get. And Everlivings are never more powerful than directly after a Feed."

"But . . . that's ninety-nine years away."

Max sighed. "The band and I are going to participate in an underground Feed. And when I say 'underground,' I don't mean in the Feed caverns; I mean 'underground' in that the queen doesn't know about it. The kind of Feed that takes place on the outskirts of the Everneath, at the discretion of the criminals in our world. It's an accelerated Feed for those of us who waste too much energy between Feeds, or, in this case, for those of us mounting a revolution."

My mouth dropped open. A raindrop hit my cheek. The dark clouds above were about to open up. I looked skyward, trying to understand what he was saying.

"So you were planning on taking Tara. And Gavin, Ariel. And Oliver . . . ?"

"Brooke Chase," Max filled in.

"Huh. Brooke. You were planning on taking these girls as Forfeits in your accelerated Feed, to, what, bulk up for battle?"

He nodded. "That was the general idea."

"Why not take more Daughters of Persephone? Why look for innocent girls?"

"It's an accelerated Feed, outside of the rules. The Daughters don't get mixed up with that, although there are other groups of Forfeits who would be willing to go. But we want to find the strongest."

My heart sank as I realized what he meant, and when I spoke, I looked at Jack. "You're looking for people with earthly attachments. You want them to survive."

Max nodded.

"If one of them survives, then why can't you use *her* to take over the throne?"

"Because it's an accelerated Feed." At my confused expression, he elaborated. "Imagine a marathon—it takes years of intense training. Surviving the accelerated Feed would be like depending on a sugar rush to get you through the race. They wouldn't be strong enough to take over the throne because it's not a full Feed. But they'll add to the strength of our army."

"That's . . . that's despicable." I held my stomach for fear I would lose my coffee. "Will they have to go to the Tunnels after the Feed?"

"Unless we take over the throne, they'll have to go to the Tunnels like every other Forfeit. Well, most every other Forfeit." Max put his hand on my shoulder, which was more voluntary contact than he'd ever made with me before. "But that's not going to happen. This is how much faith we have in you. You will be our queen."

Jack swatted Max's hand away. "Don't touch her. Don't ever touch her."

Max held up his hands. He started to walk back into Grounds&Ink, but Jack stepped in front of him. "Turn around and go somewhere else. Anywhere else. Now."

Max narrowed his eyes and hesitated for a moment. "I'll see you soon," he said.

I shook my head as he walked away. He crossed the parking lot to his motorcycle, kicked it to life, and roared away. As soon as he had disappeared from view, I turned to Jack.

"You know what this means?"

"I know, Becks."

"They're going after innocent girls. Girls with earthly attachments. Girls like Ariel, who has a boyfriend."

"But Tara doesn't have a boyfriend," Jack said.

"It doesn't have to be a boyfriend. The tether between a mother and a daughter could probably save a Forfeit just as easily." I pressed my lips together and shook my head. "Innocent people are going to die, all to make me queen."

Jack took me in his arms. "It's not your fault, Becks."

"Then why does it feel like my fault?" I stepped back, looked at the ground for a moment, took a deep breath, and raised my eyes to meet Jack's. "We've got to go find Ariel. Jules will take care of Tara, I think. Now we have to find Ariel and get her back together with Luke, who I'm sure never cheated on her. And then we have to find Brooke Chase, because she's going with Oliver. . . ."

"We have to find the girl he's homed in on and get her away from him. Then we have to watch them to see who they're going to go after next—"

"Becks," Jack interrupted.

"We have to." I looked away toward the mountain, blinking rapidly.

He put his hands on my shoulders and leaned down so we were eye to eye and I would have to look at him. "We can't do it all. Maybe we can save Tara and then Ariel, but what's to stop the Deads from going somewhere else and finding more girls?"

I sniffed. "You're right. There will always be more girls. Even after this, word will get out about how to survive a Feed, and there will be more innocent lives lost, and Everlivings will prey on ordinary human beings with all sorts of attachments and . . . and . . ." I grabbed my hair, pulling at it, and paced to the end of the parking lot, where I turned around. "We have to destroy it."

"What?"

I walked back to him. "We have to destroy the entire thing. It's the only way."

Jack dropped his hands. "No. We have to save you first. We have to focus on finding the cure for you."

"That's not as important."

Jack grabbed my shoulders again, strong enough to make me wince. "Don't you dare say that. Saving you is the *only* important thing."

Slowly I brought my hands up and placed them on either side of his face. "But I can't live with blood on my hands. I can't live knowing I'm the reason that girls like Tara and Ariel will become targets of the immortals. I can't. Saving me will mean nothing if more people die. The only way to save me . . . really save me . . . is to destroy the Everneath."

He closed his eyes and then hesitantly released his grip on my arms. "Okay. Then we destroy the Everneath."

EIGHT

NOW

The Surface. In Jack's car.

Jack and I dropped off Jules and Tara at Tara's house. Tara didn't say anything on the way, but Jules sat next to her and told her that everything would be okay. I wasn't sure if she believed us or if she thought we were all crazy, but regardless, Tara was safe for now. Jules was going to stay with her.

Once we were alone, Jack pulled over to the side of the road. He threw the car into park. I wasn't sure what he was doing.

He looked into my eyes. "We will try to take down the Everneath," he said.

I gave him a confused look. "I know."

"But promise me, Becks. Promise me it won't get in the way of keeping you alive. Promise you will do whatever it takes to survive."

"Why are you saying this?" I said.

"Because I can see the switch in your eyes. The second you

found out about the accelerated Feed, you went from survival to martyr mode."

"I'm not planning on martyring myself," I said, shaking my head.

"I know you," Jack said. "So here's the deal. You make it through this. You feed on Cole. We both make it to the other side of this. Okay?"

I nodded, knowing this was a promise that I couldn't guarantee, but also realizing that, at this moment, it was a promise I needed to make to Jack.

"I swear. I will."

Since it was nearly dinnertime, Jack dropped me off at my house. He wouldn't have left me alone, but it was Monday night, and my dad had this archaic rule that Monday nights were strictly reserved for family. Heaven help the telemarketer who dared interrupt family night.

That night my dad brought home Chinese takeout for dinner. I picked at the ham fried rice, anxious about where I was going tonight. Luckily, Tommy was excited about an extra-credit summer project for school for which he had to bake a cake in the shape of Utah and decorate the geography of it using brown sugar for the deserts and chocolate Kisses for the mountainous regions.

It was enough of a distraction that my father didn't notice I was preoccupied with something else, namely the fact that at midnight, Jack and I were going to Cole's condo so Cole could feed me. And tomorrow I was going to start my mission to blow up the Underworld.

But for now I had to focus on surviving a night with Jack watching while Cole fed me. Suddenly this feat seemed the more difficult of the two.

The Surface. My bedroom.

I climbed out my window and ran down the street to where Jack's car was parked. Jack was leaning against the driver's-side door, waiting for me. When he saw me, he opened the door wide.

I climbed in. "Have you been waiting long?"

"My entire life," he said.

I smiled. He used to say that all the time, that he had loved me ever since he'd known me, and until we got together he was just waiting. Then I would make a joke about how he spent his time waiting by dating everything in a skirt.

But I didn't make those jokes anymore.

We were quiet on the drive to Deer Valley. Jack's hold on the steering wheel was relaxed, and I wondered how many trees he had pummeled to reach this state of zen. I stayed quiet, not wanting to do anything to mess that up, especially by talking about what was going to happen tonight.

If I could feed off Cole without our lips touching . . .

If I could feed off Cole from across the room . . . even better.

From across the Earth . . . best.

I knew that what we were doing would save me, but I couldn't help feeling as if I were participating in a death march.

When we got there, we stood in front of the door for a while. It looked like it had been recently repaired. Jack looked at me and grabbed my hand.

"We'll be okay," he said.

I leaned toward him, and he put his arm around me. "Sometimes I actually believe it," I said.

"We will," he insisted. "We survive until we can strike."

He pulled me close. "Hold on to me. This storm will pass, and until then I'm leaning into the wind."

I settled into his chest, inhaling his clean-boy smell. "Are you going to be okay tonight? I mean, my lips have to get really close to his."

"It doesn't mean anything," Jack said. "Nothing will convince me it does."

Too soon, and before we had a chance to knock, the door swung open, and Cole stood in the threshold. He saw our embrace, and for a moment his confident smirk faltered, but he recovered quickly.

He looked at Jack. Took in the sheer size of him. "Damn, you're huge," he said. "I mean, I knew that would happen, but—"

"What do you mean?" I asked. "What *did* happen to him?"

Cole raised an eyebrow. "He climbed out of the Tunnels. The energy it took to do that was massive. Each inch would've been the equivalent of, I don't know, say a hundred weight-lifting sessions. So someone who was beefy before would become . . . extra beefy." He seemed suddenly bored with the explanation. "So, Nik," he said. "On to more exciting things than Jack's biceps. Where do you want to . . . *consummate—*"

Jack stepped in between us, effectively cutting Cole off. "Say 'consummate' again. Please." He clenched his fists, his knuckles turning white.

"Anywhere," I said. I reached for one of Jack's hands and urged it open, and then laced my fingers through his.

If he was this tense now, how would he last the night?

We followed Cole into the living room, and that was when I saw that we weren't alone. Gavin was there, on one of the chairs; and sitting next to him, running her fingers through his hair, was Ariel Hughes. Jules was right.

Yesterday she'd been head over heels for Luke, but tonight she was groping an immortal from the Underworld. She had no idea what she was getting into.

"Hi, Nikki," Gavin said. Ariel didn't even bother looking up from Gavin's neck.

"Hey, Gavin," I said. "I thought that latest STD test came back positive?" Ariel's head shot up. Good, I had her attention. I kept my eyes on Gavin. "I'm happy to be wrong, though."

Ariel pushed herself up off Gavin and stood there.

"It's not true," Gavin said, a disbelieving smile on his face.

"I've never even *been* tested."

"I'm out of here," Ariel said. She grabbed her purse and stalked past me and Jack and out the front door.

Gavin shot me a dirty look. "Thanks a lot, Nikki."

Cole's lips twitched, obviously amused at what had just happened.

"You'll find someone else," Cole said. He gestured for us to follow him. "Let's go to my room. Privacy."

The last place I wanted to go was Cole's bedroom, but no setting would make what was about to happen less awkward. Jack and I followed Cole down the hallway. As we walked in, I noticed there was still a giant hole in the wall where Jack had ripped the safe out.

"Don't worry," Cole said. "I'll cover the expenses."

He sat on the edge of his bed, but Jack and I stayed standing.

Crap. We were finally here, the moment I'd been dreading. Neither of us moved. I knew I needed to feed off Cole. I could feel it in my weak muscles; the exhaustion that had been building all day had reached all the way to my bones. I could only imagine how I'd have felt if a full day had gone by. And now that I was so close to getting energy, my body could no longer support itself.

"You'd better put your arm around her, Jack," Cole said.

Jack turned toward me, surprised. He hadn't realized I was sinking. He put his arm around my waist and held me up, and yet he made no move to help me get over to Cole. I tried to assemble my frayed thoughts enough to give Jack my speech about how this was the only way to keep me alive, but I couldn't get the pieces together to form the words.

"Look," Cole said, leveling his gaze on Jack. "I know you love her. I know what that looks like on a person. You would do anything for her. You want everything for her. And so do I. The problem is, we disagree on what her future should look like. But no matter which path she ends up on, she needs to survive the night. Right here. Right now. That's something we both can agree on, right?"

Jack frowned and closed his eyes. I couldn't believe it. Cole was making perfect sense, and he had said probably the one thing that would make Jack move.

Jack hesitated for just a moment and then helped me over to the bed. I collapsed next to Cole, unable to keep my eyes open.

"Just sleep, Becks," Jack said, running his fingers over my closed eyelids and down my cheeks "Sleep through the whole thing. I'll be here the entire time."

I couldn't have stayed awake if I'd tried.

SOPHOMORE YEAR
The Surface. Rock Garden Climbing Gym.

One blink. That was all it took, and suddenly I was somewhere else. A place I recognized. It was the cavernous inside of the

Rock Garden Climbing Gym. The cement floors matched the cement ceiling, and rock-climbing walls stood at different angles for all levels of climbers.

I'd been here once before, for a PE field trip sophomore year. I remembered it vividly because I had been dreading it. I'd always had a slight fear of heights, but the fresh loss of my mother had somehow increased the terror for me.

I remembered standing at the base of the beginner's wall, staring up the shallow slope as if it were the face of Mount Everest.

I turned toward the beginner's wall and saw a girl in black yoga pants and a green tank top with a negative photograph of the Beatles walking across Abbey Road on the front.

I knew that tank top. My dad had given it to me for my birthday. I was looking at . . . myself. But if that was me, then . . . I glanced down at the hands by my sides and saw black tattoos encircling each finger. These were Cole's hands. This was Cole's memory. I'd had no idea he'd been there that day, probably because I was so consumed by my fear.

He watched the memory-Nikki staring up at the top of the wall. The harness was attached to her waist, the rope strung through the pulley. Nate Pinnock, a junior, held the other end of the rope, ready to belay. He watched the frozen girl in the green tank top and rolled his eyes impatiently.

I could feel what Cole was feeling as he watched it all unfold. He couldn't tear his eyes away. He had to find out if the frozen girl would ever gather the courage to try.

Suddenly Jack appeared behind the memory-Nikki. Cole took a few steps toward them so he could hear what they were saying.

Jack placed his hands on her waist and put his lips to her ear.

"Don't look at the top, Becks. You don't have to figure out how to get way up there. You only have to figure out how to get here." He placed his hand on the foothold nearest her right foot. "Never focus on the end. Only focus on your first step."

She took a deep breath, unable to tear her eyes off the highest platform. "And then what?" the memory-Nikki whispered.

From Cole's perspective, I could see Jack's face. The way he closed his eyes as if my fears were his fears. The way he held memory-Nikki's waist as if he were holding something more precious than his own life.

He leaned closer to her. "Then you take the next step."

Nate waved the rope back and forth. "Please, give me something to do."

Jack turned and glared at Nate. Nate stopped moving the rope and sank a little lower against the floor.

Memory-Nikki hadn't even noticed Nate's impatience. She closed her eyes, took another deep breath, and whispered, "Just one step."

She stepped closer to the wall and placed her hands on the two nearest rocks; but when she went to lift her foot, Jack's hands at her waist got in her way. "Um, Jack?" she said.

"Yes?"

"Do your little bits of wisdom include a part about you actually having to let me go?"

He gave a wide smile and kissed her shoulder. "You take the first step, and I'll let go."

She turned her head slightly toward him. "You let go, and I'll take the first step."

He sighed, and with a reluctant expression that he kept hidden from her, he dropped his hands. She climbed.

Cole backed away, carrying a heaviness in his chest that I couldn't quite understand, but the only word that came to mind was *wistfulness*.

NOW

The Surface. Cole's bedroom.

I woke the next morning to hushed voices and the lingering images from the memory Cole had shared with me. I wondered if he could control what he did and didn't share; the more I thought about it, the more I believed Cole couldn't control them. He'd shared memories purposely before, such as his perspective on our first meeting at Harry O's club. But last night's memory . . . it showed our love. Mine and Jack's. I had a feeling he wouldn't have purposely shared it.

I didn't get much of a chance to focus on the memory, though. Jack's and Cole's voices began to cut through the sleep, and I listened in.

"There could be a place for you," Cole was saying. "Once she's queen, we'll make you an Everliving in the High Court. You two could be together forever."

Jack scoffed. "You'd stand aside and let us be together. Ruling the Underworld."

"Not ruling together," Cole said. "She and I would rule together. But there's no reason the two of you can't . . ."

I opened my eyes briefly just in time to see him wave his hands in a finish-the-sentence kind of way. I wasn't awake enough to actually finish it.

"I can't believe I'm having this conversation. It's all pointless," Jack said. "First off, I would never become an Everliving. But more importantly, when it comes down to it, Nikki will never feed on another human being. You may have your band, and whoever else you can recruit to your side, and maybe they'll feed on innocent girls to bulk up for battle. You might have all the other pieces in place, but Nikki will never do the Century Feed."

Never do the Century Feed. My eyelids fluttered open again as that phrase triggered a memory. Cole had once told me that one of the reasons he wanted to rule the Everneath was because it would mean he'd never have to do the hundred-year Feed again. His search for Forfeits would be over. His "subjects" would do it for him. The Everneath itself would provide all the sustenance he would need.

An important piece of Cole's puzzle had just popped into place in my head.

"That's part of his plan," I mumbled.

Cole and Jack turned toward me. Jack rushed to my side. "Becks, you're awake."

I tried to sit up, but my head felt like a balloon.

"Here," Jack said, handing me a cup of water. "Cole said it would be like you had an energy hangover."

He was right. I might be a little lightheaded, but I felt as if I could pummel a few trees myself.

I gulped the water, slammed down the cup, and wiped my lips. "Me refusing to feed is part of his plan."

Jack crinkled his eyebrows. "What?"

Cole's face was blank, but he didn't deny it.

"Because the queen doesn't have to feed." I shook my head. "All this time, you and I thought I had two choices. Century Feed on a Forfeit or die. Which would mean there's only one choice for me. To die. But Cole is giving us a third choice. If I become queen, I won't have to Century Feed. And I won't die."

I kept my eyes on Jack's face, and I saw it. The tiniest reflection of a smile.

And then I realized what I had just done. I had given Jack motive to make me queen. I frowned. "Don't even think it, Jack."

"What?" Jack said.

"I'm not becoming queen."

"Of course not, Becks."

But I could see it in his eyes. I could see it on his face.

"But . . . ?" I said, waiting for him to fill in the rest.

He shook his head. "But if it comes down to it, if it comes down to your life, then you becoming queen might buy us some time."

I closed my eyes, my breath caught in my throat.

Cole clapped.

I opened my eyes and narrowed them at him.

"I'm sorry," Cole said, obviously not sorry. "I just thought this monumental occasion, when Jack and I both agreed on your future, should be marked with some sort of applause."

I put my head in my hands. "This can't be happening."

"I don't agree with you," Jack growled. "I only want to keep her alive."

"Me too!" Cole said, excited. "I want to keep her alive forever and ever. Just like in the fairy tales. Happily ever after . . . forever!"

"Enough!" I said, standing. I held up a finger. "You two don't get to decide. I've made my decision. Listen closely. I. Won't. Do. It." I took a step closer to both of them and enunciated my next word carefully. "Ever."

With that, I stormed out of the condo.

Jack chased me down the stairs and across the parking lot. When I reached his car, I turned on him, and he nearly ran into me.

I shoved my hand into his chest. "You do *not* get to decide how I stay alive!"

"I know. I know." He took my hand off his chest and pulled me close. "I'm with you. You will *never* be queen. We'll destroy the Everneath."

"But . . ." My lower lip trembled against his shirt. "But what you said—"

"Cole doesn't need to know how I really feel now, does he?"

I tilted my head back to look at him. "You mean . . ."

He shrugged. "I'd say Cole's feeling pretty confident right now. He thinks that if it came down to it, I'd try my best to force you to become queen rather than see you die. If we're going to destroy the Underworld, we need him believing he has the upper hand. Don't you think?"

I let out a giant sigh of relief and leaned my head all the way back, letting the morning sun shine full on my face.

"I thought I'd lost you in there," I said.

Jack pressed his lips against my forehead. "Never," he said. I nodded, and we got into the car. Before he started it, though, he opened his phone and checked his email. Once the most recent ones loaded, he smiled.

"What is it?" I asked.

"Professor Spears," he said.

"What?"

"I've been emailing him every day, hoping to convince him it wasn't all one big joke. I didn't want to tell you because I didn't want to get your hopes up. But early this morning he said he'd found something that might help us. I asked to meet with him, and he just said yes."

I threw my arms around Jack's neck.

"It might not be anything," Jack said.

"I don't care. It's hope."

NINE

NOW

The Surface. Parley's Canyon.

On the drive down Parley's Canyon, I told Jack about the rock-climbing memory that Cole had leaked to me during the Feed.

"I remember that day," Jack said. "But I can't believe Cole was there. You'd think we would've noticed the Dead Elvises' lead singer just hanging out in the corner of the gym."

I shrugged. "Maybe he was there in his Neal form." I tried to remember if he had the same tattoos on his fingers in his Neal form that he had in his Cole form.

"The question is, why was he there in the first place? Did he follow you there?"

I shrugged. "I don't know. The rock-climbing field trip was right after I'd met him."

"He was obsessed from the start."

I stared out the window. Considering how Cole had felt

during that memory, I realized that Jack was probably right.

We were mostly quiet for the rest of the drive to the university campus. My dad was going to give me a lecture if he found out I was already missing my Creative Writing class, but it couldn't be helped. Once we reached his office, Professor Spears ushered us inside.

"Do you have the documents?" he said by way of greeting.

I turned to Jack, my eyebrows raised. He dug into his backpack, pulled out a manila folder, and placed it on the professor's desk. The professor opened it. Inside was the most ancient-looking page from Mrs. Jenkins's collection of documents, the page we never could translate. I didn't know he'd had it with him. He shrugged. "I wanted to encourage him to hurry, so I scanned the page and emailed it to him. Told him he could see the original if he helped us."

The professor lifted the folder and brought the page closer to his face, careful not to touch it with his fingers. I didn't bother telling him we'd already left our prints all over it.

"It's incredible," he said, holding it under the light on his desk.

Jack stepped forward. "You said you had something for us?"

The professor kept his eyes on the page when he answered. "After you left my office last time, I decided to contact my colleague, Professor Frank Sheldon. He's sort of an Akh ghost aficionado."

I remembered that "Akh ghost" was the term the professor had used before to refer to an Everliving.

"Frank said he had gathered numerous articles and documents. Made notes on the world of the Akh ghosts. He gave me this." The professor opened the bottom right drawer of his desk and pulled out a large, leather-bound journal of sorts. "All the research Frank's ever done." He gingerly flipped through the pages, some of which were completely covered in scratchy writing, others with articles and drawings taped on them. Some showed hastily drawn figures and maps. Some had symbols like the ones on the bracelet Meredith had left me: the five parts of the human soul, as the Egyptians saw it.

And it was all in English.

"Frank says this is the bible of the Akh universe. I went through it. All of it. I decided this would be a diverting exercise in hypotheticals. So, kids, you brought me the ancient text. What can I help you with?"

I looked at Jack. His mouth hung open for a moment. Then he shut it. Then opened it again.

I leaned forward. "Does that book"—I rested my hand on the open journal—"give you a good idea as to what their world looks like? Its structure? Its strengths? Its weaknesses?"

The professor narrowed his eyes. "Yes. Why?"

"Because I . . . *we* . . . want to destroy it."

He looked from me to Jack and then to me again. "Destroy what?"

"The Underworld," I said. "The whole thing."

A few long moments later. Professor Spears's office.

"You want to destroy the Underworld," Professor Spears repeated. He spoke as if he couldn't understand the words coming out of his mouth.

"It's called the Everneath," I said.

He ignored me. "Why?"

"Are we still talking in hypotheticals?" Jack asked.

The professor nodded.

"Then, hypothetically, destroying the Everneath will save lives. Nikki's included."

The professor glanced at me. "What's wrong with Nikki?"

Jack leaned forward. "I'm going to stop saying the word 'hypothetical,' just to make things easy. Nikki is halfway to becoming an Akh ghost. We want to save her first and foremost." I glanced at him sideways, but he ignored me. "Then we want to destroy the Everneath. So please, Professor Spears, tell us what you know about the Underworld."

The professor looked from Jack to me. "Seriously?"

"We brought you what you wanted," Jack said.

"I know, I know." The professor walked over to the whiteboard on the wall and used the sleeve of his tweed jacket to wipe it down. He popped the lid on a dry-erase marker and proceeded to write.

He waved the marker around as he began to explain.

"Let's talk logistics. The Everneath has a few distinct things that hold its shape." He drew three concentric circles. "The first is the boundary between the Everneath and the Surface. The membrane between the two worlds. The pressure of the energy inside is part of what holds the membrane together."

My face must have looked even more blank, because once he had taken in my expression, he waved his hand as if he were wiping an imaginary blackboard in front of him.

"Imagine a balloon. Now when it's deflated, the latex doesn't hold any particular shape. But inflated with air, the balloon takes on a three-dimensional shape, held in place by the pressure inside. It's the same thing with the Everneath. All the energy inside is what gives the world its shape. It's also why there are only a few entrances. You wouldn't want to poke too many holes in a balloon, right?"

I nodded.

He got a small smile on his face and shook his head, as if he still couldn't believe we were talking about this.

"Any attempt to destroy the Everneath would have to take into account destroying the membrane."

"How do we do that?" I asked.

He frowned. "I have no idea." He wrote the number one on the whiteboard and then wrote the word *membrane* beside it.

He let that sink in for a moment. I glanced at Jack, who stared at the board. "So, if we figure out a way to destroy the membrane—"

"Oh, I'm not done," the professor interrupted. "That's just the first obstacle. The second obstacle would be beings known as the Shades. Have you heard of them?"

I rolled my eyes. "Yes."

"What about them?" Jack asked.

"They're connected. Every single Shade is connected to every other Shade, creating a web of . . . power. So imagine our balloon, and then imagine a web-like fibrous layer inside the latex, basically there to make it stronger. Almost like chain mail under the armor of a knight."

I sighed. "A chain mail balloon?" Maybe we should've come up with a different analogy than a balloon. A balloon seemed so . . . poppable.

The professor wrote the number two on the board, followed by the words *Shades connected*.

"You said there were three things holding it together?" Jack said.

The professor nodded. "I saved the most important one for last. Every Everliving has a Surface heart and an Everneath heart. Does this sound familiar?"

Jack and I both nodded.

"Again, all these hearts are connected. To destroy the Everneath, every heart would need to be destroyed."

He wrote the number three, followed by the words *destroy every heart*.

I looked at Jack. "I think I remember Cole telling me the Everneath hearts are kept hidden in the High Court."

"That may be true," the professor said. "But according to

this"—he patted the journal—"the problem would be with the other hearts. The Surface hearts. The ones every single Ever-living has on him or her at all times."

Jack leaned back in his chair as what the professor was saying sank in. "Shit." He shook his head. "How could we possibly get hold of every single heart?"

"We can't," I said. I closed my eyes and put my head in my hands. "We can't. He's basically saying it's impossible."

Jack pried one of my hands away from my face. "Look at me." I kept my eyes squeezed shut and shook my head. "Becks, look at me."

I raised my head.

"It's not impossible. This Underworld shouldn't exist in the first place. It's an anomaly. Against nature. Which means it's not meant to be here, and that makes it vulnerable." He walked over to the board and pointed to the outermost circle the professor had drawn. "We'll focus our energy on weakening the Shade network and the membrane. By then, hopefully, we'll have figured out a way to get the hearts."

I closed my eyes as I realized what he was saying. "We'd have to destroy my hearts." I turned to the professor. "What would happen then? I'd be human, right?"

"I don't know," he said, still looking stunned at our discussion.

I thought back to the story of how Cole had become an Everliving. "Cole once told me that breaking both of his hearts would kill him. But he just meant that it would make him mortal again. Because the woman who turned Cole—Gynna—she turned him so she could use his heart to trade for her own, so she could break both of her hearts. And become human again. Breaking both hearts should just mean that I would become human again."

Human again. Fully human again. I didn't want to let myself hope that one day soon I could leave the Everneath behind. It seemed too much to wish for, especially considering that Cole was guarding my Surface heart, and my Everneath heart was tucked away in a vault somewhere in the Underworld.

"You're only halfway to becoming an Everliving," Jack said. "What if that means you only have one of your hearts? What if you get your Everneath heart when you Century Feed the first time?"

We looked toward the professor, but he just shrugged.

"I still think we should try to break your compass," Jack said.

The professor tilted his head.

"It's her heart. It's in the shape of a compass," Jack explained.

"We don't know if that would cure me," I said, not caring anymore if the professor thought we were lying. "No, we have to destroy it."

"Hypothetically," the professor whispered, as if that word didn't mean what he thought it meant anymore. "When are you two planning on starting this . . . Everneath coup?"

"As soon as possible. Becks only has until the shackle on

her other wrist appears. Then she'll have to Century Feed or she'll die. She's got anywhere from a few days to a week."

The professor raised his eyebrows. "You have a few days to a week, maybe, to weaken the membrane, undo the Shade network, and find and destroy every Everliving heart?"

Jack nodded. "That's the plan."

The professor scratched the back of his head. "Hypothetically, I don't think that's enough time."

Jack clasped my hand. "It has to be."

After our meeting, Jack rushed me back up the canyon and straight to school so I could make it in time for the last half of Creative Writing. We didn't want Cole to know we were up to anything, which was the only reason I was going to class. On the way, we discussed the meeting with the professor.

"I think we should tackle the easier stuff first," I said. I couldn't believe I was referring to the task of figuring out the bond holding the Shades together and then destroying it as the "easier stuff," but I knew it would be nothing compared to rounding up thousands and thousands of hearts.

"What do you suggest?" Jack said.

"I say we go down to the Everneath. Rustle up a few Shades. You can beat the crap out of them until they tell us how they're bound together."

Jack raised an eyebrow. "'Rustle up a few Shades'? Get them to talk? From what I remember, they don't talk. Except to each other."

"I know, I know. My point is, I think any real information about the Everneath will be found *in* the Everneath. And now that I'm half Everliving, I wouldn't be leaking energy out everywhere like I did last time, which means I could go unnoticed."

"What about me?"

I shrugged and then softly said, "Maybe I should go alone."

He slammed on the brakes—not a very safe move, considering that we were on the freeway.

"Hell, no. As in it will rain fire before I let you do that. As in the sun will rise in the west before that happens."

"Okay, okay."

"The NFL will commission the use of Nerf balls."

"Okay! It was just a suggestion. We will go together. And maybe I can absorb any excess energy you have, just like Cole did for me."

"Maybe I don't have any excess energy after my months in the Tunnels."

I thought about it. They did drain him so dry. . . . What was I thinking? He was so full of emotions right now. But maybe I could absorb his extra energy. Even if I couldn't feed on him on the Surface, maybe I could in the Everneath.

It was reckless what we were talking about doing. The Everneath was not a place to visit without a lot of planning, but our frame of mind had shifted. We were going up against the Everneath. We were talking about destroying a world. Each step along the way would have to be reckless. If it wasn't, we weren't taking the right step.

"We need to get one of Cole's hairs," I said. Jack raised an eyebrow. "I don't have my Surface heart. I can't move between worlds on my own without it."

Jack sighed. "When are you going to do it?"

"In class."

Jack took a deep breath in. "So soon?"

"We don't know how long we have, but it's not long. Is there a better time?"

There was no argument from him. And why would there be? We were out of time from the moment we began.

As he pulled up in the school's roundabout, he opened the door and said, "Remember, don't let on to Cole."

I couldn't help a smile. "I won't," I said. "That's like the only thing on my mind. If I forgot that, we'd have bigger problems, namely that my brain was broken or something."

I stepped out of the car. Jack grabbed my hand. "How are you feeling?"

"Fine, right now." Though according to Cole, by tonight I would be weak again.

"Good." He let go of my hand. "Now, go get that hair."

I raised my eyebrows. "In what will forever be the strangest send-off ever spoken . . ."

He gave a laugh as I slammed the door shut behind me and waved.

Maybe this would be easy. Everybody sheds hair at school, right? Maybe there would be a little blond hair just sitting there on Cole's desk, waiting for someone to reach over and grab it, only it would be a dark hair because he would be there disguised as Neal. Would that disguise reach all the way to the hairs that fell out of his head? Would they turn blond as they made their way to the ground? I couldn't think of a reason why they wouldn't work the same as Cole's blond hair, but I never got the chance to find out. When I got to Mrs. Stone's class, the seat where Cole had sat the day before was empty.

Mrs. Stone paused whatever she was reading. "Miss Beckett? I hope this isn't the start of a bad habit."

I shook my head, scanning the rest of the classroom, looking for Cole. But he was most definitely not in class.

"Are you going to join us?" Mrs. Stone said.

I thought about answering honestly. *No, because if I can't pluck a hair off Cole's head, what's the point of summer school?* "Um, I'm not feeling well. I'll be here tomorrow," I said, and turned around and left before she could say anything else.

I ran out of the school and met Jack outside.

"That was fast," he said as I climbed into his car.

"He wasn't there." I shut the door. "It's inconvenient, but I can get a hair tonight when he feeds me." I tried not to sound worried, but Jack pressed his lips together.

"He was probably in school yesterday only so he could give me the bad news about feeding on him every night. Now that he's delivered it, there's really no reason for him to be here at all."

Jack nodded. "I know. But it seems like he would take every opportunity to be with you, especially without me."

"We'll get it tonight."

We spent the rest of the day throwing out other ideas for our next step, but everything came back to getting to the Everneath, and whereas last night I was dreading meeting up with Cole, tonight I couldn't wait to see him.

It wouldn't be the first time I'd stolen a hair from Cole, and since he was always one step ahead of us, I worried that he would see it coming. So after dinner, when Jack and I were in my room, I made a suggestion.

"I think I should go to Cole's alone tonight."

Jack was sitting at my desk, thumbing through Mrs. Jenkins's papers for the thousandth time. When he heard my suggestion, he froze.

"Hear me out," I said. "Cole has an annoying habit of anticipating our next moves. He always guesses what we're going to do. If I go alone, and if we pretend we're still fighting about whether I should take the throne to save my life—then don't you think he'll be more confident?"

"I think you're overthinking this."

I clasped my hands together and sat on the edge of my bed, across from his chair. "I'm thinking that every step of the way, we can't blow any chance to get it right. We might not get another one. And I want to increase our odds any way I can. I think it would be best if we looked like we needed some space from each other. For a night. I'd rather overthink than underthink."

He frowned. "I don't like this."

"Of course you don't like this. I'm going to spend the night with Cole. Nobody likes this. Well, except Cole. But when I wake up with new energy tomorrow, I want to be able to grab a hair and run without a fight. Take him completely by surprise. I don't want him on edge because you're there. I want him to feel safe enough to close his eyes. I want him comfortable and pliant."

He nodded. "I see what you're saying, but—"

"You saw how it went last night. I slept through the entire thing. Easy peasy. I'll just drive there, go inside, feed, grab the hair, and get out. We'll meet up in the morning."

Jack smiled. "You have your stubborn face on."

I put my hand up to my cheek. "I don't know about that. It feels like my 'clarity of thought' face."

He took a deep breath. "Okay. But you are in my arms until the moment you leave."

"And in them again the moment I get back," I said.

For the next few hours I dozed off and on against Jack's shoulder. At eleven thirty, I kissed his cheek. "See you early in the morning. And get ready, because we're taking a trip to the Underworld."

Jack smiled. "It's a date."

I scooched out of bed, but when I stood upright, I had to hold the bedpost to steady myself.

Jack shot up next to me. "You okay?"

"Mm-hmm," I said. "Just a little wobbly. Nothing a little energy won't fix."

"Let me drive you."

"I'm fine. Really."

I grabbed my car keys, and we both climbed out the window. Jack walked me to my car, kissing me as if he'd never see me again.

The lights were off at Cole's place. I'd been there before when the lights were off, but usually there was some light coming from somewhere. I scanned the balcony from where I'd parked my car and figured out why it looked so much darker. The porch light outside his front door was off, which was strange because it usually went on automatically in the dark.

It had probably just burned out.

Still, I climbed the outside stairs on my tiptoes, an unexplainable chill running down my back. It wasn't until I got close to the front door that I knew something was wrong. The door was ajar, the newly repaired lock smashed.

I turned around and ran into the chest of a tall man.

"'Scuse me, I—" My voice cut off when I saw his face. Black eyes. Cracked lips smiling around a black hole of a mouth.

I shuddered. It was the man from the other night.

But this time there was nowhere to run.

I tried to scream, but he clamped a large hand over my mouth, spun me so I was facing away from him, and wrapped his other arm across my chest. He began to drag me toward the stairs. I kicked against the cement, flailing against him. It didn't do any good. Each failed attempt drained me of more energy, as if I had only one good kick left in each leg.

I opened my mouth and chomped down hard on one of his fingers, but he didn't even flinch.

I couldn't breathe with his hand over my mouth. I clawed against the arm across my chest, but he had me by at least a hundred pounds.

Air. I needed air.

I raised my hands above my head and tried to claw at his face, aiming for where his eyeballs should be; but everything around me was getting darker, and whatever energy I'd come there with was now gone.

I went limp in his arms. He didn't even break stride.

TEN

NOW

The Surface. Outside Cole's condo.

My feet smacked against every step as he hauled me down the stairs. I gave a feeble push against the cement, hoping to throw him off balance, but my strength was gone. I wasn't sure I even moved my feet.

When he reached the bottom, he kicked the metal door open and took a couple of steps outside, and then I heard the sound of glass shattering.

His arm across my chest loosened, but only for a moment.

Another sound, this time like a fist making contact with a face.

His grip loosened just enough for me to slip out and down to the ground. Strong hands lifted me up.

"Becks! Can you hear me?" I opened my eyes to see Jack's face, but it was only for a split second. The man with the black eyes grabbed him from behind, forcing him to let me go.

I sank to the ground again. The man was almost as tall as

Jack, and just as thick. I couldn't believe he was still standing, considering Jack had smashed something over his head.

Jack punched him in the face. The man stumbled back a few steps and then lunged at Jack, who anticipated the move and stepped to the side just in time. The man went past him, and Jack kicked him in his back as he went. This time he didn't let up. He threw punches again and again until finally the man fell backward.

Jack rushed to my side.

"Becks. Are you hurt?"

I shook my head. At least I thought I shook my head. I had no energy left. Jack crouched down next to me, and that was when I saw the dark shadow of the man stagger up off the ground.

"Behind you," I whispered.

Jack turned and kicked the man away before he had a chance to stand up fully. Then he wasted no time. He gathered me in his arms and took off.

I closed my eyes and let the darkness close in around me.

Intense sunlight urged my eyelids open. Too intense for morning. I blinked back the haze, and when my eyes focused, I saw Jack's face.

He was sitting on the edge of my bed, and he was so pale it looked as if he hadn't slept in a week.

"Becks," he said, his voice cracking. "You came back to me."

"I didn't go anywhere," I said. Then I thought about the

sunlight. "What time is it?"

"Four o'clock. You've been out for more than fifteen hours."

I tried to sit up but lost any arm strength halfway through the motion. Jack helped me the rest of the way.

"Why didn't you wake me up?"

He grimaced. "I tried. Every hour. I even splashed your face with cold water."

He gestured toward my nightstand, where there was a nearly empty bowl and small puddles of water everywhere. "It didn't work."

I realized I wasn't sitting up on my own; I was propped up against Jack. If he let me go, I'd fall back on the bed.

"What's wrong with me?"

Jack closed his eyes for a few long moments and then opened them again. "You missed a Feed."

My breathing became rapid. "We have to find Cole."

"I know."

"Where do you think he is?"

"I don't know."

"Where's my dad?"

Jack nodded toward the door. "He left a note this morning saying he had an early meeting. It's a good thing, too, because if he had seen your face . . ."

My hand flew up to my cheek. "What's wrong with it?"

"Nothing. It's just, you have the dark circles again. And you look like . . . Well, it's just a good thing he didn't see you."

He ran his hand through his hair. "You're black and blue." He glanced down at my arms. "Look. It's the same on your arms."

I followed his gaze. The skin looked almost translucent, with purple and blue patches starting near my wrist line. They grew denser as they traveled upward to my biceps.

Jack touched my inner arm, just below the elbow, and the skin reacted like water-soaked paper, as if it were on the verge of falling apart.

The sight of it made bile creep up my throat. I looked as if I were wearing someone else's skin.

"I thought about taking you to the hospital, calling 911, anything. But I knew they'd check for a heartbeat first. . . ."

"They can't do anything to help me."

The events of last night came crashing back into my head. The man with the black eyes and mouth who wouldn't stay down after a severe beating. The lights out at Cole's place. The front door that looked as if it had been kicked in.

"We have to go to Cole's. What if he's been . . . ?" I couldn't finish the sentence.

Jack's face was grim. "I know. Now that you're awake, we'll go."

"Together."

He tightened his embrace. "Do you think I'm ever going to let you out of my sight again?"

With those words, I sighed and melted into his chest for a moment.

Jack didn't put voice to the consequences if we couldn't

find Cole. We both got out of bed, though Jack moved much faster than I could. My yoga pants and hoodie were hugging my body before I knew it, and I realized that Jack was ushering me around the room, pulling things out of drawers, dressing me. Spinning circles around me.

Frantic.

But everything for me was moving slower. I started to tell Jack he didn't need to go so fast, but it took several seconds at least for my brain to send the message to my mouth. Jack bounced around the room like a movie on fast-forward.

"Jack . . . ," I said, wanting to warn him that my muscles weren't working properly, and definitely not when I wanted them to.

"I know, Becks. I can see it. I'll help."

His words spilled out of his mouth like tiny pieces of paper in front of an industrial fan. I had to concentrate hard to understand them as they tumbled to the ground.

"Ready?" he asked.

I tried to smile, but the way things were going, it wouldn't show up until sometime next week.

He pulled me tight against him, and with congruent movements, we were out the door, my backpack perched on Jack's shoulder.

The house seemed to melt away behind us, swirling in a colorful mass as we sped away in Jack's car. The vibration from the acceleration rattled my teeth, and I gripped the door handle to steady myself.

Jack's eyes were hard brown circles bouncing back and forth between my face and the road in front of us.

His fingers gripped the steering wheel so tightly that I worried he'd rip the whole thing off.

In a deliberate move, I raised my hand and placed it limply over his fingertips.

"Don't break . . . ," I said, quicker than I realized I could but still unable to finish my sentence.

He smiled sadly at me. "I'm trying not to."

Of course my words reached deeper than mere concern over the steering wheel. Right now, we were doing everything we could not to splinter our souls. Again.

We made it to Cole's, with Jack only running two and a half red lights. Half because he swore it was still yellow. Not that I had the capacity to call him on it, but he knew what I'd been thinking.

Jack pulled into the handicapped parking stall closest to the stairwell. I almost expected him to dive over the hood of the car to get to me, but he didn't. Barely.

He threw my door open, then gently, but quickly, scooped me up in his arms.

"Faster this way," he said.

He was strong. I mean, I'd known it all along; but feeling his strength as he ran up the steps with me in his arms, it was unearthly. My bulk was nothing to him. He gracefully skipped the top three steps, bounded smoothly down the hall and around the first corner.

He stopped only for a moment to peek around the corner and make sure there weren't any more black-eyed crazy people. When he seemed sure the coast was clear, he took us to the door.

I raised my head from its cushion against his chest and followed his gaze. The door to Cole's condo still lay ajar. Wooden splinters jutted out in all directions where the lock had once been.

Jack set me down, his eyes looking right and left, cautiously. I took a step toward the door; and with an exasperated grunt, Jack picked me up again, turned around, and placed me behind him, as if he were moving a fragile piece of art out of the way of a wrecking ball.

"Stay behind me, Becks." His eyes burned.

I took in a deep breath. The man who had broken in had to have been someone from the Everneath, but what kind of someone? Everlivings didn't have black eyes, and he wasn't a Shade or a Wanderer. What if he was still here? What if he wasn't alone? Jack took care of him, but he had taken a good beating and was still coming after us. If he had had a friend last night . . .

I shook my head violently, but it came off as a mild tilt. Jack still knew what I meant. His lips quirked up.

"I can take care of anything waiting for me in there. But you *will* stay safe."

Jack crept toward the door and stepped lightly over the threshold. Despite his size, Jack could move like a cat. It's what made him a good quarterback.

He disappeared into the condo, and the moment he was gone, the hairs on my arms stood on end. Something dark in the shadows of the courtyard caught my eye; but when I turned to look, I couldn't see anything unusual. Except that the shadows themselves seemed to be bigger and blacker than they should.

Was it the direction of the sun that made the shadows feel so out of place? I squinted, still seeing nothing. Maybe it was the state of Cole's condo, but my stomach twisted with the feeling that we weren't alone.

We were being watched.

Jack shouldn't have left me outside by myself. At this moment I believed any danger here was no longer inside Cole's apartment. It was outside.

With a final glance toward th   shadows in the northeast corner of the co   ide the condo after Jack. When I s   . Chunks of what had once been   ll over the floor. Someone had bro   e or six pieces. Whoever it was ha   ooking for something. But what could   for that was small enough to fit in the leg of a co   able?

Nothing longer than a foot in length was left intact. Whoever had been here left no object untouched.

"Becks!" Jack stood in the hallway that led toward the bedrooms. "I told you to stay outside."

I couldn't put into words the sudden fear that had washed over me in the courtyard, so I took a few shaky steps and buried myself in Jack's chest. What I wanted to say was that I'd just gotten him back, and I couldn't lose him again. We'd promised each other we wouldn't be apart.

As if he could hear my thoughts, Jack wrapped his arms around me. "Okay, okay. There's nothing here anyway."

I realized he was whispering, and his eyes darted back and forth as if he were expecting something to jump out of the shadows.

He held my face, simultaneously brushing some strands of hair out of my eyes. "The band's not here. And whoever trashed this place didn't hold back." Jack grabbed my hand and navigated us through the carnage of the living room and out the door.

"What were they . . . ?" I couldn't finish the question, but Jack did.

"What were they looking for? I have no idea. I didn't see anything that could give me a clue. Everything was destroyed. Even the clock on the nightstand. It was shattered." He sighed. "Whoever was here did a thorough job, and they probably got what they came for. There wasn't one square inch left untouched."

Thorough job. Not a square inch left undisturbed. If the intruders had actually found what they were looking for, wouldn't they have stopped searching at that point? Which would mean that unless they'd found it in the last place available, there would be at least one corner of the condo untouched.

Jack seemed to reach the conclusion at the same time I did. "They didn't find it, did they? Whatever it was they were looking for?"

I shook my head and stumbled over the threshold of the door, hitting the ground before I had a chance to right myself. Jack swept me into his arms again. He set me down gently on the floor.

"I'm going to look for a stray hair of Cole's. Just in case."

He left me for a few long moments, which could have lasted seconds or hours, and then returned.

"What do they do? Scrub the place down every time they leave?" He sighed. "I didn't find any stray hairs. Let's get you out of here."

He carried me down to his car, opened the door for me, and gently placed me inside. He buckled me in, and I weakly rolled my eyes at the gesture.

"Hey, I'm not going to defeat the Underworld only to lose you in a car accident." He got in on the driver's side and started the ignition. I shivered, and he switched on the heater. He kept the car in park and shook his head. "Cole's place . . . it's the level of destruction that has me confused. I'd sooner believe someone had a vendetta against him and just wanted to trash the place instead of someone looking for something. I mean, what would Cole have that's valuable but small enough to hide in an alarm clock?"

Something valuable. Something small. Everlivings didn't place very much value on Surface things, such as money or diamonds; but Surface things weren't the only small things of value.

I'd seen Cole protect one small thing in his life. So had Jack. His eyes narrowed, and he became as still as a statue.

I managed one word. "Hearts."

"Everliving hearts," he said. "Cole's heart is a pick. Max's is—what did you tell me? A guitar string?"

I nodded.

"But why would anyone go after their hearts? I mean, why now?"

Jack had a point. The only time I'd heard of conflict or fighting among the Everlivings was at the hands of the queen. Or when someone was trying to take over the throne.

I closed my eyes. Is that what this was about? Did someone find out what Cole had planned? Did someone find out that I had survived the Feed?

"Jack."

"What?"

I took a deep breath and put together two sentences. "What if they weren't looking for Cole's heart? What if they were looking for mine?"

Jack's mouth went slack. His eyes got a manic look.

I gathered the energy to speak. Energy I didn't have. But the words still came. "Don't worry," I said. "Cole said they kept my identity a secret. He made sure there wasn't any connection in the Everneath between him and me."

"But people on the Surface know you're connected to the Dead Elvises," he said, bitterness lacing his voice.

"But most other Everlivings don't know about the Deads." Cole had told me they made sure they spent most of their time up on the Surface. "He wanted to stay anonymous."

"Obviously it's not working!" Jack snapped. "Someone found him. It's only a matter of time before they find you too."

Jack took his eyes off the steering wheel and glanced at me as if to say more; but seeing my face, his stony expression immediately softened.

"Sorry, Becks."

"It's okay," I said quietly. "You're right. Of course you're right. Someone has found Cole."

And with those words, I put voice to the very thing we were most scared of. Cole was gone. My salvation, my lifeline, had disappeared; and if we didn't find him by tonight, or sooner, I would probably die.

Jack grabbed my hand and brought my fingers to his lips.

"I'm not going to let that happen, Becks."

"But what if we don't find him?" I said the words before I could stop them, an audible desperation in my voice.

Jack didn't answer right away. I turned his hand over and caressed the lines, the calluses, the knuckles . . . skin to skin. I'd been close to death before, and it always amazed me how there was a moment of realization when all the extraneous things melted away and my awareness became only about simple things. The details of Jack's skin. The sound of his breath. The way Jack's lips bent around his words.

These were the things that transcended death. These were the things I was sure the real afterlife was made of.

But was I ready to find out if I was right?

No. I was ready to fight for life. My own, and the countless future Forfeits who would succumb to the Tunnels if we didn't destroy the place.

"We'll find him," I said.

"We will," Jack said. "We'll look everywhere. We'll find him."

"And if we don't, we'll go all Thelma and Louise and drive off a cliff together."

He didn't even smile. In fact, he frowned. And then nodded. "Let's just make sure it doesn't come to that."

ELEVEN

NOW

The Surface. Searching for Cole.

Jack drove all around Park City as we tried to remember all the places we'd seen Cole before. He stopped by Harry O's and bounded up the steps, but returned to the car shaking his head. We went to the Dead Goat Saloon, but nobody there knew anything about the whereabouts of the band. We tried the usual blogs that always seemed to have the pulse of the Deads, but there was no news.

"Give me your phone," Jack said once he was back in the car. "We'll call him again."

I handed it over, knowing no one would answer. When the silence confirmed my suspicion, he handed it back to me. "Text Jules," he said. "Just to make sure Cole wasn't in class today."

I raised my eyebrows. "He disappears last night, his apartment is ransacked, but he shows up for school?"

"We have to check everything."

I nodded and typed in the text to Jules. She responded

moments later. No, Neal hadn't been in class.

Jack pulled over to the side of the road and looked at me with a resolute expression.

"Can you think of anywhere we can look?"

"The Everneath," I said.

"We can't get there without a hair."

"Maybe we don't need a hair of Cole's. I'm half Everliving. Maybe if you eat one of my hairs . . ."

Jack nodded and put the car in drive, turning toward the Shop-n-Go.

When he pulled into the parking lot of the convenience store, my heart sank. The lights were off, and a black-and-red CLOSED sign hung on the inside of the door.

"It's never closed," I said. "It's open twenty-four hours a day."

Jack turned into a parking place and shut off the ignition. "Let's go in anyway."

"How?"

He held up his fists. "These babies."

Apparently he wasn't joking, because he got out of the car. I followed him. With two shoves of his shoulder, he forced the door open.

"Quick," he said, taking my hand.

Jack ran, and I stumbled, to the back, to the spot where I'd ingested Cole's hair before to get to the Everneath. The place where I'd first seen that sad woman sink through the floor.

Jack took my hand. "Try it on your own first."

"I don't know what to try," I said. I closed my eyes and pictured the two of us sinking below the ground.

When I'd eaten Cole's hair before, I'd felt an immediate, distinct pull. Same with when I'd grabbed Cole's hand and he'd taken us both under.

Right now there was no pull. There was nothing except our feet standing on the hard industrial-tile floor.

"It's not working," I said.

Jack engulfed me in his arms, and I rested my head on his shoulder. "Just relax," he said. "Think of the Ring of Earth. Think of the streets of Ouros. Imagine yourself there, with me."

I did as he instructed, picturing the tall gray wall that surrounded the Ouros Common, remembering the mad dash we'd made through the alleyways when Cole, Ashe, Max, and I were trying to get to the labyrinth.

I willed there to be a pull at my feet. But there wasn't.

I imagined the sound of the thousands of Everlivings cheering in the central square at Ouros while the queen ordered Shades to vaporize a line of criminals.

But I heard nothing except the sound of sirens. "The police are coming," Jack said.

I opened my eyes and plucked out a strand of my hair. "Eat it," I said.

He took the hair, placed it on his tongue, and swallowed purposefully. His grip around my hand tightened.

I held my breath, but nothing happened. The sirens got louder.

"It's not going to work," Jack said. He rubbed his forehead, frustrated, and then lifted me in his arms and ran out of the store. We drove out of the parking lot just as the first squad car came around the corner.

The sudden burst of adrenaline was gone, and now my hands lay limp in my lap. Jack steered the car over a speed bump. The jolt whipped my head back and then forward. If I'd had any energy, I would've been able to resist it, but I had nothing left in me.

"Sorry," Jack said. He pulled the car over.

Cole had said I couldn't go a day without feeding on him. I was beginning to feel the truth of those words. I felt it from my spaghetti muscles to my brittle bones.

"What are we going to do?" I said.

"Hospital." It wasn't a question.

"You know they can't help." I didn't want to spend my last moments—if these were my last moments—in a hospital gown with doctors running pointless tests and turning over rocks looking for stray hearts.

Jack closed his eyes and sighed. "Can you think of anywhere else he would be? Has he ever mentioned any hiding places? Anything?"

For the first time, Jack's voice cracked almost beyond recognition. I raised my hand to his face and ran my fingertips down his cheek. A single teardrop followed the trail I'd just traced.

I racked my brain trying to remember any old haunts of Cole's. But the band traveled around so much that whenever they were in town, they were either playing a concert or they were in their condo.

I looked at Jack and shook my head. Just then my phone buzzed. Jack grabbed it out of my bag, his eyes wide with hope.

"Is it Cole?" I said.

Jack's face fell. "No. It's Jules. She wants to know if you're feeling better. I told her you weren't in class because you were sick."

Jack set down the phone and looked at me.

"Take me home," I said.

We were quiet on the drive home. The sun was sinking behind the mountain, and reflecting the sinking hope in my chest. I had no idea how it had come to this. How the end was coming at me so quickly.

I tried texting Cole for the hundredth time and again got no response.

"Should we check his place again?" Jack asked.

I shook my head. "Just take me home," I said. "I'm tired. And I want to be with you."

Jack's lips thinned into a tight, white line. "This isn't it, Becks. It isn't."

"I know," I said. We'd never openly admit to each other that our fight was over. We didn't operate that way. "I just want to rest for a little bit, and then we can start looking again. But listen. If Cole doesn't make it back in time—"

"Don't say that, Becks."

"I know. It's going to work out. But if something happens, don't try to destroy anything. Just stay far away. Stay safe."

Jack's lips relaxed and formed a deep frown, his brow furrowed, his chest heaving in and out with the pain of a heart that was breaking. He took my hand and pressed it against his chest.

"Do you feel that?" he said.

I blinked and nodded.

"This heart is yours. It belongs to you. It beats only for you. And somewhere out there is a heart without a home, and it beats for me; and we're not giving up until we find it."

"Nobody's giving up."

He nodded almost imperceptibly and then turned the car back onto the road and in the direction of my house.

When we got there, Jack stared straight ahead out the windshield at . . . nothing. He put the car in park and let it idle, an automatic reaction. He made no move to cut the ignition.

I decided there was no hurry to get inside. We'd do this at our own pace. My dad and Tommy were probably eating dinner, and I was in no hurry for anything resembling a last meal.

No. I would treat this night like any other. It was the only way to have hope. Besides, I'd learned long ago that good-byes were useless. The time would slip away too quickly with too many things left unsaid and too many chances for the wrong words to escape my lips.

"Let's go to your room then," Jack said. "We'll rest. And then we'll look again."

I nodded, knowing that once we were inside, we'd probably never leave.

I tried to make it to my house using my own legs, but I only made it a few steps before Jack had to pick me up once again.

Jack squeezed me tight. "I can't ever seem to get close enough to you," he said. "It's impossible."

"I used to want to fill every nook and cranny," I said sleepily. "My nooks were made for your crannies."

I felt Jack's cheek pull up in a smile. "That they were."

He carried me inside quickly and quietly, my head resting against the crook between his shoulder and his neck. As we passed the kitchen, I heard my dad ask Tommy a question, but I couldn't make out the specific words.

Then we were on the bed, face-to-face.

I never wanted to stop staring at his face, but before I knew it, my eyes had shut involuntarily.

Jack's fingers stroked my cheeks. "Don't worry about anything. Just rest. And when you're up to it, we'll go looking again."

I nodded, relieved that he wasn't trying to leave me to go search for Cole on his own. If he did, and I slipped away while he was gone . . .

We lay like that for a long time. I kept drifting off to sleep, fevered dreams forcing their way into my head. Dreams of worlds crumbling all around me, pieces of lives deposited at my feet.

Each time, I forced myself awake, and each time, the interval between my waking moments grew.

"Don't let me fall asleep again," I said to Jack.

"I won't," he answered. But I could've guessed that was something neither of us could control, and just after I'd said it, I was out.

My bedroom.

I dream . . .

But this time my dream is not fragmented.

I walk into a large room, the walls of which are lined with shelves and shelves of knickknacks: miniature figurines and thimbles and tin toys that look as if they were made in a different century. I don't get a closer look, because a woman with long, flowing red hair steps out from behind one of the walls of shelves.

The queen. Adonia.

I back up and then turn to run out of the room, but the door has disappeared. I turn to face her.

"I see you," the queen says. She said those same words the first time I dreamed of her.

I shake my head furiously. "No, you don't."

She steps forward and lowers her head until it is level with mine. I try to move, but my muscles don't obey my brain. She

brings a long, red fingernail up to my cheek, just under my eye,
and traces downward. It feels like a paring knife against my skin,
carving as she goes. I try to scream, but no sound comes out.

Her red lips form the next words as if she is inventing the
language as she is speaking it.

"I see you. Nikki Beckett."

She knows my name. The queen of the Underworld knows
my name.

"Becks!" Someone was shaking my shoulders. Someone strong
and loud.

"It's just a dream," Jack said. "Wake up. It's just a dream."

I opened my eyes to find Jack's face inches from mine.
Once he saw that my eyes were opened, he sighed and briefly
kissed my lips. Then he pulled back and got a look at my face.

"What happened here?" he said, lightly touching my cheek
with his finger.

"What is it?" I said.

"It looks like a fresh scratch."

I shook my head and thought back to the nightmare about
the queen. Cole had always said dreams were a connection
between the Surface and the Everneath, but she couldn't literally invade my dreams, could she? More than that, I didn't
think she could hurt me, physically, in a dream. . . . The thought
frightened me.

I wanted to tell Jack about my nightmare, but my eyes were
falling shut again. I wondered if this next time would be the

time I didn't wake up.

Through the haze of my cloudy brain, I heard a buzzing noise. Jack dug through my bag and took out my phone.

"Is it Cole?" I asked hopefully.

"No. It's . . . Christopher? From the soup kitchen?"

He handed me the phone, and I checked the screen. "Yeah. That's Christopher."

"What does it say?"

I squinted, the symbols on my phone seeming smaller than they ever had before. "He says 'A man showed up at the shelter, speaks no English except to say your name. Do you want to come look at him before I call social services?'"

Jack stared at my phone warily. "No, you don't," he said as if the answer should've been obvious.

I tilted my head to look up at him. "A stranger who knows my name and shows up at the soup kitchen the day after Cole disappears? What if they're connected? We have to go."

He looked at me with a conflicted expression, as if he felt hope but didn't want to put his faith in it.

I placed my hand over his. "At this point we have nothing to lose."

He looked away and nodded. "You're right. Let's go."

TWELVE

NOW
The Surface. The soup kitchen.

Twenty minutes later, we were parked at the soup kitchen, which was adjacent to the homeless shelter. It was nearly ten o'clock now. Cole had been missing for almost two days.

I was used to seeing the line to get food stretched out the front door and around the corner of the old redbrick building that used to be part of a mine-processing facility. Today was no exception.

We walked past the soup kitchen entrance and entered the main lobby of the shelter. The place was filled with all sorts of people, from a table with four elderly men playing cards to a family with small children waiting at the check-in counter.

Christopher must've been watching the door, because as soon as we were inside, he nodded a greeting and jerked his head over toward the far back corner of the giant room.

We turned toward the direction he'd indicated. In the

corner, one of the shelter volunteers—Dan, I thought—was sitting on a bench, his arm around another man. He was talking to the other man softly. The man's clothes were in shreds. His hair was coal black, and he rocked back and forth while wringing his hands.

I took one more step inside the room, and the man's head shot up. Clear blue eyes locked with mine, even though the place was filled and there was commotion all around us. It was as if he heard my footstep and was waiting for it.

Even with black, sooty stuff all over his face and in his hair, I knew who it was.

Jack looked from the man to me and waited expectantly.

I turned toward him without taking my eyes off of the man. "It's Cole," I said.

Cole didn't wait for us to make our way over to him. With an intense gaze, he shot out of his seat and sprinted across the room, leaving Dan scrambling after him.

He barreled toward me quickly. Jack pulled me behind him to shield me from the impact, and only then did Cole even notice Jack was there. He slowed his gait and looked at Jack quizzically, then stared at me again.

"Nikki." He said it with a long expulsion of air, as if he'd been holding his breath for years. The next sounds that came out of his mouth didn't resemble words at all, and it took me a moment to remember that Christopher said the strange man didn't speak English. Whatever the words meant, they sounded frantic.

Jack looked back at me and raised an eyebrow.

"It's okay," I said, moving out from behind Jack. "Cole?"

At the sound of my voice, the tension eased out of Cole's body; and lightning quick, he closed the gap between us, wrapped his arms around me, and smashed his lips against mine.

For a moment I could breathe again. It felt as if the blood that had been slowing and coagulating in my veins began to thin out and move inside me again, and my feet began to tingle with renewed sensation. For the first time since this morning, I thought I might survive the night.

Unlike the last time I'd fed on Cole, I received no distinct memories of his to accompany the kiss. Just a jumble of faces with no distinct features and unfamiliar buildings that could've been anywhere in the world.

In the next moment, he was torn away from me and lay sprawled on the floor.

Jack stood above him, his fist clenched. The lobby went silent.

"Jack!" I said. "No!"

Using the energy Cole had just given me, I ran to Jack and yanked hard on his arm. He stared back at me with blank eyes that slowly came back into focus, and when they did, he bowed his head.

"Sorry, Becks."

He bent forward and held a hand out to Cole, who was rubbing his jaw and looking suspiciously at the newly proffered hand.

"It's okay, Cole," I said in my most soothing voice.

Cole took the hand, and Jack hoisted him to his feet again. With a glance toward Jack to make sure he wasn't going to get hit again, Cole came toward me and again brought his lips to mine.

I tried not to think about the time I'd voluntarily kissed him in the Everneath to save him from the Sirens. Not just because I'd been so fooled back then, but also because I didn't want to remember how I'd thought he was a friend.

After several moments, when I could feel Jack's eyes boring holes into our heads, I pulled back. It was amazing how quickly I felt rejuvenated. Cole, on the other hand, looked like hell. Whatever he'd been through in the past two days, it wasn't good.

And yet as he stared at my face, he smiled and spoke again in a language I didn't understand.

"Cole, why aren't you speaking English?"

He shook his head and said some more stuff. The last word sounded like "*Engelsk*."

"You can't speak English," I said skeptically, guessing at the meaning behind his foreign explanation.

Cole nodded.

I glanced at Jack, who shrugged at me in an I-have-no-idea kind of way.

I looked back at Cole. "Uh, yes, you can. What happened to you?"

He watched my mouth as I spoke, and then looked at my eyes and shook his head, shrugging. He'd obviously understood my question, so what the hell was he talking about?

I looked back at Jack. "We have to get him out of here."

Jack nodded. "Do you feel strong enough to go tell Christopher we can take it from here?"

"Yeah." I smiled. "I feel like I could leap tall buildings in at least a double bound."

Jack smiled, the relief that I was alive—at least for now—evident in his eyes. "Okay, I'll get Cole to the car."

We split up so I could tell Christopher that we would take the strange foreign guy with us, but Cole started to follow me instead. "Cole, go with Jack."

He glanced at Jack and then looked at me warily.

"It will be okay," I said, and then I realized that I was comforting the guy to whom I had been pledging my undying hate only hours before. It was as if my body wasn't big enough for the two conflicting emotions. "Just go with Jack."

I could tell that he understood me, but he didn't budge. I'd have to reconcile my feelings toward him later. For now we just needed to get him out of here.

"Okay. Come on." I waved to Jack, indicating that I would take Cole with me. From the time I found Christopher to the time we got to the car, Cole didn't let me get more than two yards away from him. Even in the car he sat in the backseat but leaned forward so his head was resting on the side of my backrest.

Somehow, Jack drove the car while keeping one eye on the road, one eye on me, and a third narrowed and on Cole.

I turned in my seat so I could face him. "Cole, tell me what happened." I spoke slowly, hoping that would help him understand.

He shrugged. *"Jeg vet ikke hva som skjedde."*

I looked at Jack to see if he had any clue what that meant, but Jack shook his head.

"Okay, Cole, I'm going to ask you questions, and you just nod for yes and shake your head for no."

Cole nodded. Jack rolled his eyes. "He understands. Just speak English!"

"Shh," I said, putting my hand on Jack's arm. "He's obviously freaked out right now." I turned to see Cole staring at my hand. I dropped it. "Do you know who I am?"

He nodded.

"Do you know what happened to you?"

He closed his eyes for an extended blink, then opened them and shook his head. He looked so sad, but I knew from all the ways he'd betrayed me before that his looks could be deceiving.

I told myself I wouldn't let it happen again. I would get to the bottom of this, but I would not be taken in.

"Okay, Cole. You're okay now. You understand English. Now we just need to get you to speak it. Repeat after me. My name is Cole Stockton."

"My name is Cole Stockton." He said it with a thick accent, but at least he said it.

By the time we'd almost reached my house, he was speaking in full sentences. It took him a few tries and imitating my own words for something inside his head to click; and even when he spoke English, he still did it with an accent. The accent sounded Scandinavian, and I remembered that Cole had been born in Norway. Was he speaking Norwegian?

Jack pulled over about a block before he reached my house. "I don't feel good about going back to your house."

"Why?" I asked.

He shrugged. "Obviously, something has happened to Cole. Someone ransacked his condo. You almost got nabbed by a guy with black eyes. We don't know where the band is. I just don't feel very . . . safe."

"What do you suggest? We can't go to your house."

Cole leaned forward even more. "We can search for an inn. A place to lodge."

Jack and I both looked at him. "A *place to lodge*?" Jack said.

"Yes," Cole said. "To board."

Jack shook his head at me, obviously noticing the strange words such as *lodge* and *board*. "We'll figure out why Sir Cole is talking like a knight later. Right now, let's find a hotel."

"Hotel?" Cole said with a questioning expression.

Jack ignored him and turned the car back toward the center of town. He pulled over when he saw an ATM and got out of the car.

When he returned, he said, "I drained my savings. That should give us enough for at least a couple of nights. I want to avoid using my emergency credit cards."

"I don't want you to waste your money. Are you sure we're not overreacting?"

"I'm sure," Jack said.

"What do we do after we find a hotel?" I asked.

"We sleep. We get you feeling better. Then tomorrow we'll continue on with . . . our plan."

"What plan?" Cole said.

I narrowed my eyes at Jack. Maybe Cole was faking his memory loss so that he could spy on us.

"Nothing," I said.

We ended up at the Silver King Lodge. It was the largest hotel in the area, which meant it was our best chance to go unnoticed. Jack checked us in using his cash. I stayed out of sight of the front desk. It wasn't as if my face was familiar enough for anyone to notice that the mayor's daughter was spending the night in a hotel with two guys, but I didn't want to take any chances. I could just imagine that phone call to my dad.

While Jack checked us in, I texted Jules to see if she could cover for me so I could tell my dad I was sleeping over at her house. She responded and said she would and then asked if I was okay. I told her yes and thanked her, then I texted my dad so he wouldn't worry about me.

Cole stayed by my side, seeming confused but following

my every move. Shadowing everything I did, much like a child would a parent. Once we had our room, I ushered him in, Jack following behind us, and shut the door. Cole sat down on one of the beds and then flopped onto his back, rubbing his eyes.

"What's happening to me?" he said.

Jack narrowed his eyes skeptically and leaned against the closed door.

I sat by Cole and brushed a clump of dirty hair out of his eyes. His blond strands were barely visible underneath inches of what looked like caked mud. His eyes looked so blank, as if they were windows to an empty room.

But *was* it empty inside? I yanked my hand away.

"Cole . . . look at me," I said. He obeyed. "You remember my name?"

He frowned. "You're Nikki."

"But do you know who I *am*?" I said. I didn't mention the fact that he had so naturally kissed me or that since then he'd stuck to me like glue.

He tilted his head sideways as if he were trying to remember what had happened only twenty minutes ago. His lower lip started to tremble. "I only know that I had to find you. I'm supposed to be with you."

"Shhh," I said, taking his hand in mine. "You're okay now. We were supposed to meet up last night, but something happened. Do you know where Max, Oliver, and Gavin are?"

"Who?"

"The rest of the band."

"What band?"

I sighed. "The Dead Elvises. Your band. You, Max, Oliver, and Gavin." I said the names slowly.

He furrowed his brow and looked from Jack back to me, as if he were waiting for one of us to tell him this was all a big joke.

Jack shoved his hands into his pockets and shook his head. "I don't think he's faking," he said.

"Everything he does is fake!" My outburst surprised me. Cole flinched at the venom in my voice. I took a few deep breaths. "Sorry. We'll figure it out later. Can you get some rest?"

Cole nodded; and as if all he needed was my permission, he rolled over toward me onto his side, taking the bedspread with him. He didn't even bother to orient himself toward the head of the bed. His eyelids sagged shut, and within moments he was asleep.

I looked up at Jack. "We can't let him out of our sight like this."

"I know," Jack said.

"But I don't want to be stupid either. If it *is* a trick."

Jack pulled me over to his bed and clasped my hand. "We can't afford . . . *You* can't afford to lose him. If he was faking . . . what purpose would it serve? Especially considering what we saw at his condo."

"Who's to say the black-eyed man doesn't work for Cole?" I said.

I knew I was being completely unreasonable with that

accusation, but I couldn't help it. It was the product of my recent spiral of hate for him.

Jack put his arms around me and held me tight. "But why would Cole do it? He was getting everything he wanted, namely you. Every night. He was in the power position. They were building an army. So why would he fake amnesia?"

"I don't know. I just can't think about anything else."

Jack glanced at Cole, making sure he was asleep, and then he put his lips at my ear. "Do you want me to help you think about something else?"

I looked into his chocolate-brown eyes and let Jack's calm nature wash over me. What was the danger? We had Cole back. I was safe for now. We had a plan to take down the Everneath. I didn't know if it was my renewed energy or the fact that neither of us had been able to relax in what seemed like a long time. Or maybe it was the fact that Cole was more than asleep—he was passed out on the other bed.

"I bet I can make *you* forget about Cole before you make *me* forget about him."

Jack's lips twitched. "Betcha can't."

"Hmmm." I looked again at Cole. He had the bedspread over his face and was snoring softly. I turned back to Jack. "I think I'll take this hot hoodie off," I said in a fake-breathy voice.

For a moment Jack stood transfixed, a worried look in his eyes. But he couldn't help a smile. "The way you say 'hoodie' . . ." He glanced at Cole.

"Don't worry," I said with a grin. "He's out cold. Plus I have a T-shirt on underneath. And a tank on under that."

"You and your many layers."

When I crossed my arms and grabbed the hem of my sweatshirt, I moved slowly and deliberately, pulling up on the fabric until I turned it inside out and ripped it off. My hair fell in messy curls all around me.

I heard Jack's intake of breath.

But then a quick movement from the other bed caught my eye. Cole had ripped off the bedcovers, sat up, and was now staring at me. "You're beautiful," Cole said. "Do that again."

The blood rushed to my cheeks. I searched for something to throw at him, but then I caught the look on his face. It was pure, innocent joy.

I waited for his smile to slip into a smirk or for one hint that he was faking, but nothing happened. He never would've said that in front of Jack—with such a complete lack of guile—if he remembered the beating Jack had given him.

"Stop looking at her," Jack warned.

"I'm in a T-shirt!" I said. These guys were acting as if I had stripped down to a teddy or something.

"I can't," Cole said. "She's glorious, isn't she?"

Jack tensed, and I rushed to his side to hold him. "Let it go," I said.

Cole looked up at us, confused. "What? She is, isn't she?" He looked to Jack as if expecting confirmation.

Jack's previous patience with Cole had been eradicated.

The lines around his lips and eyes tightened, and he clenched a fist.

I handed Jack the room service menu to occupy his mind with something else, and to give him something to tear apart if he needed to.

"Cole, go to sleep. You're obviously exhausted. Jack, order room service. Extra French fries."

Jack raised an eyebrow—he knew I only used French fries for extreme emergencies—and then nodded and sat at the desk.

Cole just watched me from the bed.

"What?" I said.

He grinned expectantly. "What comes off next? The T-shirt?"

Suddenly a pillow hit him in the face with enough force to sound like a gloved fist. The seam of the pillow split on impact, and feathers went flying.

"So . . ." Cole blew a feather off of his shoulder. "No?"

Jack tried to give me an accusatory look, but the tight lines around his mouth faltered.

I held up my hands, palms out, in my best innocent gesture. "It's a T-shirt. And jeans."

He bit his lip. "You could be wearing a garbage bag and . . ."

"Next time I will."

Jack ordered room service, with extra fries; and after we had finished eating, we fell asleep in each other's arms.

We could do this. We had to do this.

It was a long night, punctuated by a few tense moments when Cole woke up screaming because of some nightmare. Each time I reached out from my bed to his and put my hand on his arm, which seemed to settle him down.

In the morning, I woke long before either of the guys. I went to the kitchenette and put a pot of coffee on to brew and then sat down by the window to think about what to do next.

Yes, we had Cole back, and therefore my life was not in imminent danger; but I wasn't 100 percent sure Cole wasn't playing us. There was still that tiny bit of doubt that the guy who tricked me in the Everneath might be trying to pull a fast one again. And I didn't know where the rest of the band was, but up until two nights ago their plan had been to take Forfeits to an accelerated Feed, and soon.

Not only that, but now we were technically on the run. I still wasn't sure anyone from the Everneath had connected me to Cole, but what if they had? Would they consider me a threat to the queen? Would they come after me? Would they come after my family?

I was worried about my dad and Tommy. I couldn't take them on the run with us and simultaneously try to destroy the Everneath. If only going on the lam with me were as simple as packing a few bags and not as complicated as convincing the mayor of Park City to run away with his teenage half-Everliving–half-human daughter because monsters from the Underworld were coming for them.

Jack and I needed to get to the Everneath to investigate the Shade connection; but what if Cole really was lying, and he was waiting for us to make a move?

I needed to know for sure that Cole was telling the truth about his amnesia. But how?

The coffeemaker clicked off just as something clicked on in my brain.

I had just jumped out of my chair to go wake up Jack when he appeared from around the corner and I ran into him.

He used his hands to cushion the impact. "Whoa. Where's the fire?"

"Jack." I couldn't hide my enthusiasm. "We need to take Cole to Professor Spears."

"Wait. Slow down. What do you mean?"

"I think I have a way we can figure out if Cole's lying or not, but we'd need the professor."

Jack backed against the wall. "But we went to the professor so he could help us destroy the Everneath. Cole wouldn't want to cooperate."

"That's the beautiful thing. Cole doesn't know that." I poured a mug of coffee for Jack and then one for myself. I felt so excited finally to be one step ahead of Cole, to be manipulating *him* instead of him manipulating me. "Right now, Cole is a blank slate. And we can fill that blank slate with whatever backstory we want."

And I had just the story in mind.

THIRTEEN

NOW

The Surface. The hotel.

$\mathcal{J}$ack tilted his head. "What kind of backstory?"

"The kind that convinces Cole he wants the same thing we do." I handed Jack his coffee. "The kind where he wants to destroy the Everneath just as much as we do. Maybe even more."

Jack raised his eyebrows as he brought the mug to his mouth. He blew on the steaming coffee and then took a sip and swallowed. "If he's faking this whole amnesia thing . . ."

"He'd never keep up the ruse if he thought he was helping us destroy the Everneath."

Jack set his mug down on the counter and smiled. "Do you have a story in mind?"

I nodded. "I've got a tragic one."

Twenty minutes later, Cole was seated on one bed, Jack and I on the other. We had told him about how he was an Everliving, but we also added a fictional backstory, hopefully one that would make him want to help us. He was staring at me with a frown on his face. "So these Everlivings . . . they killed my family? My extended family? Cousins and aunts and uncles? The entire thing?"

I nodded.

"And then they . . . *burned* my village?" he said, shaking his head in disbelief.

Jack glanced sideways at me. Okay, I admit I embellished our original story by adding the part about a burned village. But I wanted to make sure Cole was on our side totally and completely.

I nodded again. "Yes. You and I met because we were both trying to destroy the Everneath. I have certain . . . abilities that can help us."

"What kind of abilities?" he said.

"I can make things appear."

Cole squinted one eye at me. "How? Do it."

"I can't do it here. But in the Everneath I can think about an object and then make it appear. You noticed my ability, and you thought it would come in handy for taking down our mutual enemies."

Cole looked at me, deep in thought. Jack shifted uncomfortably beside me. There was a knock at the door.

"Housekeeping" came a woman's voice.

"Later!" Jack and I both yelled in unison.

Finally, Cole sighed. "Okay. This makes sense."

"It does?" I said.

"Yes. The fact that I'm depending on you to seek revenge for the people I used to love? It explains why I'm so attached to you. Why I feel like lives depend on me being near you. Why everything around you seems made of . . . light."

His face was earnest. Here Cole was, thinking I was the source of light right after I'd told him the biggest lie. At his words, guilt edged out my hate for a moment. My resolve faltered, and Jack stepped in.

"So now, Cole, we need to go see a man named Professor Spears. Hopefully, even though you can't remember anything, something will come to you."

Cole held out his hand. Jack eyed me and then took it, and Cole shook it vigorously. "I will meet this professor. I will help you."

He left to go use the bathroom, and Jack looked at me with an eyebrow raised. "If he's faking it . . . ."

"Well, then we'll know for sure, won't we?"

Two hours later, we were sitting in Professor Spears's office, waiting for him to get back from a class. The three of us sat facing the professor's desk, a marble bust of Poseidon staring back at us.

The door swung open, and Professor Spears blew in.

"Nikki. Jack. I didn't expect to see you again so quickly. And you have a friend?"

Cole stood and said formally, "Yes. Coleson Stockflet. Pleased to meet you, Professor Spears."

Jack and I exchanged looks. *Coleson Stockflet?* Maybe it was an old name. I'd only known him as Cole Stockton.

The professor took his hand. "Nice to meet you too," he said, giving me a confused look.

"Cole is an Akh ghost," I said. "Hypothetically. He's here to help us."

"Ah. Okay. Why would an Akh ghost want to take down the Everneath?"

"Because Everlivings killed my family," Cole said, his voice fierce. "And burned my village."

I gave the professor a shaky smile. Our story must have stuck. "So, Professor, Cole here is on our side. But he has some sort of amnesia. He and his Everliving friends disappeared two nights ago. A large guy with black eyes may have been involved. When Cole returned, he had amnesia. And his friends still haven't shown up. For all we know, they might have started their accelerated Feed early. But Cole here can't remember. Do you have any idea what could have happened to him?"

The professor frowned and took a couple of steps closer to Cole. He put his finger on Cole's collar bone, pointing to a deep scratch I hadn't noticed before. The scratch got bigger as it disappeared underneath the collar of his shirt. "Do you mind, Cole, lifting your shirt?

Feeling suddenly protective, I took a step toward Cole, but Jack held me back. "He'll be fine, Becks."

Cole looked at me questioningly, and when I nodded, he slowly lifted his shirt, revealing his belly and chest.

And my breath caught in my throat. Scattered across his torso were deep purple welts with torn skin in the center of each one. I couldn't imagine what would make such wounds. Maybe a hot poker? I raised my finger, and Cole flinched. I didn't touch him.

"Cole," I said, my voice soft.

The professor frowned, a grim look on his face. "I wouldn't presume to know what happened, but this looks like . . . torture. And it looks fresh. Maybe not within the past day, but it surely happened within the past week."

I closed my mouth, which had been hanging open. "Time moves slowly in the Everneath. It still could've happened yesterday but healed a little bit before he got back to the Surface."

I pulled at the hem of Cole's shirt and softly urged it back down, my breath catching in my throat.

"It's okay," Cole said. "I don't remember it."

Jack's face had turned ashen. He looked away, almost as if he wanted to give me and Cole some privacy. I loved him for it at that moment.

I squeezed Cole's hand. "You're going to be okay." Then I turned to Professor Spears. "How can we get his memory back?"

He shook his head. "I'm not sure. The best way would probably be to share memories of him. Also, he might still have some lingering instinctual behaviors." At our confused expressions, Professor Spears continued. "I have a degree in psychology too. Sometimes people suffering from amnesia will drive to places they know, like the post office, or a favorite takeout haunt, even though they don't technically remember them. Cole might exhibit this type of behavior."

Once the professor had finished talking, the four of us sat there in silence for a while. Now that I knew Cole had been tortured . . . I don't know. It didn't change our course of action necessarily. But who would torture him?

I could only think of one person. The queen. Or someone acting on her orders.

"We'll try to help him with his memories," I said. "But in the meantime, does seeing him, or being around an actual Everliving, give you any further ideas about our plan?"

He shrugged. "I'm sorry, but I don't know anything more than what I already told you. And meeting Cole hasn't really done anything to change that. But I'm still looking through the journal from Sheldon."

Jack let out a breath. "If we can't figure out a way to destroy the Everneath in time, Nikki will die. You know this, right?"

The professor raised his eyebrows. "But all she would have to do is feed."

"She won't feed. Ever," Jack said. "Because that would mean taking a life."

The professor looked down. "Right. I'm still coming to terms with the fact that this isn't just mythology. We're not dealing in hypotheticals anymore."

Jack's and Cole's faces were glum, and I could only assume they matched my own expression.

"Look, I'll work on it," the professor said. "I have your number. I'll text you the second I find anything."

On the drive back to the hotel Cole had a strange expression on his face. "I didn't know you were going to die."

I shifted in my seat so I could see him. I considered lying to him and coming up with another grandiose story about how hundreds or thousands of people would also die if we failed, but at this moment the truth seemed to be the best course of action. "I am. If we don't destroy the Everneath, I'll die."

"How?"

I shook my head, momentarily caught off guard by the fact that I was explaining my death sentence to the very person who had given it to me. "Because you . . . because someone stole my heart. Which means I'm halfway to becoming an Everliving. And I'm getting weaker. I can survive by feeding on you, but that's only a temporary solution." I glanced involuntarily at the shackle on my one wrist and then looked at the other. Did I see the faint shadow of a line? I closed my eyes and went on. "And eventually I'll have to take a human sacrifice to the Everneath and feed on him . . . or her . . . for a century. But the thing is, that sacrifice, that Forfeit, would then be condemned to the Tunnels, where he or she would die a slow death. And I would never do that to someone."

"But if it would save you . . ." Cole paused and seemed to think about it for a moment. "Jack would do that for you.

Wouldn't you, Jack?" Cole said it as if he were telling me Jack would loan me a dollar.

I laughed disbelievingly. "It doesn't matter. We're talking about death here."

Cole frowned. "I'm sorry. I don't remember all the details, but for some reason . . . I don't know. I feel like death isn't as big as we all think it is."

Jack snorted. "Coming from someone who did everything he could to stay alive forever."

Cole shook his head as if unsure of which side he wanted to take in this debate. "I don't know what I did before. Maybe it's because I'm hundreds of years old, as you say. Maybe my subconscious knows I'm supposed to be dead. Maybe that's why death feels so natural. So inevitable."

For a long while silence fell upon us, only broken when Jack flipped on the turn signal for our exit at Kimball Junction.

As he checked his blind spot, he caught my gaze and shrugged, as if to say *You still believe the amnesia is an act?*

The harder question was, What do you do with someone who doesn't remember all the bad things he's done? How do you hold him responsible when he doesn't even remember who he is?

If this were all an act, I think he would've played his hand by now. That being said, I know neither of us trusted him. I didn't owe Cole forgiveness. But did I owe it to this amnesiac in the backseat?

Jack finally broke the silence. "What do we do now, Becks?"

What *were* we going to do? I stared out the window for a moment. We'd done everything we could to make sure Cole wasn't lying, so there was only one thing left to do.

"Pull over at that café here," I said, pointing to a little place near the strip mall.

"Why?" Jack asked.

"I think it's time we go to the Everneath. But first we need to eat."

Ten minutes later. At Sunrise Café.

We ordered giant plates of eggs, bacon, and toast; and when the waitress left to put in the order, I pulled out a pen from my backpack and handed it to Jack, along with a napkin.

"Let's go over what we know from Professor Spears," I said.

Jack nodded and began to write. *According to the professor, we have three obstacles we have to bring down in order to destroy the Everneath. Number one is the membrane. Number two is the link between the Shades. Number three is the hearts.* He rubbed his forehead so hard, I thought he would rub off his eyebrows.

"I think number one and number two are related. I think the membrane will be more easily destroyed if we go after the link between the Shades first."

Jack nodded. "That makes sense. As much as any of this makes sense. What do you have in mind?"

"There's someone who might be able to help us with the Shades."

"Who?" Jack and Cole said in unison.

"When Cole and I were searching for you in the Everneath, we had help from an old friend of Cole's. Named Ashe." I checked Cole's face for any signs of recognition at the name, but there wasn't anything I could see. "Ashe looked different from other Everlivings. He was gray all over. Looked as if he was made of smoke. Cole had seemed surprised by Ashe's appearance. Apparently he hadn't always looked like that. At one point when we'd almost made it to the Tunnels, we were attacked by Shades. We couldn't touch them, but Ashe . . ." I sighed. "Ashe's fists made contact with the Shades. He could connect with them when we couldn't. He'd missed the last Feed, and that made him look more like a smoky version of a Shade. I'm sure he's least part Shade."

Both Jack and Cole were listening intently. I kept waiting for Cole to jump in, or at least reach the conclusion I was trying to guide him toward, but he looked as though he had never heard this story before.

"So," I continued, "maybe if Ashe is part Shade, he'll know how they're all connected. He's very loyal to you, Cole."

"Why?" Cole asked.

Oh jeez. How did I explain that Ashe's Forfeit, Adonia, had survived the Feed; and when she decided not to become an Everliving, Cole hunted her down so Ashe could turn her over to the current queen? And then Adonia *became* the queen?

"You helped him find something once. Something he had lost." I shook my head. Cole had once used the same generic phrasing with me to explain Ashe's loyalty.

Cole hung on every word as if he had no idea where I was going with this but couldn't wait to find out.

"So," I said again, "we'll probably need to go to the Everneath. Find Ashe."

Jack crumpled the napkin. "But why would Ashe help us? Why would he betray what the Shade connection is if he knew we wanted to destroy it?"

The waitress set down a plate of eggs in front of me, and I put a forkful in my mouth while I thought for a moment.

"We won't tell him we want to destroy it," I said. "We'll tell him we're there to try to jog Cole's memory. But really you and I will be investigating the Shade link."

Cole sat back, lacing his fingers together and bringing them up to his chin. "We could do that. Question, though: How do we get to this . . . 'Everneath'?"

Jack rolled his eyes, then looked at me. "To the Shop-n-Go?"

I nodded.

Technically, Cole could take us down to the Everneath from anywhere, but in the state he was in and the way he'd forgotten everything, I didn't want to make it harder than it already would be.

So we headed to the Shop-n-Go.

When we got to the store, it was open again, the busted lock fixed. But another clerk, not Ezra, stood behind the counter. The new clerk looked barely out of high school and very bored.

"Crap," I said.

"What is it?" Cole asked.

"It's not Ezra." At Cole's confused expression, I explained. "Ezra is the clerk you and your band paid to keep watch over the entrance to the Everneath." I shook my head. "It just seems like a sign that something is wrong."

I walked up to the new clerk. "Where's Ezra?" I asked.

"Don't know," he said. "He sorta had a breakdown."

"What do you mean?"

The clerk narrowed his eyes. "Why?"

"Ezra's my cousin. I'm worried."

The clerk shrugged, as if he couldn't be bothered being suspicious of me anymore. "He called me to replace him. When I got here, he was freaking out. Looked scared. Said he wasn't coming back. That's all I know."

Jack pulled me away from the counter, and we went to the back of the store. I tried not to think about how ominous Ezra's actions sounded. Once we were in the back, we all three faced one another, forming a triangle around the spot where I'd first seen that woman slip through the floor. Where I'd slipped through the floor myself after I'd ingested a hair of Cole's.

"Let's take each other's hands," I said.

Cole took one of mine, Jack took the other, and then, reluctantly, Jack took Cole's hand. We formed a ring. I briefly thought about all the ways this could go wrong. We could land in the middle of the city square of Ouros. Worst case scenario, we'd appear during one of the queen's Feasts. We could drop into the middle of a Shade convention or something. At least we couldn't land anywhere in the labyrinth. Direct teleportation inside the three rings was impossible without an Everliving already there to grab your hand.

"Okay, Cole. We want to land in Ouros. But not in the main square. Anywhere but there," I said, referring to the Common where Ashe lived. "Does that name mean anything to you? Ouros?"

He shook his head.

"Imagine . . . an ancient city. Surrounded by a circular wall. Single-level dwellings on the outside that give way to larger buildings toward the center." I closed my eyes, trying to think of something that would set Ouros apart from the other Commons, but I couldn't come up with anything. I would just have to rely on the fact that Ouros was Cole's home, and hopefully it would be the most familiar to him.

I closed my eyes. "Okay, Cole. Let's go."

He squeezed my hand. I waited for that feeling of falling through space, of being tossed around in a washing machine.

But it never came.

I squeezed one eye open and looked at Cole. His eyes were

closed, and he had a peaceful look on his face. I opened both of my eyes and caught the new clerk giving the three of us a very strange look.

"Cole. Are you doing anything?" I whispered.

He leaned toward me and spoke out of the side of his mouth, keeping his eyes shut. "What am I supposed to be doing?"

"I don't know. Can't you . . . think downward?" I'd been in his position recently enough that I realized the futility of how it felt.

He pressed his lips together and then began to sink lower. But he was only bending his knees.

Jack sighed and opened his eyes. "It isn't working."

I released Cole's hand. "Give me a strand of your hair," I said.

"What?"

"No humans can get to the Everneath unless they have a ferryman to take them there. You, as an Everliving, are supposed to be able to come and go as you please, from anywhere; but that obviously isn't working. Maybe your body just doesn't remember what to do. In the absence of an Everliving escort, a human can go to the Everneath if he or she ingests part of an Everliving."

Cole's eyebrows shot up.

"Maybe if I do that, it will kick-start the process. Which means I need to swallow one of your hairs."

He looked relieved, as if he'd thought I was going to ask

for a finger or something. He plucked a hair off his head and handed it to me.

I put the hair on my tongue, cringing, and said, "Once we get going, Cole, think of Ouros."

I grabbed both of their hands again and swallowed.

And then the turbulence began.

FOURTEEN

NOW

The Everneath. Outside Ouros.

When the turmoil finally stopped, I opened my eyes and stared at a sky that was too blue, as if it had gotten itself confused with the sea. Instinctively, I raised a hand to shade my eyes from the sun, but of course there was no sun, because this was a fake sky. A sky I'd hoped never to see again.

I turned my head. Jack was flat on his back on one side of me. Cole was on the other, sitting up, his knees drawn against his chest and his elbows resting on them as if he were sitting somewhere on a beach. He was staring straight ahead, frowning.

"What's wrong?"

He flinched at the sound of my voice and shook his head. "Nothing. I keep waiting for something here to click."

I sat up and squinted my eyes at him. "Does anything look familiar?"

"No. But I'm still hoping."

He smiled at me, but something about the smile seemed sad. I reached for his hand, then caught Jack watching right before I closed my fingers around Cole's. I stared at Cole's eyes. "Are you okay?"

"Yeah," Cole said, pulling his hand away.

"Where are we?" Jack said. His face looked tense.

That's when I noticed a faint, colorful mist coming from Jack. His energy was leaking out around him, although it wasn't very strong. Maybe that was because of all the time he'd spent in the Tunnels. I realized this was his first time coming back to the Everneath since that day he'd clawed his way out of the Tunnels.

I put my hand on his cheek. "Do you feel well?"

He nodded and closed his eyes. "I'm not sure." He opened them again and looked around. "What's with the air here?"

"That's your energy. Leaking out. Stay next to Cole, because he'll soak it up."

Jack eyed Cole and then looked at me again. "Why can't *you* soak it up?"

I stepped close to him, but the energy only floated around me too. I didn't absorb any of it. "You know why. I can only feed off Cole."

Jack sighed and scooted closer to Cole.

I looked around. We were at the base of a giant gray wall. I knew that wall. It surrounded the Common areas. Opposite the wall were flat, single-level, ancient-looking buildings.

As long as this was Ouros, we were on our way to finding Ashe. I looked at Cole and smiled. "You did it, Cole. I think we're inside Ouros. I think we're good."

"We're not quite good," Jack said.

He was looking at a poster hanging on the nearest building. Cole's picture was front and center on the poster, and underneath it were the words:

ESCAPED
THREAT TO THE QUEEN
REWARD:
TWO DAYS IN THE ELYSIAN FIELDS

Cole looked at the poster with a clueless smile on his face. Jack pulled Cole's hoodie up and forward, covering as much as he could.

He turned to me. "Which way do we go?

I looked down the several passageways that branched out from where we stood and, with a sinking feeling, realized that nothing looked familiar. "I don't know. The streets all look the same. I don't even know if we're starting in the same place I did before."

Jack pulled me aside. "Sometimes, during football practice, Coach would leave it to me to call the plays. I struggled in practice because there wasn't anything on the line. But during the games, when the adrenaline was high and victory was at risk, I always made the right call. Maybe Cole needs a little bit of adrenaline."

"What did you have in mind?"

He glanced toward Cole to make sure he wasn't looking and then gave me a tiny nod.

"I think I hear something . . . ," Jack said.

"What is it?" Cole asked, starting to turn around.

"Shades!" Jack shouted.

Cole flinched and then just took off in a flat-out sprint. We followed as close as we could. He darted right and left, down alleyways and narrow spaces between buildings, and I realized that his instincts were directing us toward the most clandestine route.

Finally, Cole pulled up outside a familiar door. He raised his fist and pounded on the door.

"Where are the Shades?" he asked, panting.

Jack smiled. "Nowhere. I was just trying to jog your memory."

I raised an eyebrow. "You know what happened to the boy who cried wolf too many times. . . .?"

Cole waited with an expectant look on his face. "What happened?"

I rolled my eyes.

"Remember," Jack said to Cole. "Don't let on about our plan."

"What plan?" Cole said.

Jack took a deep breath and gritted his teeth. "The one about destroying the Everneath." We'd gone over this countless times. "I didn't think the amnesia affected the short-term memory," he muttered.

"Oh, yeah. The plan," Cole said just as Ashe's door swung open.

When I caught sight of Ashe, my mouth dropped open. He had changed. He'd looked strange before, with his gray coloring and smoky texture. But even in the relatively short time since I'd seen him last, his coloring had settled into a deep-black hue. Black hair lay flat against matching black skin on his head and face. I could no longer discern any white in his eyes. Every part of his body was black. It was as if he was now made of oil. I knew the Everneath ran on a different time frame, but the extent of the change was shocking.

He must be closer to a Shade now than ever. The sight sent chills down my neck and back. He so resembled the Shades that had attacked me in the Ouros square the first time I'd come down on my own. Suddenly I wasn't sure this was a good idea. But at least Ashe was still shaped like a man and not like the fluid forms of the full Shades.

As for Ashe, he couldn't stop staring at Cole. As he spoke, strands of an oil-like substance connected his upper and lower lips, and his voice sounded like he was speaking under thick water.

"Cole," he said. "You're okay." He sounded relieved and surprised, and then he glanced nervously down the street.

"Come in, come in. Quickly."

We filed in, one by one; and as I passed by, Ashe finally seemed to realize who I was. "Nikki. I wasn't sure I'd ever see you again," he said. I couldn't tell how he felt about the prospect.

"It's a long story."

"I bet." He shut the door behind us. Cole couldn't stop staring at Ashe's strange appearance, and I wondered if he would all of a sudden run away.

Ashe ushered us toward the table in the middle of his room. His place hadn't changed much. The long rectangular room was broken up by the large round table in the middle and several rugs lining the ground in the corners, and there was a back door in the middle of the opposite wall.

Once we were all seated at the table, he stared at Cole. "How did you escape?"

Cole glanced at me nervously before answering. "Escape what?"

"The queen." Ashe looked at me with a questioning expression.

"He has amnesia," I explained. "He can't remember."

"Amnesia," Ashe said. He looked at Cole again, this time a little critically. "You're lucky."

"Why?" I asked. "Do you know what happened to him?"

Ashe sighed, then stood and grabbed some glasses from his cupboard, turned a spout that emerged from the wall, and filled the glasses with water. I remembered the water here wasn't ordinary water. It had powers to make you forget. He poured four glasses and set down one in front of each of us.

I pushed mine away. "No, thanks. I want a clear head."

"Keep it nearby," Ashe said. "You might change your mind once you hear what I have to say."

Neither Jack nor I touched our glasses, but Cole—the one who needed a clear head the most—took a giant gulp and set the empty glass down with a thud.

Ashe sipped his own water and then set it down. He turned toward Cole. "There's been a bounty on your head ever since your run-in with the queen. When you were here with Nikki. At the end of the maze."

Cole turned to me with raised eyebrows.

"It's a long story," I said.

"Nobody knew who you were, and I didn't tell anyone." Again he glanced at me. "But apparently a Delphinian ratted you guys out. He traded the information so his exile could be revoked. Does any of this make any sense to you?"

Cole frowned and shook his head.

"What's a Delphinian?" I asked.

Ashe looked at me. "The Delphinians were banned from the Everneath centuries ago, and they live in hiding on the Surface. They're a scary group. You don't want to mess with them." He gestured toward his window and addressed Cole again. "You know those posters plastering the streets? Well, those used to show pictures of you and your band. Once the Delphinian gave them a name to go with the face, they sent bounty hunters after you specifically. I guess they found you."

"Bounty hunters?" Jack said.

Ashe nodded. "Ten-Shade bounty hunters. Shades aren't very strong on the Surface because of their makeup. So ten of them will join together and find a human body to inhabit."

Jack and I exchanged glances. His eyes were wide. "The man with the black eyes," he said.

I nodded.

Ashe looked from Jack to me. "You ran into a bounty hunter and survived?"

"Jack's strong," I said.

"Still," Ashe said, seeming impressed. "Anyway, the bounty hunters brought you and the band to the queen." At this point in the story, Ashe paused and looked intently at the wooden table. "The queen . . . she tortured you. And the others. Trying to find out about Nikki. I only know because the Shades share certain knowledge among themselves, and as you've probably guessed by the change in how I look, I'm part Shade. I saw the torture through their eyes."

He shook his head, refusing to look up.

Cole leaned forward. "Don't worry about it. I don't remember anything. Not anymore."

Ashe raised his head and squinted his eyes, in an almost-disbelieving way. "You'd better hope that memory never comes back."

My stomach turned at the thought of Cole being tortured.

How bad must it have been if he had blocked out everything before and after?

"What about the band?" Cole asked. "Does the queen still have them?"

I was ashamed I hadn't thought of the other band members.

Ashe shook his head. "I don't know. If she does, she's keeping it quiet. The Shades don't know either, because I haven't heard or seen any solid information. There were some rumors coming from the more criminal element here—rumors that the band escaped and were arranging for an illegal accelerated Feed; but I haven't been able confirm anything. Since I'm part Shade, nobody seems to want to talk to me about criminal activities."

I took in a breath. "But if that's true, the band could already be bulking up for battle?"

"I don't know for sure."

"And you don't know how I escaped?" Cole said.

Ashe lowered his head into his hands. "That information was kept from the Shade network."

Shade network. The first words that sounded as if they could have something to do with the link between the Shades.

"What is the Shade network?" I said, avoiding eye contact with Jack.

Ashe sat up but hesitated before answering. "In the simplest terms, it's like a hub where information is shared." He shook his head. "I didn't believe you had escaped, even when the posters appeared. I didn't believe it until I saw you at my door." He looked at Cole again.

"This Shade network," I said. "If the queen's looking for Cole—"

Ashe put up a hand. "The Shades' loyalty is to the Everneath, not the queen. I can keep Cole's presence here a secret. So why are you here? Do you want to try to get your memory back?"

I looked at Cole warily, hoping he would say yes and remember not to divulge the real reason why we had come.

Cole nodded toward me infinitesimally. "There's a professor on the Surface who thinks I might be able to kick-start my brain if others share memories they have of me. Do you have any of these?"

Ashe lifted his head. "I've got a million."

"It would help if it was something with some sort of emotional attachment," I said.

Ashe nodded. "I have the one. It happened a long time ago, when I was in South Africa. . . ."

FIFTEEN YEARS AGO
The Surface. South Africa.

Ashe looked down at the river from more than seven hundred feet above it. He stood at the center of the Bloukrans Bridge— one of the highest bridges in the world, or at least in South Africa—and leaned out over the ledge.

Every Everliving would eventually suffer the equivalent of a human midlife crisis. It was inevitable in the life of an immortal. When the price of immortality was as low as finding a Forfeit every hundred years, one could be in danger of growing bored.

Except boredom for an immortal felt more eternal, and more constricting, than it did for his human counterparts.

But this was no typical midlife crisis.

"Mr. Campbell?" A man with headphones and a clipboard said.

Ashe blinked and then nodded.

"Ready to jump?"

Ashe nodded again, his toes venturing beyond the edge.

"In three . . . two . . . one . . . Go!"

Ashe stepped off the ledge and went into a free fall, and the only thing on his mind was the face of the woman he was trying to forget. She had blond hair and blue eyes, and looked like sunshine after a summer storm.

When the bungee contracted, so did his heart. Or it would have if he had had one.

Safely back on the surface, Ashe climbed in his car just as his phone rang. A big, clunky phone. Not like the kinds they have now.

Ashe pressed the green button. "Hello?"

"Did it work?" The voice on the other end of the phone asked. Ashe knew that voice. It was Cole. "Did you forget her?"

"No," Ashe said. "I've climbed the pyramids, I've walked

hundreds of miles across Spain on the Camino de Santiago, I've climbed Mount Kilimanjaro and dived the Great Barrier Reef. I didn't forget her. I don't know why I thought throwing myself off the world's highest bridge would be any different."

"Maybe that's because the Bloukrans Bridge isn't the world's highest bridge."

"Or maybe it's because Sheree is unforgettable," Ashe said. "I thought we weren't supposed to be able to feel this way about a human."

"Obviously, there are some exceptions to the rule." Cole sighed on the other end of the phone. "You could always go to the Everneath. Drink from the Fountains of Lethe. Forget her completely."

Ashe was silent as he thought about this. He was about to agree when Cole cleared his throat.

"Or you can admit that you haven't felt this way since Adonia, and you'd be stupid to let her go."

"She'll never come over to our side," Ashe said. "She'll never become an Everliving."

"Then go be with her for a human lifetime."

NOW

The Everneath. Ashe's house.

"And I did," Ashe said. "I stayed with Sheree until she died of cancer. When she left me, I stayed in the Everneath for a long time. I didn't leave my house. That's why I missed the last Feed. Missing the Feed is what started my transition into becoming a Shade."

I was watching Ashe, but all I could think about was the fact that an Everliving had just admitted he'd been in love with a human. And Cole supported that love. He'd always told me it was impossible for Everlivings to love. For *him* specifically to love. And now to hear his part in what was essentially a love story? To know that at one point in his life, he recommended that his friend choose love?

These stories didn't seem to fit the Cole I knew, but they were real. Why had he been so determined to hide this side of himself? Did it scare him to be vulnerable to human emotions?

Cole sniffed beside me, and I finally looked at him. His eyes were wet.

"Do you remember something?" I said.

"No," Cole said, sniffing again. "But that story is so beautiful."

I pressed my lips together. I didn't know what to do with this version of Cole, and the uncertainty of how I should treat him was unbearable. Were these stories supposed to make me feel sorry for him? Could I be stupid enough to trust him *again*?

I chose anger. "The old you hated love. *Hated* it. Those who made decisions based on love were weak. Those who wanted a life surrounded by loved ones were ignorant. To you, it wasn't beautiful at all. It was never beautiful!"

"Becks," Jack said, his voice calming.

"Don't pretend you know anything about love," I said.

Cole's face cracked and crumpled before me. I could see what my outburst had done to him. I immediately regretted everything I'd said.

"If that's true," Cole said, "then why, after I've forgotten everything . . . *everything* . . . why do I still know I love you?"

FIFTEEN

NOW

The Everneath. Ashe's house.

The air rushed out of my lungs. "What?"

"I love you," Cole said. "Right now, despite all the things you said I've done and all the ways we've tried to get my memory back, loving you is still the only thing I know."

I looked at Jack, who was frowning—but in pity, not anger. I turned back to Cole. "I'm sorry. For what I said."

Cole frowned with his entire body; then a strange, wild look appeared in his eyes, and suddenly I worried what he would say next. He took a deep breath. "The truth is, Ashe, the entire reason we're here is because we want to take down the Everneath."

I froze, my mouth hanging slightly open. Jack sprang up from his chair. The one thing we were supposed to keep secret, and Cole blurts it out. To a part Shade, no less.

Ashe looked from Cole, to me, and back to Cole again. "No way."

Cole gave him a blank stare. "No. It's time. Don't you think? How many centuries have you been alive? Don't you want to see what's on the other side?"

"Are you insane?" Ashe looked at me again and then at Jack, desperately searching for someone to validate him. "Is this a joke?"

"No," Cole said. He motioned with his hand for Jack to sit back down. Jack did, but his expression looked murderous. "Look at the life you're living right now, if you can call it a life. You have nobody. And literally no *body*. You lost the love of your life. Both of them. What do you have to live for now? You want to be a Shade? You want your only reason for existing to be to work for the survival of the Everneath?"

Ashe still looked at him as if he weren't talking normally. I just sat back, worried that our plan was all going up in smoke. Why would Ashe ever be convinced to end his own life? And if he felt as if Cole was telling the truth and his home was in danger, would Ashe's loyalty to Cole be enough to prevent him from turning us in to the queen?

Cole gave me a look as if to say *Trust me*. But how could I trust someone who didn't even know his own name? Who didn't even really know what it meant to be an Everliving? And now he was talking like everyone would agree with him. It would be like me going to my neighbor and being all *Hey, let's destroy the world! We've lived long enough. Are you in?*

"Tell me, Ashe. What do you live for?" Cole said.

"Immortality," Ashe said. "It's what we all live for. We

chose this life because immortality is the *only* important thing. It's the everything."

Cole softened his voice. "Immortality is time. It's not something you live for. That's like saying you live for living longer. Don't you see the fault in that thinking? You just told me *when* you live for. But I want to know, Ashe, *what* do you live for?"

Ashe froze for a moment, his eyes on Cole's face. Maybe he was waiting to see if he would crack a smile. Maybe he was waiting for some *Candid Camera* crew to come in. Whatever he was waiting for, it didn't happen. Nobody did anything.

"I don't know," Ashe said. "Do I have to have an answer?"

"Yes!" Cole nodded. "Yes, everyone who is alive has to have an answer to that question. What are you living for?"

"I'm living to live."

"That's not enough. It's not enough anymore, is it?"

Jack and I exchanged glances. This didn't sound like Cole. This sounded like something I would've said to Cole while we were trying to find Jack. Could his amnesia have given him a new soul? A new reason for being?

I didn't know. But it would never work on Ashe. At least, I assumed it wouldn't. But then Cole said, "What if you could have Sheree back? What if she's waiting on the other side for you to follow her?"

"What if she's not?"

"So then she's not. If there is no afterlife, what will you care? You'll be dead and gone then. But here's what I can promise you: You'll never find her in this world. And you won't have to miss her for one more day. You won't have to live with that gaping hole in your chest. You know the one I'm talking about."

A giant, oily black tear escaped one of Ashe's eye sockets. Was it working? I couldn't believe it.

"I think there's another place for us, and another way." Cole looked up at the ceiling momentarily, as if he were just figuring something out. "And the only way we can reach it is through a mortal death."

At this point my mouth dropped open as I stared at Cole.

Ashe stood up. "I've got to go. I've got to go for a walk or something."

Cole reached for his arm, but he couldn't grab onto anything; Ashe was that close to being a full Shade. "Just promise you'll ponder it. If you can't think of a reason to live, will you consider dying with me? Can you promise me you'll really think about it?"

Ashe nodded. Then he walked out the doorway.

When we were alone, all I could do was just stare at Cole. "What was *that*?"

Jack picked up his chair and threw it against the wall. It shattered and fell to the floor in pieces.

But Cole ignored both of us. The second the door closed behind Ashe, he got up and went to the window.

"Answer me, Cole!" I said. "You gave away our plan. How could you do that?" I put my hands on my head and pulled at my hair. "I knew it. I knew you weren't on our side. This whole amnesia thing is bullshit, and I let you trick me again!"

Jack crossed the room and stood in Cole's face. He clenched his hands into tight fists. "Say something, Cole."

I shot out of my chair and stood next to them. Cole didn't even seem to notice Jack. He just stared out the window.

"Cole! What's going on?" I asked.

Finally, he looked at us. "Ashe turned right at the end of the street. He's going to turn us in."

"Of course he is," I said. "And it's your fault!"

"Do you want to follow him to see how he communicates with the rest of the Shades?" Cole asked. "Or do you want to sit here yelling at me?"

"Sit here yelling at you," I said before his words had completely sunken in. "Wait. Did you say follow Ashe?"

Cole nodded.

In the blink of an eye Jack was two steps ahead of us, opening the door and shooing us out into the street.

SIXTEEN

NOW

The Everneath. The streets of Ouros.

We stayed hidden as well as we could as we followed Ashe. I remembered back to the day of the Everneath blackout, right before Cole and I had entered the labyrinth. We'd had to hide in the cellar.

I'd slept that night against Cole. I'd thought he was my friend.

We followed Ashe all the way to the edge of the Common. I wondered why Ashe was walking and not flying like the rest of the Shades would do. Maybe it was because he wasn't a full Shade yet. Either way, I was grateful we didn't have to try to follow a flying Shade right now. We headed toward the entrance to the labyrinth, and I thought for a moment, with a sinking feeling, that we would be going inside. I fought to keep my feet going, but suddenly they felt like they were made of cement.

I couldn't face that three-ring circus of death again.

But he walked past the entrance to the labyrinth. Instead,

he went behind a wall; and the moment he entered there, the outline of a door appeared, angled downward. Ashe pushed through it and descended.

"Do we follow?" Jack asked.

"If we don't, we may never have another chance," Cole said.

Before the entrance could fade away again, the three of us leaped in.

I landed with a thud on what felt like hard-packed dirt. My spine compressed with the impact.

"Ow!"

Cole and Jack landed in a heap next to me, kicking up a cloud of dust. Jack covered his mouth to try to suppress a coughing attack.

What little light there was quickly vanished as the entrance closed off behind us.

I heard someone brushing off his pants. I thought it came from where Jack had landed. "Where are we?" he said.

"Um . . . Underneath the Everneath?" I said.

"Under where?" Cole said, then snickered.

"Are you twelve?" I asked.

Something clicked near me, and suddenly there was a little circle of light. Cole's lighter. We were in a dark tunnel—not like the spacious caves of the actual Tunnels; this was more obviously a passageway somewhere.

As my eyes adjusted, an icy chill ran down my back. The walls looked like they were made of strands of oil, and those strands seemed to be moving and churning as if they were alive: contracting and relaxing, creating a wavelike movement.

The effect made it seem as if we were in the belly of a black snake, about to be digested. I felt the waves of movement under my knees. With each wave, the tunnel seemed to get smaller.

I stayed crouched down. There was no way I'd be able to stand up in here. The entrance to the tunnel was maybe five feet high and five feet wide, but farther down it looked more like three by three.

"This must've been how Jonah felt in the belly of the whale," I said.

Cole gave me a blank stare, but Jack started to shake next to me. I could feel it. I put my hand on his arm, but he threw it off immediately. I knew it was just a reflexive move. "What's wrong?" I asked.

But then I realized I already knew the answer. Jack had spent decades buried alive in the Tunnels. As bad as I thought the Feed was for me, Jack had had it worse. I was merely cocooned with Cole for a hundred years while he stole my energy. Jack had been surrounded by dirt, the earth pressing in on him, stealing his breath. He'd felt as if he was suffocating the entire time. And just when he thought he would die from the lack of oxygen, he somehow kept going.

"I'm sorry," I said. "You should go. Don't do this."

"I'm not leaving you alone with him," he said. Now that he was distressed, he was unable to mask his suspicion of Cole.

"We have no idea how far this tunnel goes," I said. "You

can't do this. Aside from the fact that you can barely fit . . . no. I won't let you."

"You don't have a choice," he said. "I'm not leaving you. I'm not. We promised, and I'm not about to break my promise. Not for this."

I sighed. Cole just held his lighter, his face showing he didn't want to get in the middle of anything.

"Listen. What if something happens to us?" I said. "What if we can't get back out? Somebody has to be on the outside. We should've thought of this before. But somebody has to know where we are."

Even in the dim glow of the lighter, Jack's face looked pale and ashen. He would be useless to us in this condition, but I wasn't about to tell him that.

"You might be our only chance," I said. "Go outside. Put your ear to the ground. Try to figure out if anything is going on."

"What about my leaking energy?" Jack asked.

Cole pointed toward Jack's feet. "It wasn't very strong to begin with. Now it's barely visible. You'll be okay as long as you stick to the shadows."

Jack nodded. Thankfully he was agreeing with us, because there was no way he'd survive in a place this small. In fact, just seeing him made me wonder if any of us would survive it. But Cole and I were skinnier than Jack, and we hadn't been traumatized as he had.

Jack reached up to where the entrance had been. I wondered for a split second if it would really open again or if we were all trapped here, but it opened under the pressure from his hand.

"Okay. How long before I should start to worry?" Jack said.

"Now." I smiled. Jack looked at my face and instantly relaxed a bit, to the point where he even smiled.

"Okay, I'll start worrying right now." He grabbed my shoulders and brought me close and pressed his lips against mine. I threw my arms around his neck and lost myself in the kiss. His lips parted, and mine did too. I felt the kiss everywhere. And suddenly we weren't in a snake belly anymore. We were on the Surface, and we both had our hearts, and we were standing in real sunlight. And we were whole and together.

It was that kind of kiss.

Cole cleared his throat.

Finally, we pulled apart. "I'll see you soon," Jack said.

"So soon," I said.

Then Jack leaped out of the hole and closed the door behind him, and Cole and I were alone.

Cole was looking at me with a curious expression.

"What?" I said.

He shook his head. "I just . . . you and Jack. How long have you been together?"

"Years. But it's felt like an eternity." I used my hands to shoo him forward. "Why?"

"Because I don't see it. The two of you."

I sighed, remembering when he'd said nearly the same thing that day we silk-screened Dead Elvises T-shirts in the

GraphX Shop. And now we were being digested by an oily tunnel, and we were still talking about it.

"What?" he said. As he inched farther down the tunnel, he resorted to army crawling after a few yards. I followed suit.

"We've had this conversation before," I said. "When we first met. Right before you . . ." My voice faded away.

"Before I what?"

I looked away. "Let's get going."

"No. Finish what you were saying." He stopped moving, and I knew he wouldn't start again until I talked.

So I blurted out the answer. "Right before I went to the Feed with you."

He was quiet for a moment. "Why *did* you go to the Feed with me?"

"I don't know. It doesn't matter now. We have to go."

"Yes, it does," he said, his voice a whisper. "It matters to me."

I sighed and then looked beyond him to where the tunnel disappeared in darkness. "We don't have time."

"In a hundred words or less."

A hundred words to explain how my mother had died, how her murderer had gotten off on a technicality, and then how I thought Jack had cheated on me. And Cole was there for me. "I made a series of bad decisions. I thought nothing could be worse than feeling so much pain. But I was wrong."

I finally glanced up at him. He frowned. "And coming with me ended up being worse than the worst pain you could bear."

I nodded slowly.

"I'm sorry." The words hung in the cramped air of that tiny hole for a long time. "I'm sorry I did that to you."

I didn't know what to say. Cole had never been apologetic for anything that he had ever done. In fact, he'd always believed that being an Everliving, and sucking the life out of someone, was morally defensible. Because it was the Forfeit's choice. Because it was about life triumphing over the absence of life.

I couldn't believe he was apologizing now. And suddenly, knowing that he held my heart, knowing that he had tricked me into giving it up, knowing that he had betrayed me . . . now that he was apologizing, I was furious.

"You took everything from me," I said, my voice shaking. "You tricked me into becoming an Everliving. You did this to me."

"I'm sorry," he said again. He put his hand over his heart as if he needed to keep it from spilling out. But he had no heart.

"Stop apologizing!" The words were loud, but they were digested quickly in the pulsating walls. "There are some things that you just can't apologize for. Some things are too big for an apology. Some things . . ." My voice trailed off as I remembered saying something similar to Jack when I'd first Returned.

Sometimes, when someone keeps forgiving someone else, it becomes too much.

"Look, this is not going anywhere," I said. "Let's just go."

Cole nodded as if there were nothing in the world he

wanted more at that moment than to get out of the current conversation.

He pointed ahead of him. "Do you want to go first or last?"

I thought about it. If I went last, all I would be thinking about was that if someone was chasing us, they'd get me first. Maybe the same was true if I was in front, but at least in front I knew I was facing the danger.

"First," I said.

He moved to the side and then held his arms out in an "after you" kind of way. I scooted past him and started to crawl.

SEVENTEEN

NOW

The Everneath. The crawlway to the Shade network.

The only illumination came intermittently from Cole's lighter behind me. And even when it was lit, I was blocking most of it.

"Just keep it off," I said. "It doesn't help."

Cole clicked it off. I could see, far up in the distance, a spot of light moving up and down. But the more I focused on it, the more I realized that it wasn't the light moving. It was the wave of the tunnel moving me up and down.

"What are we going to do when we get there?" I said.

Cole grunted as he navigated through a particularly narrow part of the passageway. "I don't know. I hadn't thought that far ahead."

"What do you mean?"

"Well, the moment I thought about spilling the beans about our plan to Ashe, I assumed that getting him to believe us would take longer than it did. It wasn't part of the plan for Ashe to actually take the bait so quickly."

"So, what, your plan was to, A, get Ashe to take the bait, and then there was no B?"

"Basically."

"Suddenly I don't want to be first in the tunnel."

We kept crawling. The waves started to take a toll on my stomach, and pretty soon my goal was not only to emerge at the end, but also not to puke along the way. It didn't help that I kept picturing digestive juices along the walls and floor. Juices that were slowly disintegrating my skin.

But the light got closer. And the air in the tunnel became colder.

"When we get there," Cole said, "don't do anything. We're just going to get a glimpse of where their headquarters is located and see if we can see anything that will help. Don't take any chances."

I rolled my eyes, even though Cole couldn't see me. "What did you think I was going to do? Announce our arrival?"

As we approached the opening, I could see that the light wasn't coming from outside. Instead, it was coming from a giant, glowing ball shaped like an egg. Shadows danced back and forth in front of it. Shades. Gathering around the ball as humans would gather around a campfire.

The walls of the room were round and pulsating. If the tunnel had been the esophagus of the snake, this was the stomach.

"What do you see?" Cole asked.

"A glowing ball. In the center of . . . a cavernous . . . stomach."

"What?"

I focused on describing the scene. "It's as large as the Feed caverns. The Shades are gathered around the ball, touching it. And where they touch it, the light from the ball condenses against their fingers. It's like they're drawing power from the ball."

Suddenly a denser figure approached the ball and placed a more defined hand on its surface. Instead of drawing the light toward his hand, the contact thrust the light farther away.

"It's Ashe," I said. "He's touching the ball. But the light is going away from his touch."

Ripples of light emanated from the point of contact, and suddenly, above the ball, an image appeared. Three dimensional, like a hologram.

At the sight, every Shade in the place froze. They turned toward the hologram expectantly, as if whatever was about to appear would be big news.

Inside the image a face began to take shape. Someone with short hair. Blond.

It was Cole's face. Then my face. Then Jack's face. There for every Shade to see.

"We've got to get out of here. Now!"

I started to crawl backward, my feet smushing into Cole's face.

"Watch it, Nik!"

"Move, move!"

We crawled backward until we reached a place that was

large enough for us to turn around. Maybe it was because I was so much smaller, but I was moving faster than Cole could. I pushed against his feet, trying to give him extra leverage to springboard from.

The light from behind us grew faint, as if someone were blocking the exit point.

"Faster!" I said. "I think someone's coming."

That lit a fire under Cole. He scrambled onward. Since the entrance at the other end was closed, we couldn't tell how close we were until Cole actually fell into the dirt anteroom.

He threw his shoulder upward against the door, and we fell in a heap outside on the ground. Jack wasn't there, but I didn't have time to wonder where he was. Whoever was behind us was right on our tails. Dark tendrils of oil-like fluid reached around the edge of the door.

Shades. I desperately wanted a railroad tie or something to throw across the entrance, to lock them inside.

The second I thought of it, a stream of mist emanated from my chest, forming a large, rectangular object. It floated toward the entrance, and as it solidified, I could see it became a railroad tie. It lay across the entrance in slots on either side, bolting it shut.

Cole staggered to his feet, looked at the railroad tie, and then helped me up. We both started running.

"How did you do that?" he said.

I shook my head. "Keep running!"

The signs around the streets changed to show both Cole's

face and my own, and underneath the image were the words *Traitors to the nation.*

Cole grabbed my hand roughly and closed his eyes, and it took me a split second when my feet lifted from the ground to realize what he was doing.

"No!" I yanked my hand away. "We're not leaving Jack."

He looked as if he might try to grab my hand again, but then he closed his eyes and nodded quickly.

We bounded down the street. A couple of Everlivings saw us coming and jumped out of the way. I took my first right and then a left and then another right, trying to make our movements as random as possible. Why hadn't we discussed another meeting place?

I concentrated on Jack. His face. His cheekbones. His shaggy brown hair. The lines of his body. The way he moved. The way he flicked his ring finger. The divot on his forehead.

A small rod appeared at my feet, exactly like the tether that had led me to Jack when he was stuck in the Tunnels.

"This way!" I shouted to Cole.

We darted around corners, going whichever way the tether pointed us. Brushing past Everlivings, most of whom gave us strange looks. Obviously, the change on the posters hadn't quite sunk in, because no one tackled us.

At one point we saw a couple of Shades blocking our path, so we cut through a dark alley. But when we reached the end, there was no way out. We turned around and nearly ran smack into Ashe.

He had us trapped. There was nowhere to go and no way we could outrun him. Panicked, I turned to Cole.

"Ashe," Cole said, a pleading tone to his voice.

Ashe reached for a door in the building on the right wall. He shoved it open. Was he going to lock us inside?

"Follow the hallway, then take a right," he said. "You can get past the Shades that way."

I stared at him, suspicious.

Ashe noted my expression. "If I wanted to turn you in right now, I would. And there's something else," Ashe said. "When I shared your intentions with the network, that was before I thought of something that could help you. If you get your hands on—" His voice cut off, and he froze midsentence. His mouth hung open as if he were in pain. I almost looked behind him to make sure someone hadn't stabbed him or something.

"Ashe?" I said.

He shook his head and started again. "Find the—" Again he stopped. Closed his eyes. "I can't say it."

Cole stepped forward. "Because it would betray the Everneath?"

Ashe lowered his head, took a deep breath, raised it again, and said, "Cronus." He gritted his black teeth, and the next word came out as an almost indistinguishable grunt. "Tantalus." The moment the word left his lips, he collapsed onto the ground.

Cole grabbed my hand. "We're out of time!" He pulled me into the building. We followed Ashe's instructions and stumbled out into an empty street, at the end of which was Jack, tearing down one of the thousands of posters of Cole's face.

"Jack!" I said.

He saw us barreling toward him, and he held out his hands. Cole grabbed one and I grabbed the other, and we froze, waiting to leave the ground.

And nothing happened.

"Cole," I said, staring at the way we'd come. "Do something."

"I know," Cole said. "I'm trying to concentrate. I'm thinking upward."

He raised himself up on his tiptoes.

Tentacles of black oil appeared around the edge of the building that stood on the corner we'd just come from.

"They're here!" I said. Jack tried to let go of my hand, and I knew he was going to charge them. "No!" I said, grabbing him even tighter. "You won't be able to touch them. Stay still."

The Shades moved like a cloud, or more like a tornado, coming down the road.

"Cole!" I dug my nails into his hand.

"I'm trying!"

"Think of a place. A calm place. If you can picture it, then I'd bet it's a real place you've been. Think of it. Put yourself there."

Cole's eyes were closed. I would've closed mine, but I couldn't help staring at the Shades coming for us. We were moments away from being swallowed.

"You know how to do this," I said. "You just have to remember."

At the possibility that this was the end, I had one thought.

"I love you guys," I said. I had only an instant to realize, with surprise, that I indeed loved both of them, in their own way.

A rush of cold wind washed over my face.

"Hang on," Cole said.

Just as the first Shade wrapped a swirl of oil around Jack's arm, our feet lifted simultaneously off the ground. And then we were tumbling upward, the Shades screaming behind us.

We crashed into the earth, a heap of limbs and torsos. Cole's arm had fallen across my face. I couldn't see a thing.

"Ow," I said.

"Sorry," he said. He removed his arm, and daylight, real daylight, blinded me. Above me was clear blue sky. I pushed myself up into a sitting position and looked around. We were on a dirt road surrounded by green fields for miles and miles. The land was flat, the horizon distinctly clear on all sides of us. The place didn't look familiar at all.

"Where are we?" I said.

Cole was sitting beside me. He shook his head as if he had a headache. "I don't know."

Jack was already standing. He turned around in a full circle. "I don't see anything, besides— What are those, cornstalks?

No people. No structures." He looked at Cole and narrowed his eyes. "Where the hell are we?"

Cole frowned. "I'll tell you where we're not. We're not being chased by Shades."

"The Shades wouldn't have been chasing us if you hadn't given up our real plans to Ashe." Jack's nostrils were flaring.

Cole didn't back down. "We wouldn't have found out anything if I hadn't followed my instincts."

"It was a gamble! With my life and Nikki's!" Jack's fists were clenched tightly. "If I were placing bets, I'd say you just got away with a nice bit of sabotage back there."

"Hey, I didn't have to bring you here. I could've just grabbed Nik and zoomed away, leaving you to deal with the Shades."

"Yeah, we all saw how well you *zoom*."

I stepped between them. "Okay, boys, settle down. It wasn't all for nothing. We saw the Shade network, and Ashe helped us at the very end—he gave us our next step."

"How?" Jack said.

"He said there was something that could help us." I looked to Cole for confirmation. "A Cronus Tantalus."

Cole nodded.

Jack narrowed his eyes. "What's a Cronus Tantalus?"

Cole and I both shrugged. "We'll work that out later," I said. "We're safe, for now. We just have to figure out where we are."

Cole looked around too. "This place feels familiar."

Jack folded his arms. "Can't you just . . . zap us somewhere else again?"

Cole shrugged, but I actually knew the answer to this one. "He would have to take us to the Everneath again first. And in the shape he's in, we're not guaranteed we'd get any closer to home. And not only that, it takes massive amounts of his energy."

Cole nodded. "Yeah. What she said."

Jack sighed. "So what did you guys see down there? What did the network look like?"

I explained to Jack about the giant glowing egg-like thing we'd seen Ashe touching, and the Shade convention that seemed to be going on.

Jack squinted one eye in a thoughtful kind of way. "I think I saw something like that in Mrs. Jenkins's papers."

"What did it say?" I said.

"I don't know. At the time, I wasn't sure a glowing egg would mean anything. The papers are in the back of my car."

Cole looked from me to Jack and back again. "So, what do we do now?"

Jack sighed. "We start walking."

"Which way?" Cole said.

Jack squinted as he turned slowly around. He stopped. "There. Something on the horizon. It's a ways from here, but probably a farmhouse or something. Let's just hope we're in the United States. We didn't exactly pack our passports."

We started walking toward the black dot. I began to wonder if Cole had ever really been here. It seemed very remote, and cornfields weren't exactly Cole's scene.

I watched Jack out of the corner of my eye as we walked. His face was smooth and unruffled, and I was amazed by how well he was dealing with all the crazy. A girlfriend who'd left him to spend a century in the Everneath with another guy. A girlfriend who was always on the verge of dying. A girlfriend who basically had to kiss another guy every night, while all he could do was watch.

It took me only a second to realize—or remember—that all the crazy revolved around me.

Jack saw me staring. "Don't even think it, Becks."

"Think what?" I said.

The corner of his mouth turned up. "I know that look. It comes in the quiet moments, like this one. I know you're thinking that this is all your fault and that I would be better off without you. But here's the thing you need to understand." He stopped walking and grabbed my shoulders. "You are my peace and my home. You are the everything. The pain isn't real. The hearts are."

I held my breath. I blinked rapidly. If I'd had a heart, it would've sprouted wings and flown out of my chest and into the blue sky.

"Breathe, Becks."

I breathed. "How were you ever a football player?"

His lips twitched. "Not all football players are stupid."

Then the words spilled out, like they always did when my pulse was racing. "But they're big, and they tackle each other, and they smack bottoms, and say things like 'pigskin' and 'blitz.'"

Jack stepped closer and raised an eyebrow. "And 'forward pass.' And 'holding.'" He wrapped his arms around me.

"Ugh." Cole made an actual gagging sound.

We both turned to look at him.

"Sorry," Cole said, looking horrified. "I have no idea where that came from."

"I do," Jack said. "I think your natural instincts are getting stronger."

Cole frowned, and the lines around his mouth became tight.

"What is it?" I said.

Cole tried for a smile, but the effort was faint. "You both have these histories, and you can cling to them at times like this. But me . . . I'm just feeling a little homesick for my memories."

I glanced at Jack, who tilted his head and nodded. I sighed. "How about I tell you a story?"

Cole stopped walking. "I would love it."

I nodded again. Memories. So many memories, many of which I would've liked to forget forever, such as waking up after a century of Cole feeding on me.

"What do you want to know?"

Cole chuckled. "If I knew that, I wouldn't have this

problem. Do you have any memories that would tell me about . . . myself?"

I wasn't sure I could objectively tell a story about my history with Cole. Every memory was tainted with all the stuff I knew about him now but didn't know then. Not making things any easier was the fact that Jack was listening, and many of the more positive memories I had of Cole took place during the time Jack was away at football camp and ended with me following Cole to the Underworld. I didn't think any of those stories were safe.

But I knew other stories. In particular, I knew the memory that had accompanied that first kiss in the courtyard during Creative Writing, when I discovered exactly how Cole would keep me alive. I hadn't thought about it since then, but now that I focused on it, the entire story came into my head with such clarity, it was as if I'd lived it myself.

"You used to live on a farm, in Norway," I said. "Imagine a young man working a field."

1186

The Surface. Norway.

A young man with blond hair raised an iron-shod spade above his head and thrust it downward into the ditch. The summer sun shone behind him, giving his hair a haloed look. During these months the sun wouldn't set until late in the evening, making the work hours long.

The man was young to be working the fields on his own, and his shoulders ached from the new weight of responsibility placed upon them after his father had succumbed to the fever. As the elder male, the young man took his place in the fields, his younger brother, Edgar, assuming the farm apprentice position that the young man vacated.

The young man set the spade aside and grabbed a pick. He plunged it into the hard dirt, softening the soil as he went.

"Coleson!" Edgar's voice sounded out of breath.

Coleson looked up to see his sixteen-year-old brother running toward him. He plunged the pick into the dirt and left it there, standing upright.

"Edgar. What's wrong?" He picked up the spade again.

"They're coming."

Coleson stood up straight. He brushed the dirt off his trousers and shook his head.

"Which one did they send for the *skora a hólm*?" Coleson asked his brother. *Skora a hólm*. The official challenge to a duel.

Edgar looked down. "Gunnar."

Of course. Gunnar was the largest of the *Hólmgang* pack. They'd probably heard of Coleson's father's passing. They preyed on the families left behind, who were most vulnerable. It was easy to challenge survivors to a duel to steal their property.

"*Hólmgang* is supposed to be outlawed," Edgar said.

"Tell that to Gunnar."

Coleson stalked off toward the house, throwing the spade aside.

"What are you doing?" Edgar asked. "You might need that."

Coleson's frown was set. "No, I won't."

He entered the house and reached for the largest satchel he could see. "Mother!" he called out.

A striking woman with long, blond hair braided at the nape of her neck appeared from the kitchen.

"Mother, we're leaving."

Coleson set about packing the most valuable items into his satchel.

"What? Why?" his mother asked.

Edgar burst through the door. "Gunnar is coming, Mother. He's coming for the duel. And if Coleson wins, we'll get everything Gunnar owns. Those are the rules of the *Hólmgang.*"

Coleson grunted as he shoved the last of the silver goblets into the satchel. "I'm not fighting."

Edgar and his mother stared.

"What do you mean?" his mother said.

"I mean if I fight, I'll lose. And you both know Gunnar's history. He won't stop until I'm dead and he has the farm. And then where will you both be?" He shoved a plate into the satchel. As the new man of the house, Coleson knew his first obligation had to be to his family. "No, we take what we can and we run."

Edgar's mouth hung open for a moment. "What about family honor? Honor demands that we stay and fight. Without it, we will be shunned everywhere we go."

Coleson dropped the bag and turned on his brother. "This is not like the brawls that you get into at the tavern! This is sure death." He grabbed his brother's hand and brought it to his chest, just above his beating heart. "This is life. No matter if we are on the farm or . . . somewhere else."

Edgar yanked his hand away. "There is no life without honor. I will not abandon our land. And if you will not fight, then I will."

Coleson turned toward his mother, who was slowly inching her way toward Edgar. Coleson held out his hand. "Mother. You understand we have to run."

She shook her head. "I understand this is our home. And we will not flee simply because a band of thugs challenges us for our land. I will stand where your father would stand, were he with us."

Coleson looked from his mother to his brother and hesitated. It was simple for them to talk about words such as *honor* when it was Coleson's life on the line.

His brother would not make the same stand if he really had to fight.

"I'm leaving," Coleson said. "And you are both welcome

to come with me. Or you can stay here and die, with your honor."

Coleson knew that if he left, his family would soon trail after. Everyone would know that they were forced to follow. That way they would be able to keep their honor. The disgrace would then rest on Coleson alone.

He hoisted the satchel high up onto his shoulder and left, but he did not go far. Instead, he hid out just beyond the trees bordering the Stockflet property and waited. As soon as his mother and brother appeared, he would run to meet them.

But for two days they didn't appear. The only activity came from a band of four men on horses, who stormed toward the farmhouse.

Edgar came out to meet them, an ax in his hand. Coleson was not close enough to hear any of the words spoken, but he was close enough to see Gunnar's sword run through his brother's chest.

Coleson turned away, stifling a shout. And then he ran.

Two days later, word of a terrible tragedy reached the inn where Coleson was lodging. The entire Stockflet family was murdered during a *Hólmgang*. The older brother's body was never found.

When Coleson heard the news, he left the town and changed his name. He used the money from the valuables he'd collected to purchase an apprenticeship. He never spoke again of the family he'd abandoned.

NOW
The Surface. Still no idea where we are.

Cole stared at me, transfixed. I brushed my hair out of my eyes and waved him forward. I continued on with the rest of the memory Cole had shared with me. "You became obsessed with the myth of Hercules, particularly the part where he was cursed with the inability to discern right from wrong. You believed that would be a blessing."

The revelation explained so much about Cole.

Cole squeezed his eyes shut. "How do you know this story? Were you there?"

"No. It was a memory from your mind before the amnesia. You shared it with me when I fed on you. But I didn't know the details of it until I started telling it to you just now."

"I thought you said the Everlivings killed my family."

Oh, crap.

"They did," I said, flustered. "Your extended family. Not the immediate family."

For a moment I felt a little guilty about the fake backstory I'd given him for my own selfish reasons. It was becoming more difficult to remember all the reasons I hated Cole, especially now that I'd gotten this glimpse into his tragic past.

Jack was so quiet on the other side of me. I wondered if he felt sorry for Cole or if the story made him hate Cole even more.

"How could I have left them like that?" Cole asked. "It's despicable."

I cleared my throat. "You used to say that there was no such thing as good or evil. There was only life and the absence of life."

In light of this memory of Cole's, I thought that maybe I understood a little bit more about his motives. I could understand the yearning to forget. The urge to focus on something as simple as life and death, and not on wrong or right.

"Forget the past," Jack said softly from behind me. "The question is, did the memory spark any sort of recognition in you?"

Cole closed his eyes, as if he were searching his brain for something. He shook his head. "No. But somehow I know in my bones that the story is true."

We were quiet as we walked toward the dot, which now that we were closer we could tell was a house. A farmhouse.

The faint sound of running farm equipment reached us through the air. A man steered a tractor through one of the fields adjacent to the farmhouse.

Cole's eyes went wide, like a kid's eyes in a candy shop.

Ten minutes later, we were riding on a hay-bale trailer connected to the back of the tractor. The farmer had agreed to give us a ride into the nearest town, Blue Hill.

We were in Nebraska.

* * *

The tractor stopped in front of a small grocery store set back off the desolate Main Street.

"We have to call Jules," I said, hopping off the bale of hay. "If the queen knows who the Dead Elvises are, she'll find me. And that means she'll find my family. Jules can help. She can get them out of the house."

Jack's phone was dead. He flagged down a man on the other side of the street, jogged over to him, and talked for a moment. The man nodded and handed him a cell phone.

Jack ran back and handed me the phone.

I dialed Jules's number.

"Jules," I said. "It's Becks."

"Becks! Where are you? Are you okay?"

"Yes. We're in . . . Nebraska. It's a long story. But I need your help."

I explained enough of the situation so that she would know I was telling the truth, and then we devised a cover story she could use to get my dad and brother out of the house.

When we had settled on it, she asked, "Are you really okay?"

I looked at Jack. Well, I was stranded in Nebraska with an amnesiac Everliving and a claustrophobic boyfriend, having escaped nearly being smothered to death by an army of Shades. "Everything's fine," I said. "I'll explain it all later. But Jules?"

"Yeah?"

"Thank you. *Thank you*."

When I hung up, I breathed a sigh of relief. "She'll take care of it," I said. "Though I think it's safe to say that when this is all over, I'll have to go to rehab indefinitely."

Jack got a bright twinkle in his eye, and I realized that I'd made reference to a future in which both of us were whole and alive and not fighting for survival.

But in order to reach that future, there couldn't be an Everneath. And right now there was very much an Everneath.

EIGHTEEN

NOW

The Surface. Trying to get out of Nebraska.

*O*nce we found an airport, we were able fly home, but getting to the airport took a hike, another ride on a tractor, and a ride on a bus and in a taxi.

We probably really didn't need the second tractor ride, but Cole became so excited when he saw one for rent.

As we were waiting for the bus, we sat on a bench, me in between Cole and Jack. I couldn't help yawning. Cole leaned toward me.

"You're tired. Let me feed you," he said.

I looked right and left at the people around us. "Not here," I said.

Jack had gone rigid next to me, but he remained silent.

"Why not?" Cole asked. "You're exhausted."

"We all are."

Jack turned toward me. "Just do it, Becks." He sounded resigned.

I didn't know why I felt so uncomfortable about it. Was it hearing all the stories from his past? Hearing how he felt about love?

I would've preferred not to feed on Cole, but I couldn't deny the exhaustion that reached my bones. I recognized the weakness coming on now.

I closed my eyes and felt Cole move toward me, his breath on my face, his lips touching mine. I was so aware of the way Jack was watching that it took me a few minutes to realize that Cole was unintentionally sharing a memory again. A dark memory. The first memory since his amnesia that had distinct shapes and a definite story line.

MEMORY
No idea as to the place and time.

I walked up a set of stairs, the paint on either side of the walls peeling, in the plaster a hole that hadn't been fixed for decades.

I raised my hand to knock on the door and noticed tattoos on each of my fingers, making it look like I was wearing black rings. Again I was reliving things through Cole's perspective.

Cole knocked.

The door opened slowly, revealing darkness behind it. I couldn't see who had opened it. I would've hesitated at the threshold, but Cole did not. He went inside, and as his eyes adjusted to the dark room, he saw a figure sitting in the corner.

"What's with the foil?" Cole asked. It was then I noticed the aluminum foil covering the windows, letting in only one tiny sliver of light.

"The darkness reminds me of home. The one you burned." Cole nodded. "So did you really find it?"

"Yes," the man in the corner said. "Did you bring the Helmet of Hermes?"

"Yes."

"Give it here." The man held out a bony hand, extending his long, pale fingers. The longest fingers I'd ever seen.

"No," Cole said. "Show me the memory first, then I'll give you the pendant."

The man in the corner chuckled. "That's not how it works."

"I saved your ass from a napalm fire. You owe me this." Cole's mind flashed to an image of a dungeon. He was running through stone hallways, escaping from some sort of captivity. The walls were on fire.

The man was quiet for a moment. Then he said, "This is true."

He stood, and that's when I noticed his head. It was enormous, as if it housed a brain three times the normal size. It made his face appear squished. I would've leaped back at the sight, but Cole didn't move.

The man produced a wooden box. He must've been

holding it the entire time. He opened the box and took out a black square of material that swished in the air like gossamer, then balled it up in his hands and threw it against the wall. It silently shattered into millions of tiny pixels that rearranged themselves into an image against the white paint.

The image showed two women facing each other, one tall and regal, with long, black hair, the other petite and fair-haired. I recognized the latter immediately.

Adonia.

The current queen of the Everneath, before she adopted her red-haired look. But in this frozen moment she didn't seem powerful. She was cowering like a dog.

The image remained frozen only for a moment more, then it melted into action.

The dark-haired woman flicked her fingers, and a cage appeared around Adonia.

Adonia grabbed the bars and shook them, her eyes wide with the terror that comes with being trapped. The woman flicked her wrist, and a dagger appeared in her hand. She threw it at the cage. It sliced through the air between two bars, speeding toward Adonia's face. Adonia closed her eyes and threw up a hand to block it. I was worried that the dagger would slice right through her hand, but just as it reached her, a wooden shield appeared in the hand she'd held up.

The dagger glanced off the shield and hit the bars of the cage before falling to the ground.

The dark-haired woman conjured another dagger, but Adonia, her eyes squeezed shut, raised her hands above her head and began drawing circles in the air with her fingers. The air around her cage began to move, becoming windy. She touched a pendant at her neck, and immediately the storm gathered intensity. Tiny flecks of crystalline snow appeared, swirling around outside the cage, a blinding blizzard localized within a ten-foot radius.

The cage disappeared behind the wall of white flakes.

The dark-haired woman stared, dumbfounded. She threw the knife into the blizzard, but the wind sucked it into the tornado of snow.

The blizzard died down, and as it did, I could see Adonia lowering her arms. She closed her eyes again, and a long, metal club appeared in her hands. She swung the club, and when it made contact with the bars, they shattered.

That must've been the reason for the blizzard. So the iron bars would freeze, and she would be able to break them.

Adonia leveled her gaze at the dark-haired woman. She raised her hands again, and two spiked walls appeared next to Adonia's opponent, one in back and one in front. The spikes were pointed toward her.

Adonia clapped her hands together; and as if they were mirroring her hands, the walls smashed together, collapsing on the other woman.

The movie stopped playing at this point, frozen on the

image of Adonia collapsing to the ground in exhaustion.

"Oh, Nikki," Cole muttered. "We've got a long way to go."

The man with the huge head turned to Cole. "There you go. The memory you had me dig up. Now, where is the Helmet of Hermes?"

Cole reached into his satchel and pulled out a wooden box. He handed the box to the man. "It's in there."

The man took the box, an expectant smile on his lips. "Invisibility. This will get me by until my exile is revoked."

"I'll leave you alone with your prize," Cole said. He started to walk toward the door.

"Wait!" the man said.

Cole's hand froze on the doorknob.

"Remember. If this works out for you and you have a seat on the throne, you will revoke my exile."

I could almost feel Cole's pulse settle back down. "Of course."

He turned the knob, stepped out, and closed the door behind him. The second the lock latched, Cole started running. Down the stairs, to the landing, down the next set of stairs.

Then the screaming started. From the apartment he'd just left.

"Coleson Stockflet! Where's the Helmet of Hermes?"

Cole kept running, but he called out behind him. "I'll get it. I promise. I know where it is!"

As he burst through the front door of the apartment building, I heard one more faint shout. "You will pay!"

Cole ran.

NOW

The Surface. Nebraska.

I pulled back from Cole, releasing myself from the memory. Cole's head was tilted back on the bench. He had fallen asleep.

"Becks?" Jack said. "Are you okay?"

I took a few deep breaths. "I think I know how Adonia defeated the previous queen. And how Cole wants me to defeat Adonia."

NINETEEN

NOW
The Surface. Nebraska.

I told Jack all about the memory, about how Cole had gone to a strange man with a huge head and had promised him a pendant called the Helmet of Hermes in exchange for someone's memory of Adonia killing the previous queen.

"I know it was a memory of Cole's. Maybe it's still buried deep in his subconscious, and it could only come out in a dream." I thought about the timeline. "It obviously happened before Cole was captured. What if the guy with the huge head betrayed him? What if, when Cole didn't have the"—I shook my head—"Helmet of Hermes thing, what if he turned him in?" I sank into the chair and put my head in my hands. I couldn't stop obsessing over the fact that this might have been the point that got Cole in so much trouble.

Jack put his arm around me and kissed my forehead. "Shh. It's done, Becks. It's in the past. There's nothing you can do about it now."

"I know," I said softly. I leaned my head into Jack as I thought about the rest of the dream. "You know, Cole always said surviving the Feed made me different in a way that would help me take down the queen. I think I got a good look at how that would have to happen. But Adonia was conjuring up *blizzards*. When I first got to the Everneath, I conjured up the entire Fiery Furnace at Arches National Park, but once I got rid of it, I had enough of a problem conjuring up a tether and turning it into a stick. Cole said it was a problem with my focus." I grimaced as I remembered how Cole and Max had been overcome by hunger in the Ring of Fire, and the only way I could get them to move was to poke them with a hot stick I'd made out of the tether. "I doubt I could kill the queen with a twig."

"Maybe Cole was planning on teaching you how to do more. He did say you had a long way to go."

I thought back to the memory. "Right before the blizzard got really strong, Adonia touched the necklace. I think it was her heart. Maybe she got even more strength from it."

Cole stirred next to me and promptly rolled off the bench.

"Ouch!" he said. He sprang up, looking from Jack to me with a confused expression on his face.

I wondered if the recollection meant he had recovered his memories, and I grabbed Jack's hand in preparation to face a Cole who knew the truth.

"What happened?" he said.

"Cole, you have amnesia," I said slowly.

He tilted his head. "I know that. What happened just now?"

I glanced at Jack. "You fell off the bench?" he said.

Cole sighed. "Oh. Okay. Are we going to destroy the Everneath now?"

With a screech of brakes, the bus pulled up to our stop. "We're going back to Park City first," I said.

Cole nodded. "Park City. Where's that?"

Cole fed me again at the airport, and after so much continuous contact, I felt stronger than I had in a long time. Stronger I think than even before I'd lost my heart.

As we traveled, I couldn't stop thinking about how Adonia touched her necklace—her Surface heart—to get more strength. If I had to face anyone, where would I get strength without my heart?

Once we landed at the Salt Lake City airport, we took a taxi to the Shop-n-Go to retrieve Jack's car.

"My credit cards are almost maxed out," Jack said as he started his car. He had used his emergency ones to buy our airplane tickets as well. "Hopefully there's enough left to get us a hotel."

I shrugged, a little lost in thought as I stared out the window.

"Becks? You okay?"

I turned to Jack. "I think I need my heart."

"What?" Jack said.

Cole leaned forward from the backseat.

I shifted in my seat so I could see both of them. "It's the memory of the queens. If we try to take down the Everneath and we run into Adonia, I don't think I'll stand a chance fighting against her unless I have my heart."

"Well, hopefully we won't run into her," Jack said.

"But even if we get that far, to the point where we destroy all our hearts, I'm going to need to know where my heart is."

"Where do you think it is?" Cole said.

I pressed my lips together and breathed out through my nose, trying to keep my composure. "I don't know," I said. "I'm guessing *you* hid it somewhere."

"Why would I—" Cole stopped and tilted his head. "Oh, yeah. I stole it."

I closed my eyes and put my face in my hands for a moment.

Cole tapped my shoulder. "You know, if I shared a memory with you, then maybe my memory is coming back. Can't we go to my condo and see if I can—I don't know—see if I can *feel* where I hid it?"

Jack groaned. "Cole, your place was ransacked."

"But they obviously didn't find it, because they're still looking for me. I bet I hid it well."

Jack glanced out the window. "We should follow up on the Cronus lead from Ashe."

"Say we found something and destroyed the Shade network," I said. "We'd *still* need my heart."

"I just think it might be a wild-goose chase," Jack said.

Cole put his hand on my arm. "What's on your wrist?"

"What?" I said. Jack and I both looked down at my left arm, the one that hadn't had the shackle; only now, at my wrist line, the faintest black mark encircled my wrist. Not nearly as dark as the other shackle, but definitely visible.

Jack couldn't stop staring at it. "Let's go find your heart," he said.

I nodded. "We'll talk to Will and have him research anything and everything he can about Cronus. By the time we're done searching Cole's condo, hopefully he'll have something for us."

I stared at the new shackle. Was it growing darker even as I watched? I waited a few long minutes. No, I couldn't tell a difference.

But even though I couldn't see it growing darker, I knew it was.

Jack turned the car in the direction of his own house, and I called Will to give him a heads-up; but no one answered.

"He's probably passed out," Jack said, referring to his older brother's love of drinking.

When we got to Jack's house, we found Will asleep on the Caputos' couch. Jack shook his older brother awake.

"Wha—" Will startled up to a sitting position.

He looked from Jack, to me, then to Cole. The second he saw Cole's face, his eyelids narrowed into tiny slits. "You," he said accusingly. "You . . ." He jumped up from the couch, but he'd obviously been drinking, because he staggered to the side a few steps and then fell.

Jack ran to him. "It's okay, bro. He's helping us."

Will looked at him as if he were crazy. "Are you nuts? He's 'helped' us before, and we barely survived. He helped Nikki all the way into the Everneath!"

"We need him," I said.

He stared at me. "Why? What's wrong?"

I grimaced. "Um, I'm sort of turning into an Everliving. And we'd like to destroy the Underworld."

Will was silent for a moment. And then . . . "So, the usual."

Jack helped Will back up to the couch and explained the Cole situation. He also told him of our plan to destroy the Everneath.

Will looked as if he could've used a few more drinks to process everything Jack was saying. It was moments like these that made me realize how totally ridiculous the entire thing sounded.

But at the end of it all, Will stood up. "I'm in. What can I do?"

I explained our clue about Cronus Tantalus and then handed him the documents from Mrs. Jenkins.

"And try the internet," I said.

"All right. Google can destroy worlds."

We left Will with a fresh cup of coffee and an open laptop, and headed to Cole's condo.

TWENTY

NOW

The Surface. Cole's condo.

Minutes later, Jack pulled into the parking lot below Cole's condo. We all got out of the car and started jogging toward the stairs that led to Cole's balcony and the front door.

Jack led the way. But as he turned the final corner, he stopped so quickly, I had to dig my toes into the ground so as not to run into him. He put his hand back, catching me around the waist and pulling me directly behind him.

"What is it?" I whispered.

Jack turned slightly and put a finger to his lips. "I closed the door when we were here before. I'm sure of it," he whispered. "And now it's open again. Stay put."

I nodded and backed away from the corner. Cole wrapped his arm around me and pulled me so now I was directly behind *him*.

I rolled my eyes. "I don't need two bodyguards."

He grinned apologetically. "Sorry. It just felt natural to do that."

"It's fine." I couldn't help a smile. "Just . . . stop."

We peeked around the corner. Jack was a few yards away, standing with his back to the wall just to the side of Cole's door, which was hanging off its hinges.

A chill ran down my back. Jack leaned around the door-frame and apparently didn't see any immediate danger, because he crept inside.

Cole started out, but I grabbed his shirt and yanked him back. "What are you doing? The bad guys could still be there! Again!"

Cole leveled his gaze at me. "I thought you wouldn't care."

"I . . . don't. I mean, I don't want you to get hurt. In your present state . . . That is . . ."

Cole smiled sadly. "You mean, if I still had my memory, and I was the bastard of your past, the one who stole your heart, it'd be fine."

Shaking my head, I was about to protest, but then I realized . . . he was right.

I looked back toward Cole's door. There was no sign of movement. "He's been in there too long."

"It's only been a few seconds."

"I'm going."

"Then so am I."

Upon first glance inside, I couldn't see Jack. But the condo seemed to be in the same state of disarray as it had been before.

It was difficult to tell, given that it was trashed, but it didn't look *more* trashed.

"Jack?" I whispered.

There was no answer.

"Jack!" I said a little louder.

"In the back," Jack said. "There's no one here." We followed his voice toward the farthest bedroom. Cole's bedroom.

It was in worse shape than the living room. Cole walked in and righted a lamp that had been overturned.

"Does anything look familiar?" I asked.

He didn't get a chance to answer. The front door slammed shut, and immediately cold air breezed in and settled over us.

There was a frozen moment in time when I could see my own breath. Jack was the only one with a good view down the hallway. Whatever he saw made his mouth drop open.

Then he dived for me, his shoulder catching me in my stomach. I barely had time to brace for impact before we crashed to the ground. He kept his hands on my back, trying to cushion the fall, but I still heard something crack. Lightning quick, he shoved me under the bed and followed, and I had just one moment to glimpse what looked like floating black oil crossing the threshold of the room.

A Shade. It could only be a Shade.

Jack put his hand over my mouth with a warning look in his eyes. He didn't have to use words to tell me not to breathe.

But the Shades could sniff out humans so easily. I had no idea if I could ever hope to hold my breath long enough.

Cole hadn't made it under the bed with us. I saw his black boots for a split second before the Shade rushed inside. Then Cole's boots disappeared off the ground. A moment later, he landed with a *thwump* on his back on the wooden floor.

He glanced at me. I tried to call his name, but Jack held his hand over my mouth too tightly.

And then it was too late. A black, oily shroud covered Cole's face and upper chest, wrapping itself around and around, like a flat, black python. Cole's legs kicked and thrashed.

I struggled against Jack, trying to reach Cole, but Jack locked his muscles down tight. I couldn't move.

All I could do was watch Cole's feet. Finally they fell still.

But the Shade didn't let up.

My first instinct was to go to Cole. I tried again to pry Jack's hand off my mouth, but he was too strong. He held his arm around my waist even tighter, as if to tell me it would all be okay. But it wasn't. Cole wasn't moving. My lifeline was dying right in front of me.

Cole's hand had flopped underneath the bed, inches from my own. I took it, and held it, and tried to squeeze it reassuringly, even though I knew he was probably dead.

The Shade tightened around Cole's head like coiled cords being cinched. I held tight to Cole's hand. His other hand was up over his head, toward the fireplace. He was reaching for . . . something.

What if I could reach what Cole was looking for? I bit down on Jack's finger, and he finally released his death grip.

Scrambling out from under the bed, I climbed over Cole's body to where his hand was flailing. Hopefully the Shade was so busy sucking the life out of him that it wouldn't notice me.

Cole was reaching toward the poker next to the fireplace. I dived for it, grabbed it, and placed it in Cole's hand. In a move so fast I could barely see it, Cole brought the poker around toward his own face and sliced through the Shade at his throat.

With a hiss, the Shade disintegrated, turning into a dusty smoke before disappearing completely. Cole sucked in a deep breath and coughed it out, the color drained entirely from his face.

"Cole!" I threw myself at him and touched his face. His cheek cooled my fingertips.

I lowered my face until it hung inches above his so he could feed. But within a few seconds, his face changed from pale to ghastly white and then almost to gray. Yanking back my head, I realized my mistake. I was still automatically feeding off him. I'd just made it worse.

Jack had watched me try to feed Cole, and he seemed to figure out quickly why it didn't work.

I looked at him imploringly.

He registered my expression. "Uh-uh. No. No way."

"He's in bad shape, Jack. He's not even conscious."

"I don't care. There is no way I'm letting him feed off me." Jack sprang to his feet and paced across the room, running his fingers roughly through his hair.

I didn't say anything else. How could I? I was asking him

to give up part of his soul to save the guy who had destroyed our futures.

I watched as Jack's feet pounded against the carpet. He marched so forcefully that I was surprised he wasn't shredding the carpet as he went.

He walked one more time to the other side of the room, stopped, and faced the wall. Then his shoulders heaved up and down as he expelled a breath of air.

"I have to," he said.

I shook my head. "No, you don't."

He turned. "Yes. We do. It's you and me. It's us. It's 'we.' And 'we' have to survive." He managed a smile. "As long as there's no tongue."

"Your lips don't even have to touch."

With a determined blaze in his eyes, he crouched beside Cole and brought his face to within a couple of inches of Cole's mouth and breathed out. Once he had expelled all the air inside his lungs, he raised his head, took another deep breath in, lowered his head, and breathed out again.

The change was immediate in Cole's cheeks first. The slightest shade of pink returned. His face lost the sickly gray pallor. And then, after the fifth breath, Cole's eyelids fluttered open.

It took him a moment to focus on the face hanging above him, and when he did, he sprang up into a sitting position and immediately grabbed either side of his head.

"Ow." He pressed his palms against his temples as if he

were trying to hold his head together.

"Are you okay?" I asked.

He winced. "I don't know. What was that?"

Jack, who was now sitting against the bureau panting, jerked his head toward Cole. "What *was* that? A Shade attacked you. You killed it with a poker. How did you know to do that?"

Cole breathed in and out a few times before going on. "I wasn't even thinking. I just did what felt natural. I don't remember even thinking about the poker. I just let my hand do what it wanted to do."

Jack looked away, shaking his head. I think he was angrier that he'd had to resort to feeding Cole.

Cole turned the poker over in his hands. He reached toward the music stand in the corner of the room and grabbed something small and black off it. He held it against the poker. It stuck. "It's magnetic. It must be made of iron."

"So?" I said.

He looked at me. "I don't know. I just . . . feel like that should mean something. I think iron hurts Shades in their Shade form. That's why they prefer the ten-Shade bounty hunter form."

Jack looked at the spot where the Shade had disappeared. "I bet this one was left here as a lookout. He probably alerted the network, which means we don't have much time."

Cole stood up. "I'll look for your heart, but I think I'll have better luck if the two of you aren't watching over my shoulder."

I nodded, and he walked down the hallway.

"Let's call Jules," I said. "See if she's had a chance to talk to my dad. I want to know they're safe."

Jack pulled out his phone and dialed, then handed it to me. I didn't even have to ask her anything. She answered the phone and said, "Your dad's gone. I told him you'd called me from Los Angeles. I said I thought you were in trouble and that you were staying at a shelter. There are quite a few of them there, so the search should take him at least a few days."

"What about Tommy?"

"He took Tommy to your aunt's."

I released a sigh of relief, satisfied that this wild goose chase would keep my family safe. "Thank you." We hung up.

I leaned against Jack's chest and brushed some stray hairs out of my eyes. "Where do we go now? We're out of money. What are we going to do? Camp?"

Just then Cole called from somewhere in the condo. "I found something!"

We sprang up and raced out of the room and into the kitchen, only to find Cole with a handful of plastic cards in his hand. "I didn't find the heart, but look. Cards. In my name. Does that mean anything? That's good, right?"

Jack stared at the credit cards. "Yeah. That's good. Except for the part about the heart."

"At least we tried," I said. "Let's get out of here before we run into anyone else."

TWENTY-ONE

NOW

The Surface. Jack's car.

*A*fter we packed a few bags, we drove a half hour west, down Parley's Canyon, to the larger city of Salt Lake City. Just to make sure everything was as random as possible, we wove through the city center and picked the tenth hotel we saw, a place called Hotel Monaco.

Before we even got to the clerk at the desk, Cole pulled out two of the cards and held them in front of him. It was as if he'd never paid for anything with them before. Like a six-year-old would act if he'd just found them on the floor.

"I'd like to buy a room!" he announced enthusiastically.

"*Get* a room," I muttered out of the side of my mouth. "You'd like to *get* a room."

"Yes," Cole said. "A room. Please. I have these."

Cole shoved both of the cards toward the clerk, surprising him. The clerk looked at the card. "I just need one of those. And a license."

Cole's eyes widened slightly, even though his smile remained frozen in place.

I leaned closer to him, keeping my eyes on the clerk, and whispered with my teeth clamped together. "It's the one with your picture on it."

"Right," Cole said, relaxing. He handed the clerk the card. The clerk started typing on his keyboard.

"Maybe we should get two rooms," Jack said.

"We can't leave Cole alone," I said. "Who knows where he'll wander in the middle of the night."

Jack frowned but nodded.

The clerk handed Cole the key. Sixth floor. Two double beds. For now we were safe.

Once inside the room, Jack closed the door behind us, and for the first time in a long time, we all breathed a sigh of relief. Cole flopped down diagonally on the bed farther from the door as if he were at a sleepover and had no cares in the world.

Jack and I both glanced at the other bed, but then Cole scooted over. "Here, Nik. There's plenty of room."

Jack's entire body tensed, so powerfully I expected a resulting energy wave to blast through the room. "No way in hell," he said, much more calmly than his body language indicated.

Cole didn't seem to notice Jack's bulging biceps. He put his hands behind his head and wrinkled his eyebrows. "It's feeding time. And it's the most efficient way. That's obvious, isn't it?" As if purposely exacerbating the situation, he patted the mattress beside him. "The sooner the better," he said.

I knew Jack was at his breaking point already with my life on the line and us on the run. I didn't think he had anything left to hold his jealousy in check. Jack flinched toward Cole, but I put a hand on his arm and squeezed. "Jack, remember this is keeping me alive. And it means nothing."

He sighed and then did something unexpected. He turned around and stormed out of the doorway.

Ten minutes later he stormed back in, grabbed our bags, and went back to the door, holding it open. "We're switching rooms," he said. "To one with a king."

I closed my eyes. A king-size bed. For the three of us. Maybe some adult romance author somewhere was writing the beginning of a similar scene, and maybe that scene was supposed to be hot, but to me it felt like hell.

TWENTY-TWO

NOW

The Surface. Hotel Monaco.

Will met us a while later with his laptop. He glanced at the single king-size bed. "Kinky," he said.

Jack punched him lightly on the shoulder, nearly sending Will to the floor.

"What did you find?" Jack said.

Will rubbed his shoulder as he walked over to the desk and set down his laptop.

"First off, I found nothing about 'Cronus Tantalus' together. But separating the two words, I found a lot. Cronus." He pointed to his screen. "Cronus was a Titan—offspring of Uranus—Heaven—and Gaia—Earth. He was jealous of his father's power. His mother also hated Uranus because when she gave birth to this kid that had like a billion hands, or eyes, or something, Uranus hid the kid so he'd never see the light of day. To get back at Uranus, Gaia convinced her son, Cronus, to castrate his own father. She gave him a sickle, and he did the deed."

Will held up his hands as if he were expecting applause.

Cole, Jack, and I just stared.

"It's not my fault it's a horrible story," Will said. "Myths. They're all horrible stories."

"It's not that," I said. "It's just that the words 'Cronus Tantalus' were all we had to go on, and I can't figure out how that story helps us."

Will shrugged. "What was the Cronus clue in reference to?" he asked.

"Destroying the Shade network," Jack said.

Will squinted at the computer screen again. "Well, if you want to destroy something, you probably need a strong weapon. . . ." He flipped the screen so that we could all see a drawing of the sickle. "It's forged out of the toughest stone on Earth. Adamant. And it can supposedly destroy anything."

I looked at Cole. "Do you think that's what Ashe was getting at? Telling us about the only thing in the world that would be strong enough to destroy the network?"

He nodded.

"It's the best theory we've got," Jack said. "But do we know where it is?"

I looked from Jack's face to Cole's, to Will's, hoping that someone would have some sort of input; but the only sound came from the fan in Will's computer.

"What about Tantalus?" I said.

"Ah," Will said, typing something into his computer. "This one is a little more obscure. Tantalus was famous for his eternal punishment. He was made to stand in a pool of water under a fruit tree with low-hanging branches. Each time he reached up to pluck some fruit, the branches lifted out of reach. Each time he reached below for water, the water receded. Thus he was always longing for food and water but never getting it. And yes, I used the word *thus* in a sentence."

I bit my lip, trying to figure out the significance of the story, but came up with nothing. I expected blank faces all around again, but Cole's mouth hung slightly open as he stared at the computer screen.

"What is it?" I said to Cole.

"Tantalus," he said. He turned his head toward me. "I know where the sickle is."

"What are you talking about?" I said.

"Tantalus is a lake," Cole said. He squeezed his eyes shut. "It's a place not many people know about, but Ashe and I know it. I can't even remember *why* we do, but we do. I thought the name sounded familiar, but I didn't make the connection until you mentioned the water."

I held my breath for a moment, worried that the renewed memory would spark a flood more and that Cole would suddenly realize he didn't want to destroy the Everneath. But nothing happened.

"It's in the Ring of Earth," Cole continued.

"In which Common?" I asked.

"Not in a Common. In the void between Ouros and Limneo." His eyes went wide as the name Limneo just rolled off his tongue as if he'd known it all along. "Limneo. Another Common, right?"

I nodded and tried to keep his focus on Tantalus before his mind started wandering and remembering other key things.

"So Tantalus," I said. "You think the sickle might be hidden there?"

Cole smiled. "That's the thing about Tantalus. Whatever you most desire in the world will be hidden there, but you can only traverse the lake once in your lifetime. We didn't want to waste it until there was something we really needed."

Jack and I exchanged glances. "We really need the Sickle of Cronus," I said.

"Then let's go get it," Cole said.

Will wanted to come with us, but Jack convinced him to stay and email Professor Spears, to catch him up on everything we were doing.

We left Will in the hotel room, and Jack drove us to the Shop-n-Go, where the same confused clerk watched with raised eyebrows as we entered the store and walked to the back, then formed a circle, holding hands.

He was probably understanding why Ezra went a little crazy.

This time Cole didn't hand me a strand of hair.

"I know where I'm going," he said. "I've been there. I can picture it."

"Which means we should be able to land directly there since it's not in the labyrinth," I said.

We didn't waste any more time talking, and within moments we were spinning through the darkness.

I landed on my back looking at the fake azure sky, but the blue canvas was broken up by pine trees stretching high, towering above me.

I sat up on a bed of pine needles. "Are we in a forest?" I asked.

"A forest with a lake," Cole said.

I turned around and saw that we were on the edge of a huge clearing that held a giant lake, at least the size of Jenny Lake near Jackson Hole. The water was clear and blue; and except for the fact that there wasn't a single ripple on its surface, it could've been a lake anywhere in the Rocky Mountains.

I pushed myself up to a standing position and walked to the water's edge. I breathed in deeply, expecting the smell of pine; but there was no odor, although I felt the needles crunching beneath my feet.

"Don't touch the water," Cole said. "You know how the water works here. Makes you forget things."

I paused in my tracks and raised my eyebrows. "Yeah. I'm just surprised you know," I said.

I took a step back. Jack came up beside me, put his arm

around my shoulders, and stared out at the lake.

"So Cole," he said. "Where is the sickle?"

Cole shielded his eyes, even though there was no sun. "In the middle."

"Of the lake?" I said.

"Yes. In the middle. Underwater."

"What?!" I said. "How are we supposed to get it? Swim?"

Cole laughed. "No. Even if you could swim to the middle without drowning in the water—and without ingesting any, or forgetting why you're there in the first place—it's far underwater. So . . . then you would drown."

Jack's fists clenched.

I stepped purposefully between him and Cole. "What was your plan, Cole?" I said.

"I don't know. I always thought that when I wanted something bad enough to wish for it here, I would figure it out then."

I grabbed Jack's fist with both of my hands before he exploded, but he wasn't even paying attention to Cole anymore. He was staring out across the water. "There's a tree out of place," he said.

I looked all around us. "How can you tell? You know where each one belongs?"

He smiled and pointed to a spot that was maybe a quarter mile away. "That tree."

I followed his gaze and saw exactly what he was talking about. In a sea of pine trees, there was one bushy fruit tree right by the edge of the water.

The myth of Tantalus talked about a fruit tree. It had to mean something. We followed Jack as he navigated a pathway to the fruit tree, keeping us close to the water.

"Maybe the sickle will be hidden in the tree," I said.

"Yeah," Jack said, turning and shooting me a grin. "Maybe it will be that easy."

We made it to the tree. Searched the ground surrounding the trunk of the tree. Looked up in the branches. Tried to find anything that looked like a sickle. Or a scythe. Or a dagger. Or a sword.

There was nothing.

Cole didn't help search. He stood there staring at one of the branches.

"Are we boring you, Cole?" I said.

"That branch looks different," he said. He reached up and pulled on it, but it didn't budge. But he was right; it was different. The base of the branch, where it was attached to the trunk of the tree, looked as if it could pivot with the right amount of force. "Hercules, you come try it," Cole said.

Jack raised an eyebrow.

"Cole?" I said. "That sounded like the old Cole. A little bit."

"Really?" He seemed genuinely shocked. "Sorry. I didn't realize."

"No, it's okay," I said. "Anything you can remember . . . is a good thing." I tried to sound convincing, but I didn't succeed.

Jack went over to the branch and pulled. It didn't budge.

He tried again until he was hanging with his entire body weight. The branch creaked as if it thought about moving but then didn't.

"Both of you need to hang on it," I said.

Cole reached up and added his body weight, and the branch finally gave way. That's when the ground shook. And the waves started.

TWENTY-THREE

NOW

The Everneath. Lake Tantalus.

*T*he water retreated at first, revealing more of the sandy beach. Then we saw a giant swell forming in the center of the lake, growing as if the lake itself were sucking in all the water from the perimeter.

Once the water had retreated into the lake by at least the length of a football field, the gigantic swell in the center froze for a second.

"That's not good," Jack said. "We've gotta run."

"Don't let go!" I said.

"Becks. It's a mini-tsunami coming for us."

I looked all around, thinking as fast as I could. "Climb to the branch," I said.

Jack didn't waste time arguing. He swung himself over the limb, then reached down and pulled me and then Cole up just as a tidal wave of water rushed onto shore. The water rose up and barely skimmed the bottom of the branch before it fell back down.

"Was that all we did?" Jack asked. "Create a wave?"

"Look!" I said.

The water had gone back into the lake, but it began to swirl in a circle, a giant whirlpool centered in the middle. And the level was going down.

"It's like a giant toilet flushing," I said.

The water level sank enough that a small platform appeared in the center of the lake. Well, small from where we sat in the fruit tree.

"That's how we're going to get there," I said. "Once all the water's gone, one of us can just walk out."

"I hope it stops sinking soon," Jack said.

"Why?" I asked, but then I saw the problem. As the water sank, I could see that the edge of the platform dropped off on all four sides, rock walls nearly perpendicular to the surface of the water.

"Oh," I said. "Can you get off and stop it?"

Cole dropped from the branch, and the lever flipped up. Immediately, water bubbled up from the center of the platform and spilled over the sides, creating a waterfall on all four edges.

"That's not going to help," I said.

Cole climbed back up, and the branch flipped back down.

I turned to Jack. "Okay, here's what we know so far. We know that we have to keep the branch depressed while we retrieve the sickle, which we hope is on top of the platform. And we know that you and Cole are the ones who have to keep it depressed, because when Cole got off, my weight wasn't enough to keep it down. Which means . . ."

Jack looked skyward. "It means you have to go to the platform. Alone."

I nodded. Jack put his arm around me, and I leaned into his chest.

"I don't like this, Becks," Jack said, looking warily at the lake.

"What's not to like? I've been wanting a chance to rock climb again. You remember that time at the Rock Garden?"

Jack smiled. "Yes."

"I can do this." We watched as the last few feet of water disappeared. And when it did, what it left behind made my blood turn cold. A dark shadow covered the deepest part of the lake. And it appeared to be moving.

"Are those Shades?" I asked, my voice weak.

"No," Cole said. "Beetles."

TWENTY-FOUR

NOW

The Everneath. Lake Tantalus.

"*B*eetles?" I repeated.

I squinted, but the middle of the lake was far enough away that I couldn't see individual beetles. It just looked like the floor of the lake was moving.

"Yeah," Cole said, narrowing his eyes. "About the size of half of your foot."

I whipped my head around toward Cole. "Did you know they would be there?" I said.

"No. But I can see really well here. I see them."

Jack shook his head. "You're not going, Becks."

This time it was my turn to smile and look skyward. "We've faced zombies and walls of fire and a queen bent on revenge. We're not stopping because of a few bugs." My voice broke on the last couple of words.

"Becks . . . ," Jack said. He looked as if he wanted to jump off the branch, take me in his arms, and fly us out of the Underworld.

"Remember what you said at the rock-climbing gym?"

Jack closed his eyes. "You don't have to worry about the top. You just have to worry about the first step."

"And then what?"

"And then the next step," he said.

I nodded. "That's what I'm going to do. And hopefully, as I'm stepping, I'll smash a few beetles along the way."

Jack's grip tightened around me.

"And I can't take that first step unless you let me go." I smiled at him.

Jack closed his eyes, sighed deeply, and quickly dropped his arms. I hurried and hopped off the branch before he could change his mind. It stayed down with Jack's and Cole's combined weight. I walked up to the former edge of the lake.

"Are they poisonous?" I asked Cole as I stared at the black mass.

"I don't know," Cole said. "The water's not, though. I would think that if poisonous beetles lived in the lake, the water would be contaminated too."

With a deep breath, I nodded. "Good theory."

"But they could nibble you to death eventually," Cole said.

I heard the distinct sound of Jack punching Cole's shoulder.

"Ow," Cole said. "So, stay conscious," he said, as if he'd just told a small child to be safe at school.

"Step by step," I muttered.

"Becks?" Jack said.

"Yeah?"

"I'd run."

"Me too."

I took off running toward the base of the platform, counting my steps along the way. Eventually Jack's words of encouragement faded behind me. It was step one hundred and twenty-eight where I heard the crack and squish of my first beetle. I screamed and kept running.

Crunch. Crunch. Crunch. Crunch. I tried to avoid them, but eventually I was crunching several with each step. I was scared to stop or slow down, because I was sure that this many beetles could overrun me if I let them.

I was panting.

The base of the rock platform loomed ahead of me, growing ever taller as I got closer.

Thankfully the wall of it was craggy, and I could already see there were some suitable toeholds and handholds. I kept my eyes on where I would put my hands so I didn't think about the beetles scurrying at my feet.

After what felt like at least two miles of running, I reached the base and immediately started climbing. A wave of beetles tried to follow me, but they fell backward as the wall became steep. Once I was a few feet above them, I looked back to where I'd come from and saw that there was now a thicker line of black on the path I'd just taken, as if every beetle wanted to converge on it.

Maybe on the way back down I would take another path.

I started the climb, trying not to think about the facts that I wore no harness and there was no one to belay me. With sweaty fingers, I grabbed and tested each handhold, making sure it was strong enough before I made a move. Eventually the time between steps diminished as I got used to the routine of it.

I even stopped thinking about the crackling sound of the sea of beetles below me and thought instead of what waited for me on the top of the platform. If Cole was right, it would be the Sickle of Cronus, and at this rate I'd make it there in a few minutes. Once we had it in our hands, we would jump back to the Surface, regroup, and then make our first assault on the Everneath by destroying the Shade network with the sickle.

Once we succeeded, it would merely be the task of gathering every Everliving heart and destroying them.

I decided to skip that part in my daydream, because I was at the top of the platform. I'd made it. I hoisted myself over the edge and saw something lying there in the middle.

It looked ancient and made of stone, and it was shaped like a bent knife.

The sickle.

I grabbed it and turned toward the fruit tree, raising the

sickle over my head. And that's when I heard the scurrying feet behind me. I turned to see a flood of beetles coming up over the edge of the platform.

"Shit," I whispered.

TWENTY-FIVE

NOW

The Everneath. Lake Tantalus.

I put the sickle against my back in the band of my jeans and scrambled over the edge, frantically feeling for handholds as beetles from the top of the platform began falling over the edge, pelting me on my head, my shoulders, my eyes. Several got tangled in my hair, scratching against my scalp and forehead and cheeks.

I tried not to scream. I didn't want any to fall in my mouth.

I reached for my next handhold and slipped. My hands scraped along the rock as I fell a few yards. Then I did scream. I used every ounce of strength to nab a divot in the rock, and finally I slowed down the fall.

But I had accidentally put my hand on a beetle inside the divot.

Startled, I yanked it out and lost all control. I sailed through the air for what seemed like a long time and landed flat on my back.

My lungs collapsed. And a swarm of darkness and scurrying feet surrounded me.

I had the sickle. But it was the beetles that had beaten me.

I lay there for a few moments. Tried to move but nothing happened. Maybe I'd broken my back. Hundreds of beetles found their way under my shirt, down my pants, nibbling as they went. None of the bites alone would've been painful. But hundreds of bites at once . . .

The sound of splashing reached my ears, and suddenly a wall of water crashed down on me. The beetles screeched and floundered in the waves.

Maybe I would drown before I was eaten alive.

The water covered me, and within moments my face was submerged. I pressed my lips together, trying to make sure no water got inside my mouth. The last thing I needed, while drowning, was to forget who I was.

"Becks!" Jack's voice came from somewhere above through the water. "Move your arms! Paddle!"

I tried to move, and this time my arms swung a little bit, and my mouth broke the surface for only a split second. I gasped in a lungful of air before I pressed my lips tightly together and went under again.

And then strong arms grabbed me around my waist and brought me to the surface. I sucked in the air. The glorious air.

I couldn't talk. I couldn't open my eyes.

Jack squeezed my cheeks. "Becks. Talk."

"Hi," I said weakly.

"Do you remember who you are?" Jack said.

I nodded. "Nikki Beckett."

I heard him sigh, and then he was on the move, with me in his arms.

We collapsed on the beach, soaking wet and panting. Cole was there. He'd taken off his shirt and was using it to dry off my face. When he pulled it away, it was bloody.

"Damn beetles," I whispered.

Jack took the shirt out of Cole's hands and resumed wiping me down. Something under my left eye caught his attention, and he gingerly pressed the shirt against the spot. "That was a gouge," he said.

I let him fuss for a bit, then remembered why we were there in the first place. My hand flew to my back, and I felt the metal handle of the sickle.

"We got it," I said.

TWENTY-SIX

NOW
The Surface. The hotel.

*W*ill met us on the Surface at our hotel room. At the sight of me, he gasped.

"Have you been through a combine?" he asked, and I knew he wasn't being flippant.

"No," I said. "A sea of beetles."

"Long story," Jack said. "But Becks was amazing. And she got the Sickle of Cronus. Any news from the professor?"

"Yeah," Will said. "He says the Shade network, that egg-shaped ball you described, is a sacred stone called a baetylus. And he says you need one more thing, in addition to the sickle, to destroy it. That is, if you want to escape with your lives."

Knowing we had to do one more thing was too much for me at that moment. I collapsed against the bed.

My eyes closed involuntarily, and within moments I was gone.

***

When I woke, I saw Jack, Cole, and Will poring over documents at the desk next to the bed.

"What's going on?" I said.

Jack came over to the bed and sat down beside me. "Hey, Becks. How are you feeling?"

I nodded. "Fine. Tell me."

He lay down next to me, facing me. "The professor thinks that the Shade network has a fail-safe attached to it, where if we destroy it, it will set off an alarm and basically trap us in the Underworld. Like a lockdown. To give us time to escape, he thinks we need to track down the Helmet of Hermes. Sound familiar?"

"The pendant that Cole was supposed to give the guy with the big head in exchange for that memory?"

Jack nodded. "I think so. It will supposedly mask our presence until we've had a chance to get out."

I looked at Cole. "You'd told the guy you would get the pendant. Do you have it? Do you know where it is?"

Cole shook his head. "I can't remember."

I closed my eyes and sighed. "I can't swim a sea of beetles again."

Jack smoothed my hair gently with his hand. "You don't have to. Mrs. Jenkins's papers contained a log sheet that shows the chain of custody for the pendant. The last name on the list is a woman named Mildred Dorrity. She lives in

Roy. We just tracked down her phone number. We're about to call her."

I squinted. "So, this random woman has a pendant that will keep us out of an Everneath prison," I said.

"Yes," Jack said.

I nodded. "Let's get to it."

Jack put his phone on speaker and dialed her number. After several rings, a woman answered. She sounded old, her voice frail.

"Is this Mildred Dorrity?" Jack said.

She paused. "Whatever you're selling, I'm not buying."

"I'm not selling anything. I was just wondering if you know a Kathleen Jenkins?"

Another pause. "Kathleen Jenkins is dead."

With that I knew we'd found the right person.

"I was friends with Mrs. Jenkins," I said.

"Kathleen didn't have friends," Mildred said.

"We're looking for a pendant," I blurted out. "Please. We got your name from a log sheet listing possession of the Helmet of Hermes. Do you still have it?"

A longer pause.

"Please, Mrs. Dorrity. Please help us."

I could hear her breathing, even though she wasn't answering. Whatever we were saying, it wasn't working.

"Mildred," Jack said, his voice amazingly calm. "Have you ever loved someone?"

Now it was his turn to pause as we waited for an answer.

"Yes," she said.

"So you know that feeling." Jack was being so tender, so sincere. I didn't know how Mrs. Dorrity wouldn't be swayed. "The entire reason we're calling is because of love. Please. Do you have the pendant?"

"No," she said. "I passed it down to my granddaughter, but it was stolen by the Delphinians."

Delphinians. This was the second time I'd heard of the exiled group.

"The Delphinians want all the sacred artifacts for themselves," she continued. "Devon stole it back for us, but then he disappeared."

Beside me, Cole tensed. I could feel a distinct wave of anxiety roll off him. Maybe it was because he was the only person I could feed off. Whatever the reason, his reaction was strong enough that I could taste it in the air.

I turned toward him and whispered, "Does this sound familiar?"

"I'm not sure," he said.

I turned back to the phone. "Who was this Devon?"

"Millie—my granddaughter—her boyfriend."

"Where's Millie now?" I asked.

"She's dead."

I glanced at Jack. For a moment there was only the sound of some quiz show on the television in the background.

"She was named after me, you know," Mildred said.

"Thank you," I said. Jack hung up.

As we stared at the phone, a new despair blanketed our souls. Yes, she'd known about the pendant, but we were no closer to getting it.

I reached over to adjust the thermostat on the wall. Jack glanced at my hand and grabbed my arm.

"What?" I said, startled.

"Your wrist. The shackle."

I looked down. The faint line had become darker. Almost as dark as the other shackle. I pulled down my sleeve. "We already knew we had to hurry. Doesn't change anything."

But it felt as if it changed everything.

I turned to Cole, anxious to take the focus off of my wrist. "When Mildred mentioned that Devon guy, it triggered something in you. What was it?"

Cole shook his head. "I don't know. Nothing specific. Just a feeling, but then it went away."

He didn't look me in the eyes when he spoke. The emotions I'd sensed coming from him during the phone call with Mildred seemed to indicate it was something more than just a feeling.

"Are you sure that's all it was?"

"Yeah."

He leaned his head back and closed his eyes. Something

told me he was holding back. I was walking a fine line. On one hand, I wanted him to remember things that could possibly help us destroy the Everneath. On the other hand, what if he remembered his true desire? His longing for the throne?

If it came back to him, would he betray us?

TWENTY-SEVEN

NOW
The Surface. The hotel.

The sun was setting and once again I was feeling the exhaustion. It hadn't been that long since Cole had fed me, had it? I wondered if the appearance of the second shackle meant I would need more frequent feedings.

Or maybe more frequent feedings wouldn't be enough.

I tried not to think like that.

"We'll find something else," Jack said, glancing at me sideways. "I'll send an email to Professor Spears. See if he has any ideas. Maybe we'll just risk it, without the pendant."

I nodded, wishing I had the energy to sound more enthusiastic.

"You need to eat," he said.

"Let me shower first," I said. It had been two days. "I think that will perk me up a bit."

"Okay."

I went straight to the bathroom and started the water

running. The water turned warm, and I took a deep, steamy breath.

When I got dressed and came out of the bathroom, Jack was alone, on the computer.

"Where's Cole?" I said.

He didn't look up. "Playing with the ice machine."

I snorted. "I'm going to miss this side of Cole if he ever gets his memory back."

I walked over to the window to close the drapes, but a figure down by the roundabout in front of the hotel caught my eye. I squinted my eyes to get a clearer look.

It was Cole. Standing at the curb. It looked as if he were waiting for someone.

"Jack," I said.

He could hear the worry in my voice. He rushed over to me, and I pointed down at Cole.

"What's he doing?" he said.

It hit me. "He's getting a taxi. He remembers something."

Jack and I exchanged looks, and then we took off. Jack grabbed his keys on the way out the door.

We ran down the stairs. My first thought was to confront Cole, but just as I was about to burst out through the front doors, Jack pulled me back.

"If he's going somewhere, let's follow him."

I nodded. Following him would be the only way to know what exactly he remembered. My biggest fear was that he would remember his mission to make me his queen. And if he did remember, he would hide that from us, wouldn't he? Again, I was faced with the fact that I was putting a lot of trust in Cole right now. He knew our plan. And at any moment he could easily thwart it.

We ran quietly to the parking lot and reached Jack's car just as a taxi pulled up to the curb where Cole was standing. Jack waited until Cole was inside to turn on the ignition, then pulled out after the cab, his lights off.

We kept a safe distance behind the cab and followed for four or five miles out west of the city toward a more industrial part of the valley. It turned into a side road surrounded by warehouses.

"Where's he going?" I said.

Jack shrugged and turned in behind him.

The taxi stopped outside a metal gate, which opened into an asphalt parking area surrounded by storage units.

We pulled over down the road and watched as Cole entered the property.

Jack frowned. "Very deliberate move for someone who doesn't remember anything. Wait here."

"No way am I waiting," I said.

Jack sighed, but there was no time to argue. We ran across the street and made our way up to the entrance. Cole was already turning down one of the rows of units. Jack pushed through the gate and held it open for me, and then we took off to follow.

Cole stopped in front of unit 677, paused only for a moment with his finger over the keypad, and then punched in a bunch of numbers. Something metallic clicked, and Cole pulled the storage unit door open.

Cole knew the code. He knew the existence of a storage locker. Unless he had rented it in the last twenty-four hours, he hadn't been telling us the truth about remembering nothing.

"Bastard!" I said.

Cole jumped and then turned around. A wide grin broke out on his face. He looked genuinely excited to see us. "Hey! I was just about to call you."

"Bullshit," Jack said, stalking toward him, his fists clenched at his sides.

"No, I'm serious. I was going purely by instinct, telling the cab where to go as we drove. Left here, right here, that sort of thing. I swear." He put his hands up as if he couldn't figure out why Jack was angry. "Without you guys there, it was easier for me to focus."

We were all standing on the threshold of the locker at this point, Jack's nostrils flaring but his fists remaining by his sides.

"Seriously," Cole said. "I was pulling my phone out to call you. Let's go inside. See what's here."

"Why don't you tell us what's here?" Jack said.

"I told you. I don't know what's here."

I'd already glimpsed the inside, because part of me wondered if this was the type of place where the old Cole would've hidden my compass heart. But at first glance there didn't appear to be any jewelry boxes or anything that would hold a small jewelry item like my heart. Instead, it appeared the entire place was filled with old musical instruments. A couple of guitars with the signature *Les Paul* on the wooden bodies leaned against metal stands nearest the door.

As we stepped farther back, the guitars got a little bit older. There was one drum set, wrapped in plastic sheeting. A mandolin leaned against a banjo.

"Well, we're set if we wanted to start that bluegrass band we've always talked about," Jack said. "Otherwise, I don't see anything that would help us."

Cole stepped over the drum set. "I still think there's something here. Something to do with that Devon guy that Mildred mentioned. You were right, Nik. Something clicked. I just didn't want to get your hopes up without knowing for sure."

I froze, a mini-harp-like object in my hands. "You think the Helmet of Hermes could be here?" I said incredulously. "In your storage locker."

"I know; it sounds crazy. And maybe it's not the actual pendant that's here, but something that could lead us to Devon. Either way, we have to look."

Now that we knew what we were looking for, we began to tear through the contents of the locker. After twenty minutes we'd barely made a dent in the place.

"Don't break the lutes," Cole said to Jack. "Hey! I know what a lute is." He sounded so triumphant, I had to bite back a smile.

A pair of bright lights swept through the place.

We all turned toward the entrance. Jack, who was closest to the door, said, "It's just a car pulling up to the gate." He bent down again and reached for a package, but then he froze. "Wait a minute. Cole, if this storage locker is yours, does that mean it's registered under your name? Or any band members' names?"

I sucked in a breath. "If one of their names is on the register . . ."

"Bounty hunters might be watching the place," Cole said.

"If they are, why wouldn't they have just broken in?" I said.

"Maybe they're not after your heart anymore," Cole said. "Maybe they're just after me."

We heard the clink of the metal gate opening for a vehicle.

"Hurry!" Jack said. He went to stand by the door while Cole and I turned manic in our search. "It's a big black truck. Gate's opening slowly."

From the pictures Jack had found on the internet, the pendant was large, but no larger than the palm of my hand, so I skipped over any packages that looked too big. But really, we would have to rely on Cole's instincts. Otherwise we'd be here forever. We climbed up and down the piles of boxes and instruments. While I was stepping over another drum set, I accidentally put my foot through an ancient-looking bongo.

"Careful," Cole said, still showing his affinity for all musical instruments, even in his amnesiac state.

"Shut up and look!" I said.

"The gate's open," Jack said. "The truck's coming in."

"Maybe they're not for us," Cole said.

"They're turning down this row." Jack pushed up his sleeves and flexed his hands.

I heard the screech of tires.

"I'll hold them off," Jack said softly.

I saw him reach for a saxophone and step behind the front corner of the storage unit so he was out of sight of whoever was in the truck. He kept the saxophone behind his leg.

I caught sight of the driver and passenger, and there was no question they were ten-Shade bounty hunters. One of the hunters looked to be at least six and a half feet tall and as thick as a boulder. The other was only slightly shorter, and just as muscular.

Probably thinking they had us cornered, they walked side by side toward the unit. And the second they crossed the threshold, Jack stepped out from his dark corner and swung the saxophone at the hunter closest to him. The saxophone made contact with the hunter's leg, smashing his kneecap backward, turning it inside out, forcing his leg to bend ninety degrees in the opposite direction legs were supposed to bend.

The hunter dropped, an alien screech coming from his mouth. "Um, can the ten Shades escape the body?" I asked.

"No!" Cole said. Then he paused in his search. "At least no is my initial reaction, but I'm not sure—"

"Keep going!" I commanded.

With one move Jack had effectively taken out one of the

hunters. Or so I would've thought. But the one-legged hunter struggled to straighten up on his good leg as if the only thing in his way were the logistics of a busted leg and not the pain of one.

I frantically turned up my search as I heard, rather than saw, the other bounty hunter collide with Jack. The unmistakable sound of fists crunching against jaws reached my ears, and—not wanting to waste any time looking—I could only hope it was Jack's fists and the bounty hunter's jaw.

I dived into the next pile just as Cole held up a brown paper package.

"Got it!" he said.

"The pendant?" I said.

"Yes!"

I checked on Jack. The second bounty hunter had him from behind, an arm around his neck. I grabbed the nearest weapon I could find, a ukulele, and scrambled over the piles of boxes and instruments. Jack hunched forward and then exploded backward, his head cracking against the nose of the bounty hunter.

I jumped off the last pile just as the bounty hunter collapsed behind Jack, and as I landed, I brought the ukulele smashing down on the bounty hunter's black smile.

The instrument shattered into hundreds of pieces. And it didn't even wipe the black smile off the bounty hunter's face.

"You're welcome," I said to Jack as he grabbed my hand and whisked me into the passenger's side of the truck. Cole scrambled out after us and hopped into the bed of the truck just as Jack peeled out of the parking lot.

The bounty hunters, one with an extreme limp, continued after us; and even though they had no hope of catching us since we'd stolen their mode of transportation, they just kept coming.

"They're not stopping," I said.

Cole spoke through the open window that separated the cab from the bed of the truck. "They're made for one purpose. They'll never stop."

TWENTY-EIGHT

NOW

The Surface. Salt Lake City.

We ditched the truck by Jack's car and switched back to his sedan. We didn't want to risk the truck's having been reported stolen by its original owner.

Once in the car we all panted, trying to catch our breaths. Jack had a couple of spatters of blood on his cheek and his jacket, but it wasn't his. It belonged to the creepy ten-Shade bounty hunters.

"Cole, you will not sneak away again," Jack said. He sounded like a father scolding a child.

"Agreed," Cole said solemnly from the backseat.

Jack drove us back to the hotel, where he and I collapsed onto the king-size bed and Cole stood at the foot. He held the brown paper package up high by one end and let it spin toward the mattress until the pendant fell out.

It looked exactly like the picture from the internet, but it wasn't made of metal, as I'd assumed it was. It looked as if it were made of quartz or some other mineral, almost as if it had been formed naturally by the earth. But it was in the shape of a helmet, with little wings on either side.

Cole stared at it as he spoke. "There's something important knocking at the door of my brain. But I just can't grasp it."

I wanted to be patient with him, but we had no time. "Cole, you've shared memories with me while feeding me. Flashbacks I don't think you fully remembered." Jack probably wouldn't appreciate this method, but I was desperate. Cole looked at me expectantly. "Maybe if you fed me . . ."

Without hesitation, he grabbed me and kissed me, and something inside my head clicked like a key turning in a lock. I saw a memory quickly come into focus, as if someone were turning a camera lens, but I didn't have time to interpret it before he pulled away. He smiled.

"I've got it," he said. "I did time with this guy once, inside a Delphinian prison."

"Delphinian?" I said. "Like the crazy, exiled Everlivings Ashe and Mildred were talking about?"

Cole nodded. "The guy in the cell next to me was named Devon. He was a mercenary. He'd been imprisoned because the Delphinians had stolen something from the woman he loved, and he stole it back. It was a rare artifact. He hid it before he was captured. They tortured him for its location, but he never gave it up. When it seemed obvious"—Cole paused and looked down—"that Devon was going to die, he asked me to retrieve it and take care of it. At the time, I didn't know it was the Helmet of Hermes. I thought it was just a piece of jewelry." He lifted his gaze to meet mine. "But when Mildred said the name Devon, things started to click."

I gave a faint smile. "When were you in this Delphinian prison?"

He looked away. "I'm not sure. But it feels like a long, long time ago."

I grabbed the pendant and held it up to the light.

Jack was staring at Cole. "Where *exactly* did you get it? Before it ended up in the storage unit?"

Cole looked at me but answered Jack. "In a locker. Originally in Riomaggiore. Italy. Where Devon had hidden it."

Something in his expression didn't seem right. He was smiling, but it didn't seem to reach any other part of his face, including his lips.

"Are you okay?" I asked.

"I'm tired."

"Lie down," I said. "Get some rest. I won't feed on you until you're rested, okay?"

He nodded and crawled onto the side of the bed, curling away from Jack and me.

After a few moments he was breathing evenly.

"He's lying," Jack said.

"Shh," I said. I got up and motioned for Jack to follow me.

Once the room door was shut behind us, he started in. "He's lying, Becks. I know it. It all just seems so convenient. What if it's not this instinctual behaviors theory of the professor's? If he was lying, that instinct stuff is the perfect cover-up. He can reveal exactly what he wants to reveal and call it instinct."

I thought for a moment. "I believe he's telling the truth about the amnesia. But let's say I'm wrong, and he's been playing us this entire time. Whether he's lying or not, there are certain things we know for sure. One is that I need him to survive. The other is that he brought us the Helmet of Hermes. So whether he's lying or not, he's given us what we need."

Jack put his lips together and sighed. I could tell my words were making sense to him.

"Not only that, but I can't for the life of me figure out what he stands to gain from lying about this. Yes, he's lied to me in the past. But right now, I'm already dependent on finding someone to feed on. I'm dependent on him. What more could he want?"

"That's the scary part. I have no doubt he has ulterior motives for pulling this amnesia stunt, and just because we can't figure out what his ultimate goal is, that doesn't mean it doesn't exist." He shook his head. "Actually, we do know what his ultimate goal is. The throne."

"The *old* Cole's goal was the throne. The new one wants to help us. How much of the old Cole is back? I don't know." I took in a deep breath. "But right now, all I have to know is that we have the sickle—our first step to destroying the Everneath—and he holds my life in his hands." It wasn't a good position to be in, but my odds were never good in the first place.

Jack looked at me and nodded. I put a hand on either side of his face. "We have everything we need. All the pieces in place. The only thing left is following through with it. And all you need to do is trust this." I brought his face to mine and pressed my lips against his one cheek, and then the other cheek, and then finally his mouth.

The hotel door swung open, and Cole stuck his head out.

Jack looked at him sideways. "Seriously, you are begging for a beating."

"Sorry," he said. He ducked back inside.

We spent the evening with renewed energy for our mission. Jack was up half the night at the computer. I wanted to help him with whatever he was researching, but I needed to feed.

Cole woke up frequently, distressed and in a cold sweat. He wouldn't tell me what his dreams were about, but when I fed on him throughout the night, all I saw were jumbled pictures of dark, chilling images of screams that would come to life and turn into terrifying monsters. They reached inside my head and tried to steal my brain.

The images scared me, and I had to keep pulling back from Cole's face.

In the morning I woke with a feeling of dread. I wasn't sure if it came from the nightmares or from the enormity of our task. Jack made coffee for us. We sat down across from each other at the table.

Jack took my hand. "It's going to work, Becks."

I shrugged. "Even if it does . . . the chances of us destroying the network and escaping before the lockdown are about that of a snowball in the Ring of Fire; and even if it does work, what do we do then?" My lower lip trembled. "We'd still have to destroy the vault of hearts. And somehow we'd have to destroy every Everliving's heart. And the Everneath would be on lockdown."

Jack came to my side and held me. "Shh. It's going to be okay. If getting rid of the network and eliminating the bond between the Shades is the first step in destroying the Everneath, then we do it and go on faith that the next step will present itself."

"Faith?" The word popped out before I could think about it. "Faith in what? A higher power? The gods? The universe?"

My voice cracked at the end, and I realized what this whole thing had done to my faith, if I'd had any to begin with. I realized that the thought of a higher being in charge of all this made me angry.

Jack took my hand in his. "Do you want to try? Or do you want to give up?"

"It all seems so futile," I said.

He pulled me toward him, crushing me against his chest. "Right now, the other options are that you take me to the Feed, or you become queen."

"What?"

"I'm saying that if we run out of time and the only options are you dying or taking me to the Feed, you take me to the Feed."

"Hell, no," I said. "There is no way, literally no way in hell, I will feed on you."

"Then we'd better try to destroy the Everneath," Jack said. "Otherwise, we'll be facing an epic showdown, and I'm bigger and stronger than you are." The edge of his lips curled up and his eyes twinkled, but I knew that underneath it all, the threat was real. He would do everything he could to force me to feed on him.

Then I looked at Cole. The old Cole would've done anything to force me to turn into a full-fledged Everliving.

And hell, maybe he was the old Cole.

I was surrounded by a roomful of people who would both, to varying degrees, fight to make me an Everliving.

I frowned and started blinking uncontrollably. This whole thing wasn't about bringing down the Everneath. It was about me trying to survive. Maybe I'd let myself believe that it was about saving the lives of countless potential Forfeits, but wasn't it really just about saving myself?

Without me, there was no need, really, to destroy the Everneath. Forfeits weren't exactly innocent. When it came down to it, they all had to choose to go to the Feed.

Without me, the old Cole would not be trying so hard for the throne. At least, he'd only be trying in the sense that he'd be looking for the next Forfeit.

Without me, nobody would be risking his life. In fact, this whole thing had started because I'd tried to run away from my own pain. It had started because I'd thought only of myself.

"Becks?" Jack said hesitantly. He glanced at Cole. "I know what you're thinking," he said. "Don't do it."

"Do what?" Cole and I both said at the same time.

"Can't you see it in her eyes?" Jack said. "She's running."

Cole looked from my face to the spot where I was sitting on the bed, obviously taking it literally. "No, she's not. She's standing still."

Jack ignored him. "Don't do it, Becks."

"Without me, you would both be fine," I said.

"No," he said. "I would never be fine. Ever again. And if you run, I will catch you. And if I can't, I will try to take the Everneath down single-handedly."

Cole finally looked as if he'd caught up. "And I'll help him," he said.

Jack glanced at Cole, and though he didn't quite smile, the frown he gave Cole wasn't as deep as it usually was.

I couldn't think of anything to say. Would they really still try to take it down?

What if I were no longer alive?

If I were dead, there would be no point in Jack's trying so crazily to take it down.

I closed my eyes and shook my head, shaking the thought away with it. I knew my own strength. There was no way I could ever take my own life. Unless . . . unless I was saving someone else's.

"Becks, listen to me," Jack said, grabbing my shoulders. "I won't try to make you take me to the Feed. I promise. Just don't give up. However this turns out, I will be monumentally messed up if you disappear on me now. If we put up a fight and we lose . . . well, we'll have to live with it. But if I lose you here because you run . . . there would be no recovering for me."

I nodded. Again, I knew exactly how that would feel. When Jack jumped into the Tunnels for me . . . and I didn't have the option of fighting for his life . . . it was a feeling I wouldn't wish on anyone.

I nodded my head. "Okay. But promise me, if this doesn't work out . . . I cannot feed on another human being. I won't. I'll spend a century holding my breath. I. Will. Not. Feed. On. You."

He nodded slowly. "Okay. Then we're agreed. We'll fight to take down the Everneath. We'll give our last breath fighting."

I nodded. "Sounds like a plan. Now let's go destroy the network."

Jack let out a sigh. "I told the professor our plan. His first reaction was, Wait, you're only taking three people to destroy the network? You'll need an army. So I got to thinking we need at least one more person. And I have someone in mind."

TWENTY-NINE

NOW
The Surface. The hotel.

No way," I said. "No one else is going to lose their life over me."

"Silly Becks," Jack said, ruffling my hair as we walked to his car. "You're assuming that we're all going to die. When did you develop this cup-half-full kind of attitude? Will's already been helping us."

"On the Surface. It's a whole different kind of danger in the Everneath."

"Will loves danger."

I glanced at him sideways. The sun was shining through the window now, directly on Jack, making him a little too glorious for me to argue with.

"I have a good attitude."

"Sure you do," Jack said.

"I do," I insisted. "I just have to measure my attitude with reality."

"That's called having a bad attitude."

"No, it's not. It's called being realistic."

"Or pessimistic."

"Shut up."

Jack smiled. "Ah, there's that can-do spirit. Let's go start a war. And let's bring Will. This is just the type of thing he'll love to do."

Pretty soon, the four of us were sitting around the table in the hotel room, strategizing. We decided that the best time to try for the network was during one of the queen's Feasts in one of the Commons. I'd learned of the ritual the first time I'd gone to the Everneath looking for Jack. The Shades and the queen gathered in the center of whatever Common they were in and then proceeded to make a feast out of humans and Everlivings alike who had crossed the High Court one way or another.

I remembered there being thousands of Shades in attendance, so that had to mean there'd be fewer Shades to deal with around the baetylus.

Everyone agreed. We were about to get to it, but Cole raised his hand. "How are we going to destroy the vault of hearts?"

We all looked at one another.

"We'll have to figure that out later," I said.

"We should figure it out now," Cole said. "What if we get the opportunity to do something, but we can't because we don't know what that something is?"

I tilted my head, trying to decipher what he'd just said.

"He's right," Jack said. "We have to be ready for anything."

Will leaned forward. "In the war, I was in munitions for a rotation."

Jack took in a deep breath. "So?"

"So, I've got some old friends at Fort Douglas. They could help me concoct something along the lines of an incendiary device."

Jack glanced at Will and wrinkled his eyebrows.

Will rolled his eyes. "You know, something that would make stuff get blowed up."

I shook my head, thinking of my own cell phone's behavior in the Everneath. "Stuff from the Surface doesn't work right in the Everneath."

"*Electronic* stuff doesn't work. But something that is a simple elemental chemical reaction . . ."

Jack grinned. "*Elemental chemical reaction?*"

Will looked faux offended. "Hey, if I'm interested in a subject, I learn about it. And when I wanted to forget where I was in Afghanistan, I blew stuff up. It was much less destructive than other stress outlets."

Jack nodded. "Okay." He took out his phone and called Professor Spears, putting it on speaker. When the professor answered, Jack caught him up on our strategy meeting. "Will thinks that he could blow up the vault of hearts, because it would involve a basic chemical reaction. Do you think this would work?"

Professor Spears was quiet for a moment before saying, "Will's probably right."

Jack's eyes went wide.

"The problem is finding enough of a fuse . . . and an ignition made of Everneath energy that would start the chain reaction. A simple match isn't going to cut it."

Jack turned to me. "You have the ability to conjure things up, right? Isn't that what happened to you because you survived the Feed?"

I nodded, remembering the vague image of Adonia's soldier, Nathanial, I'd conjured up when we were trying to escape her clutches. And more recently the railroad tie I'd made to block the door.

Cole scoffed. "She can, but she's not very good at it."

I glared at him. "How do you know?" I said.

Cole's mouth fell open with a smile. "I remembered it! I was exasperated trying to teach you to harness your energy projection. It was a problem."

My cheeks went pink at how difficult it had been for me to control my projection. "It doesn't come naturally," I muttered. I thought about how easily Adonia had created a blizzard. She'd probably only gotten better since she'd become queen. By the time I conjured up another railroad tie, she'd probably have already sandwiched me in between two spiky walls like she did the original queen. "I need a weapon the queen is specifically vulnerable to. Killing the queen is key for me." I flinched involuntarily at the word *killing*. I couldn't believe I was speaking so flippantly about ending someone's life.

"I think if you can destroy the vault," Professor Spears said, "you'll kill the queen. Or significantly weaken her."

We hung up with more of a plan than we'd ever had before, but we still had one significant problem. Destroying the vault of hearts would get rid of all the Everneath hearts . . . but what about the Surface hearts?

We could only hope an answer would present itself before it was too late.

While Jack and Will took care of a few things at home, namely a way to disappear without causing their mother to call in a search party, Cole went to the Everneath alone to find out when the next Feast was taking place. I was worried about him going by himself—especially given that there were Wanted signs with his face on it plastered everywhere—but he seemed to need a chance to prove he could do it.

I called my aunt Grace's house and spoke to Tommy for a long time. He was enjoying spending time with our cousins and had been thrilled when my dad had taken him there.

I told him I loved him. I wished I could call my dad.

Will and Jack met me back at the hotel, and we waited for word from Cole. After what seemed like hours, there was a soft knock at the door.

I swung it open.

Cole was standing there. "Tomorrow. If we leave at ten thirty in the morning, we'll arrive in the Everneath just in time for the Feast."

It was a restless sleep that night for all of us. Jack, Cole, and I slept in the king-size bed as we had been doing the entire time. Will slept on the floor. He said his time in the army made him used to sleeping on hard floors, so being on the carpet was comfortable.

But I was up most of the night, and I could swear that I never heard the even breathing of sleep from any of the guys.

I did doze off and on while feeding on Cole; and once when I woke up, I saw that Cole was sitting up, his feet hanging over the side of the bed, his hands on the mattress on either side of him.

"Are you going somewhere?" I whispered.

"No," he said without turning his head. "I just got to thinking about the band."

"Do you remember them?" I said.

He shook his head. "No, but I feel . . . protective of them. If they're in the accelerated Feed right now, will destroying the baetylus hurt them?"

Crap. I'd been so intent on destroying the Everneath and everyone responsible for its existence that I hadn't thought about what it would do to the band if we were successful. Cole may have felt protective of them.

I didn't.

But I felt protective of Cole. I couldn't deny it anymore. I'd been so worried about letting go of my anger and my hate, but my mistake was thinking it was actually my choice. I had about as much choice in the matter as an ice sculpture on a sunny day. Drop by drop, without my permission, my anger and hate had melted away. Maybe I would get screwed because of it. But I no longer had a choice.

"I don't think it will hurt the band. Since it would break the Shade network, it might simply end their accelerated Feed. And then they'd have time to get out before we destroyed the hearts. Because we don't know how we're going to do that. So there will be time."

Cole nodded. "Thank you. I needed an out I could focus on."

I smiled. "I am familiar with the need for a way out, no matter how implausible. It can give a hopeless situation hope."

He sighed and lay back down.

There was no point in trying to sleep now.

When we got up, we packed our bags in silence. Maybe we were all focused on our shreds of hope. We hauled our bags to the car and drove up Parley's Canyon.

At ten thirty we made our way to the back of the Shop-n-Go. We clasped hands and formed a tiny circle, Jack on my right, Cole on my left and Will straight across from me.

"Any second thoughts?" I said.

"Yes," they all three said in unison.

"Um, too bad."

We stood there for a moment.

I'd come to love each of them in his own way, but it was the boy holding my right hand, the one who had nearly beheaded me with a baseball when we were twelve, who would hold my heart for the rest of my life.

I think he felt the moment too. He stared at me and then tugged on my hand to pull me near and kissed me.

I'd always loved kissing him. I remembered fantasizing about it for the entire year before we started dating. I wanted to kiss him every day until the day I died . . . which might be in a short time.

The fingers in my left hand went limp. I pulled away from Jack and looked at Cole.

"Are you ready, Nik?" Cole said, his eyes tight.

I didn't know what to say to him. So I just nodded.

This time Cole needed no prompting to get the traveling going. We were in the throes of the transfer from this world to the next. And soon we would try to destroy the baetylus.

We were quiet when we landed in Ouros. We had a purpose. Jack hung the Helmet of Hermes around his neck, and the excess energy that had been leaking out of him in a colorful mist immediately disappeared. The professor's theory was right. The pendant would hide energy.

Jack led the way toward the secret entrance that Ashe had taken to get to the baetylus, and we all followed close behind. Cole stayed next to Will, whose excess energy was much more noticeable than Jack's.

But we didn't get very far before we saw the posters. One single word was printed in the middle of them.

FEAST

And underneath that word were three faces. Max's, Oliver's, and Gavin's.

Jack, Will, and I came to a screeching halt. I turned toward Cole, who seemed confused. He looked from my face, which I'm sure had a horrified expression, to the poster, and then back to me.

"Do you know those three guys?" he asked.

I covered my mouth with my hand.

Jack stepped toward Cole. "They're the rest of your band. It's your band on the menu at the Feast."

THIRTY

We'd been wrong. Our assumptions that Max, Oliver, and Gavin had taken their Forfeits to an accelerated Feed were completely wrong. I realized then how delusional we'd been. Maybe none of us had wanted to believe that if Cole had been taken from his home and tortured, the band would have been as well.

No one was preparing for war. Instead, the inhabitants of Ouros were gathering in the center square, crowding in to watch the horrific murder of three Everlivings.

Unless we could stop it.

"When was the Feast supposed to start?" I asked.

Cole's face remained blank, as if he hadn't heard the question. He didn't take his eyes off the poster.

"Cole. Do you recognize their faces?"

He shook his head.

"When was the Feast supposed to start?" I said again.

Cole frowned. "I scheduled our arrival for right after the beginning of the Feast. So we wouldn't have to deal with the crowds rushing to the square."

Jack pulled at my arm. "We're under a deadline here. This could be our one chance to destroy the baetylus. Even if we got to the square before the Feast, we'd never be able to rescue them."

I put my hand on Cole's shoulder. "Hey, look at me."

He obeyed.

"What are you feeling right now?"

His mouth was slightly open, and he looked around him as if he were searching for what he was feeling.

"Cole. Look at me. What are you feeling?"

"I feel like I need to go home. But I don't have a home." He looked like a lost puppy.

I nodded and turned to Jack. "We have to try to save them," I said.

"Because Cole wants to go home?"

"Because the band is the only home he knows. That's what he's feeling right now." I couldn't believe I'd suggested it, but I knew that if Cole had his memories, he'd do everything he could to save his band. His family. We'd tricked him into believing he wanted to destroy the Everneath as much as we did. The least I could do for him was try.

I started to run toward the square.

"Becks!" Jack called out, but I didn't stop. I knew they would all follow.

I wasn't sure exactly where I was going, but my previous trips to the Everneath had taught me that if I wanted to reach the center of the Ouros Common, I would go in the direction where the buildings got bigger, not smaller.

We ran for a long time, the adrenaline powering my legs. If we could make it before the Feast . . . maybe there would be other Everlivings who were on the menu to be sacrificed first. Maybe the queen would save the band for last.

Maybe that would buy us some time. Jack could create a diversion. Knock over a building or something to distract everyone in the square, and then Cole, Will, and I would rush the stage and try to free the band.

The buildings lining the streets were more than four stories now, and I knew we had to be close. I could hear the crowds cheering.

One more corner and we were there. The square. It was filled with Everlivings, all focused on the stage. The swell of the noise rattled my chest.

I stood on my tiptoes, trying to get a good view of the platform, when suddenly two hands—Jack's hands—grabbed my waist and hoisted me up above the crowd.

And there they were. Max, Oliver, and Gavin. Center stage. A line of other Everliving sacrifices off to the side.

The queen was starting the Feast with the band.

Cole stood on top of the half wall I'd stood on so long ago. His mouth hung open as he watched. An army of Shades had already converged together above the platform.

"No!" I screamed.

A few confused Everlivings turned my way at the noise, but otherwise my scream seemed to get lost like a cheer at a football stadium. Except Max looked up from where he stood. He scanned the crowd as if searching for the person who had screamed. Finally, his eyes landed on mine. For a split second I thought I saw a glimmer of hope in them.

Then the Shades swirled together, forming a long spear as they had at the last Feed; and with no preamble whatsoever, the aggregation of Shades dived for the stage and shot through Oliver first, then through Gavin, and finally through Max.

In what seemed like slow motion, I turned to Cole. Jack released me, and I scrambled up the half wall and wrapped my arms around Cole, trying to interrupt his line of sight to the stage. I held him tightly as what sounded like a muffled explosion reached my ears. A pink mist appeared in the air.

"Don't breathe in," I whispered to Cole.

We held our breaths together as the entire crowd took a collective gasp and ingested the Dead Elvises.

When the pink mist had disappeared, I put my lips to Cole's ear again. "You can breathe now," I said.

He took one gasp of air and crumpled to the ground.

The rest of the sacrifices began to take the stage, one by one. Jack crouched down by Cole, grabbed an arm and a leg, and hoisted him over his shoulder. "We have to move if we want any hope of destroying the network before the end of the Feast."

I nodded, unable to form words. Maybe it was good we had a destination and a goal, because if we didn't, I wasn't sure how I would react.

In fact, I didn't know how to feel about the band dying. They wouldn't have hesitated to force me to take over the throne, but did that mean they deserved to be blown to bits? Not even to bits, but to tiny droplets? I was having a hard time processing my feelings, which was okay, because there was no time.

Again, we ran through the streets, away from the square and toward the hidden entrance to the Shade passageway. By the time we got there, Cole had woken up. Jack set him on the ground, and then we all dropped to our knees, panting.

The band. Slaughtered before our eyes. I'd known them for a long time, but for Cole . . . they were like brothers. I put my hand on Cole's cheek.

"Cole? Are you okay?"

His face was blank, but he nodded.

"Do you remember the band?"

He shook his head and put his hand on his chest. "But there's a hole right here." He squeezed his eyes shut. "I'm missing something. I've lost it. But I don't know what it is I've lost."

I dropped my hand and leaned back against the wall. Jack shook his head. "Did that really just happen?" he said.

I closed my eyes, and for a long moment we all just sat there.

Jack moved next to me, and I opened my eyes. He stood up in front of us. "We can't waste any more time. This is our chance.

Your second shackle is nearly indistinguishable from the first. The Feast is almost over. This is it. Are we doing this?"

I nodded. "Yes."

Jack opened the door to the snake belly tunnel. I put my hands on Cole's cheeks. "Look at me, Cole. We're going to be okay. We have to destroy the network, and we have to do it now. Are you with me?"

He closed his mouth—it had been hanging open—and nodded. "I'm always with you, Nik."

Nik. No matter what he'd forgotten, he'd always remembered his nickname for me. The guilt weighed heavy in my chest for a moment. How I'd tricked him into getting to this point. How I still wasn't telling him the truth—that he never wanted to destroy the Everneath. He wanted to rule it. With me by his side.

"Everyone remember where we're meeting if we get separated?" Jack asked.

We all nodded.

"Let's go!" Jack said.

Jack pulled the door open and ushered all of us inside. He followed last, shutting the door behind him.

The throat-like tube lay just in front of us, contracting and expanding in that same swallowing motion, but unlike last time, there was no echoing noise coming from deep inside. There was no noise at all.

"The clock is ticking," Jack said. This time there was no trembling, no blood draining from his face. He was the first to the mouth of the tube. "Me first. Then Becks. You have the sickle?"

I nodded. We had decided I should be the one to stab the baetylus since I supposedly had the power down here.

"Good." Jack grabbed Cole by the shoulders. "Cole, you come after Becks. She needs you. Make sure nothing gets to her. Will, you bring up the end."

Will raised his eyebrows. "You mean the most dangerous spot? Got it."

"Some people might say the front is the most dangerous," Jack said. Then he looked at the rest of us. "Ready?"

We all nodded.

The journey through the tube seemed longer than before, probably because our window of opportunity was limited and finite. The farther we got, the more I expected us to see a dim light coming from the end of the tube where the Shade network should be, but there was no light.

"What does it mean that there's no light?" I said to Cole behind me.

"I don't know," he said.

From up ahead, Jack turned slightly. "Maybe the end is blocked by something."

"But by what?" I said.

We kept going, but with each yard we immersed ourselves farther into pure darkness.

"Shouldn't we be there?" Cole asked. His voice was too

loud for the tube, and I realized that we'd all been basically holding our breaths.

"Shhh," I said.

Finally, Jack stopped. I knew because I ran into him.

"What is it?" I asked.

"Something hard is blocking it," Jack said through a grunt. "I've almost got it. . . . There!" He tumbled through, falling into the cavern that housed the baetylus. I scrambled after him, then Cole and finally Will. A round steel door hung broken at the end of the passageway. Jack had busted his way through it.

When I had righted myself, Jack was already standing, his feet apart in an athletic stance, as if he were about to get hit.

"Jack?" I said, but then I saw what he was looking at, and I froze.

There were ten Shades, at least, surrounding the orb. Swirling around it. Protecting it.

I didn't have any excess energy to attract the Shades, and Jack had the pendant around his neck, cloaking his own. Cole was an Everliving. Will was the only one of us who had anything that would draw their attention.

Just like a wave, one by one the heads of the Shades turned toward Will.

Will assessed the situation like an army officer who was used to combat strategy. "I'll divert," he said.

Before we could stop him, he waved his arms up and down.

I almost laughed, because it wasn't his movements that were attracting the Shades, but it didn't matter. Will had their full attention.

His eyes shifted toward another crevice-like opening on the opposite side of the cavern. I could see why he picked it. The hole was in the ground, going downward. Gravity would aid him. He feinted left, tricking the Shades into darting that way, and then he sprinted toward the opening. He leaped high in the air and then dropped through the chasm. The Shades hesitated for a moment and then swarmed after him, looking like a tub full of oil swirling down a drain.

"Will!" I screamed. He might be able to beat them simply by using the force of gravity, but where would the passageway deposit him?

"Nikki! Quick!" Jack said, pulling me away from the hole Will had disappeared down.

After a moment of hesitation, I ran to the baetylus, held the sickle high above it with both hands, and plunged. The sickle clashed with the orb, causing so much vibration that I had to drop it.

The orb didn't even have a dent.

I looked at Jack, alarmed.

"Shit," he said.

Cole was standing by one of the larger openings in the cavern wall. "Whatever you're gonna do, make it fast. I see something at the end. There's something coming!"

I took the sickle and plunged it again, but it was like

stabbing a granite boulder with a rubber chicken.

"Jack!" I said.

He came running over.

"Try it," I said.

He looked as if he didn't think it could possibly work, but he took the sickle from my hands. He raised it high above his head, and suddenly I flashed to a picture I'd seen in my mythology book: of Hercules holding a knife over something. Maybe this was the reason he'd come back bigger. Maybe his own journey to the Tunnels had led him to this moment. This one chance to destroy something only he and no one else could.

The frozen image gave me the chills.

He brought it down, and upon impact, the orb exploded. Shards of light burst out, implanting themselves in the rock walls.

Jack stood above the carnage, panting. He took the pendant from his neck and placed it at the center of where the orb used to be.

"I hope the pendant holds the energy long enough for us to get out of here," I said.

He nodded. "It will. If we go now."

"How do you know?" I said.

He smiled. "Faith."

Cole motioned us toward one of the crevices, and Jack went in first, followed by me. We started crawling as fast as we could. I turned behind me to make sure Cole was there, but he wasn't.

"Cole!" I shouted. "Cole!"

Jack stopped in front of me. "Where is he?"

"I don't know. Cole!" There was light from the network end of the tunnel, and suddenly shadow overcame the light. I couldn't tell if it was a human form or a Shade. My blood ran cold with the thought that the Shades had gotten Cole.

"Run!" Jack said.

"We're not leaving him!"

"He's right behind us! I'm sure of it!"

We crawled as fast as we could. The swallowing motion of the tunnel seemed to be working against us, as if the passageway itself knew we were fugitives. For every two feet forward, we seemed to move one step back.

I dug my nails in as I went, clawing my way forward. It felt like working against a strong current. Jack reached a hand back and I grasped it. With his help, we finally ended up in a heap outside the entrance.

After a few tense moments, Cole's tattooed hand appeared. Jack took it and hoisted him out. It had been him behind me the entire time.

I punched him in the arm. "What were you doing?" I said. "I thought the Shades got you!"

He shook his head. "I was just making sure everything was really destroyed."

I didn't have time to ask him questions. We had to meet Will at the rendezvous point. "Run!" I said.

We ran. A flat-out sprint. We weren't as worried this time

about drawing too much attention. We were only worried about the speed, because once we found Will, Cole would zap us out of there.

We were so close now. I started to believe we would make it. All we needed was for Will to have eluded the Shades, and when we turned the final corner and I saw Will waiting at the Fountain of Lethe, I knew we were home free. I grabbed Cole's hand and Jack's hand; but just as Jack reached out to grab Will, something strange happened, almost in slow motion. The sky above us turned from light blue to a darker blue, and then it transitioned into a deep red. The air around us seemed tinged with the deep red too, as if each air molecule were reflecting the new hue of the sky.

Jack grabbed Will's hand.

"Go!" he shouted to Cole.

I closed my eyes, waiting for that familiar feeling of being tossed about in a washing machine.

But it never came.

"Go, go!" Jack said again.

I opened my eyes and saw Cole's face, and instantly my heart sank.

"We're too late," he said. "The Everneath is on lockdown."

THIRTY-ONE

NOW

The Everneath. Streets of Ouros.

*E*verlivings poured out of buildings. Some pointed at the sky. Others stood there with knees bent and eyes squeezed shut, as if trying to propel themselves to the Surface. But they remained where they were. A few released panicked screams, looking for missing loved ones. The good thing was that with everyone worrying about being on lockdown, nobody would notice us. I wondered how often the Everneath had been on lockdown before, because the Everlivings seemed genuinely panicked.

We fought our way through the throngs of Everlivings and ran to Ashe's house, scrambling inside and shutting the door and the windows.

"Are you sure it's a lockdown?" I said.

Cole nodded. "I assume that's what the change in the sky means. Either way, I tried to jump us, but nothing happened."

Jack took a few steps closer to Cole so he was in his face. "Maybe you forgot how. Maybe you didn't try hard enough."

He grabbed Cole's hand and then mine. I grabbed Will's. "Try again."

I closed my eyes once more in the vain hope that this time it would work. But nothing happened.

"I'm telling you, it's not working," Cole insisted.

Jack threw our hands down and stormed to the opposite side of the house. He ran his fingers through his hair, pulling out more than a few strands as he did so.

"What do we do now? What do we do?"

I tried to stand next to him, but he wouldn't stand still. He just kept pacing.

"Where's Ashe?" he said.

"The Feast, I'm sure," Cole said.

Thinking of the very few war movies I'd seen, I said, "Okay, let's take inventory of what we have."

Will was the only one who responded. He emptied out his pockets. Three quarters, a poker chip, and a ball of lint.

Jack looked at it and paced even faster. I put my hands into my pockets. One cell phone that didn't work in the Everneath. And nothing else.

Cole saw what we were doing and backed up a step. He almost looked scared. Jack noticed too. He called him on it.

"What do you have, Cole?" he said.

"Nothing," Cole said.

He wasn't a very good liar. If there was one change about the new, amnesiac Cole, it was that he couldn't lie as easily.

Jack was in no mood to play games. He grabbed Cole and

dug his hands into the pockets of Cole's pants. He came up with a metal object.

The pendant.

The Helmet of Hermes was supposed to be our escape plan. It was supposed to be with the destroyed baetylus, masking its energy, allowing us to escape. Instead, it was here.

Jack threw it against the wall so hard that the edge of the pendant embedded itself in the plaster a good inch. I was definitely angry, but I thought Jack's head was about to explode.

"What the hell?" Jack growled, baring his teeth.

For the first time, I had no desire to hold him back. Cole had betrayed us. Again. I wanted Jack to rip Cole apart.

"Now, settle down," Cole said, his hands out, palms down. He walked around the table in the room so that he kept it between himself and Jack.

Jack followed around accordingly. "Settle down?" Jack said. "You raised the alarm on us. It's because of you that we didn't have time to get out. You betrayed all of us. Again!"

I just shook my head. Before, I'd needed Cole alive because I needed him to feed me, but now? There was no point in feeding on Cole anymore. This was the end. We were through.

Jack went around the table, and Cole moved to position himself the farthest distance from Jack. They went round and round. I did nothing to stop them. If I'd had the strength, I probably would have torn Cole's head off myself.

Will stepped forward. "Uh, guys?"

Jack spoke through gritted teeth. "I'm going to tear through your chest and grab the nearest thing to a heart you have inside there, and then I'm going to rip it out, and it will make that scene in *Alien* look like a kid's movie."

I almost laughed at how detailed Jack's threat was.

"Uh, guys, wait," Will said.

Jack finally spared him a glance. "What?"

"Did you empty all of Cole's pockets?"

Jack nodded.

"Then we're missing something," he said.

I looked at the contents on the table. There was my phone, three quarters, a ball of lint . . . but what was Will's point? What were we missing?

Cole looked up from the table, realization dawning on his features. "My heart. My Surface heart. My pick."

"He never goes anywhere without it, right?" Will said. We had learned that lesson when we tried to break Cole's heart.

I looked back down, trying to figure out what he was thinking. "It's gone," I said.

Jack didn't give up his position of pursuit on the side of the table, but he stopped long enough to say, "What does that mean?"

I rubbed my forehead. "So when the lockdown went into effect, suddenly Cole's Surface heart disappeared. The Surface heart is the way the Everlivings go between the worlds." I bit my lip. "What if . . . the only way the Everneath could be fully locked down is if everyone's Surface heart was somehow confiscated?"

Jack dropped both hands, and his eyes got wide.

"That means . . . ," Jack said, but he couldn't finish the sentence.

"That means all the hearts might be in one place," I said. "That means the thing we thought was impossible . . ."

"Is suddenly possible," Cole finished.

It was as if we were all so surprised that we'd lost the ability to start *and* finish a sentence. Will just smiled. Had he figured this all out before any of us?

"Ha-*ha*!" Cole exclaimed triumphantly. "See? I was following my instincts back there. Something inside me told me to take the pendant. It was a sign. That if the lockdown happened, all the Surface hearts would be stored together. And how could we expect to destroy them all if they were scattered around the universe?"

He looked up at Jack, whose ears were scorching red, as if he still really wanted to be angry with Cole and was disappointed that he wouldn't have the opportunity to beat him again.

"You're welcome," Cole said.

Jack clenched and unclenched his fist. "You forgot one thing in your brilliant plan."

"What's that?" Cole said.

"We're trapped here now. *We* can't get back to the Surface either."

Jack was right. Cole no longer had his Surface heart, which meant there would be no way to go back and forth.

Cole nodded. "Hopefully the lockdown will last only until we destroy the Everneath."

Will leaned back in his chair and put his hands behind his head. "Just like we always said. We destroy the Everneath or we die trying."

We had always said that. Only now we couldn't take it back.

Just then the door flew open, and Ashe blew in. He caught sight of us around the table and looked toward the door again as if he might run out.

"What are you doing here?" he asked.

Jack and I looked at each other.

Ashe frowned. "Don't tell me. You're the reason for the lockdown."

Cole nodded.

"Shit." Ashe looked at the windows, which were all covered by blinds, and tugged a loose one a little closer so that no one could see in.

"You're not going to turn us in again, are you?" Cole asked.

Ashe shook his head. "You destroyed the orb. Which means you destroyed the single object linking us all. Which means you've set the Shades free. Without the orb, I'm under no obligation to do what the Everneath wants."

If that was true—if Ashe was no longer tied to the Everneath—maybe he could help us locate where the queen was keeping the Surface hearts. Jack looked at me and raised his eyebrows questioningly. He must be wondering the same thing.

I nodded.

Jack turned to Ashe. "They confiscated all the Surface hearts. Which means maybe all those hearts are being stored in one place. We need to get to them."

Ashe frowned, then looked at Cole. "I know where she keeps them. All the Shades know. Now that you've destroyed the orb, I can tell you."

We all leaned toward Ashe expectantly.

"Hearts are kept in the center of the High Court. In a vault in the throne room. At least that's where she keeps the Everneath hearts. I can only think that once they confiscate the Surface hearts as well, that's where they keep them."

Ashe caught a look at Jack's smile and held up his hand. "Don't get your hopes up. If you thought getting to the Tunnels was tough . . . the throne room is Fort Knox. Yes, there won't be as many Shades around in all this chaos, but if this is all you have"—he gestured toward our knickknacks on the table—"you'll never destroy it."

Cole put his hands on the table, lacing his fingers. "But what if you took us to the throne room, and we could find our own hearts. Every Everliving has an affinity for his or her own heart. One time when I dropped my own heart, all I had to do was think about it and it came racing back to me. As long as we're close enough to the actual heart . . ."

I studied his face. "Did you just remember that?"

He seemed to wilt a tiny bit under the scrutiny. "Bits and pieces are coming to me."

I wondered if he was starting to remember because of what he'd just witnessed with the band. The professor said adrenaline would trigger memories, and I couldn't imagine more emotional turmoil than the band vaporized before our eyes. I couldn't decide if I wanted him to someday regain his memories—hopefully *after* our siege of the vault of hearts—or if I wanted him to remain clueless for the rest of his life about the pain and heartache he'd been through.

"So we go to the throne room," Jack said. "Cole's heart will do that magnet act, and then the second he touches it, we can zap to the Surface and plan our next move. Maybe we can research some sort of Everneath ammo we can use to destroy the throne room."

Cole leaned forward. "When are we planning this . . . coup?"

"There's no better time than now," Ashe said. "The Shades are newly free. They'll be all over the place, including going to the Surface to get their fill. They're not limited by hearts the way the Everliving are. Before, the existence of the network kept them in place. But now they're disorganized. The hearts are the least protected that they'll ever be."

I leaned my head back and closed my eyes. "The Shades let loose on humans." I shook my head. "Can they drain them completely?"

"Yes," Ashe said. "It's what they do."

"Then we really do have to destroy it. We have to destroy it all, now. Before anyone else dies."

Jack stood. "Let's go. Ashe, will you take us?"

Ashe nodded. He started toward the door, but Cole asked him, "Why?"

"Why what?" Ashe said.

"Why are you willing to help us destroy the Everneath?"

Ashe smiled a sad grin that dripped with oil. "You laid out a convincing argument. It turns out I have nothing to live for. And everything to die for."

THIRTY-TWO

NOW

The Everneath. Ouros.

We followed Ashe through the chaos of the streets of Ouros. Everlivings darted in all directions, probably looking for a way out and up to the Surface. Apparently the immortals were a calm bunch until their freedom was taken away. Now many reacted as any newly caged animal would.

As we followed Ashe, I caught glimpses through windows of other Everlivings, hunkering down in their homes. Maybe they were hoping this would all blow over. Some were alone, but through some windows I could see pairs of them, clinging to each other. I had only a moment to reflect on the occasional displays of love.

We followed Ashe around a corner that led to an alleyway. Tall buildings reached into the sky on either side. We'd made it several yards before I realized that it looked like a wall was blocking off the end.

I hesitated. "Dead end?" I said.

Ashe waved us forward, and that's when I noticed, in the center of the wall, a black, rectangular-shaped splotch that looked as if it had been drawn on with oil. It was about the size of a door.

"Touch me," Ashe said.

We placed our hands on Ashe's arms.

"Everyone attached?" he said.

When we all nodded, he approached the doorway. The black of the splotch seemed to reach out and engulf first Ashe and then the rest of us. It felt like a draft of cold air against my skin.

We walked through. The doorway led to a small room with no ceiling. The deep red sky hung over it.

Ashe lowered his voice. "This is the Shade entrance. Jumps to the High Court can originate only here. It's how the queen limits who goes in and out. Otherwise, we'd have to go through the labyrinth." He took a deep breath. "I just barely started being able to use it. Keep your hands on me," he ordered.

We did as he commanded. Then we rose up in the air, the chamber we had just been in growing small beneath us. The chaos of the city of Ouros shrank as we glided through the atmosphere. The outer ring of the labyrinth, the Ring of Water, came into view. I watched it move beneath me as if I were looking out the window of an airplane. We continued over the Ring of Wind and then the Ring of Fire, which was accompanied by a gust of hot air. It was the only time I could feel the effects of any of the rings.

We began our descent just as the bulls-eye of the labyrinth came into view.

Ashe guided us gently to the ground in the middle of a medieval-looking courtyard. On one side of the courtyard stood a tall, gray cinder-block wall. I recognized it as the wall surrounding the High Court, but we were on the inside, not the outside. If we had been on the outside, we would've been surrounded by the Ring of Fire.

There was no fire where we were. But unfortunately, within seconds we *were* surrounded by four Shades.

"I thought you said it was unprotected!" Jack shouted.

"I meant there wouldn't be hundreds," Ashe answered. He stood in front of us with his arms out, facing the Shades. "I'll take care of them. Go that way." He pointed one direction, along the wall. "Look for a red stained-glass door. It will lead you to the vault. And hurry!"

By the time he finished speaking, he was already fighting with the Shades and we were already running down a corridor that ran adjacent to the wall.

If we encountered any more Shades, we were screwed. Especially without Ashe. None of us could even touch them. The gray stones of the wall blended together as we sprinted. My chest burned with the exertion. Jack seemed to sense it, and he reached back to grab my hand.

Just as Ashe had promised, we came to a red stained-glass door. The wood around the door looked heavy and sturdy. An intricate iron design created a pattern in the glass. Jack tried the handle, but it didn't budge.

He took a step back and bent his knees, ready to spring.

I held my hand up. "Wait! The iron!" I said, worried he'd be hurt.

But he didn't hesitate. He crashed through the glass, tearing the iron as he went. The rest of us quickly but carefully stepped through the giant hole he had made.

"Jack, your arm!" I said.

His shoulder sported several cuts, deep enough that blood trickled down his arm.

"I'm fine," he said. "Just go!"

We followed the zigzagging corridors until we reached a giant steel door with what looked like a ship's wheel on the outside.

"Shit," Cole said. "It's a literal vault."

He tried to turn the wheel. Nothing happened. Jack grabbed two of the outer handles. But it looked as if the spindle of the wheel was welded to the door, and it wasn't possible to move it.

None of us was strong enough.

I looked at Jack, at his bulging muscles. And I formed a plan. I crouched on the ground, holding my stomach.

"Becks!" Jack dropped to my side. "What's wrong?"

I shook my head, not really proud of the lie I was about to tell. But I was desperate. "Nothing. I just feel a little . . . faint."

He put his arm around me, but I shrugged it off. "I need

Cole. I need him to feed me."

Jack tensed beside me.

Cole bent down, waiting for Jack to move aside, but Jack didn't budge. "C'mon, man," Cole said.

Jack shook his head. "The Everneath itself should be feeding her. She shouldn't need you down here."

"Obviously she does. We have no idea how the High Court operates. Maybe it's draining her."

Huh. That sounded credible. I glanced sideways at Cole, and he winked at me. He knew what I was doing.

Jack moved aside, and Cole knelt down. "Let's make it good," he whispered under his breath.

I raised my face toward his, fluttering my eyelids for effect, and Cole planted his lips on mine.

Jack watched, his face resembling a hot air balloon being blown up beyond its safe size. Veins popped out on his forehead.

Will stepped up beside him. "Hey, bro, settle down."

Jack involuntarily flung him aside, throwing him against the wall. *Just a little bit more,* I thought. I put my hands in Cole's hair.

That was it. Jack blew a gasket. He reached down to grab Cole, and as he did, I broke the kiss and said, "Jack! The door!"

He immediately directed his anger and rage against the door. He grabbed the spokes of the wheel and tore the entire thing off its hinges. It was unlike anything I'd ever seen before, even in the movies. He threw the door to the opposite side of the room, where it became embedded at least a foot into the wall.

He stood there, breathing hard.

I went to put my hand on his arm, but he shook me off. "Give me a minute," he said. I felt so bad that I had to do that, but it was necessary. Wasn't it?

I wasn't sure it was ever fair to mess with someone's emotions the way I'd just messed with Jack's, even though part of me believed the end justified the means. I'd probably be debating that move for a long time to come.

I walked into the vault, and my mouth dropped open. I don't know what I'd expected when the vault was opened, but it wasn't the giant warehouse that I saw in front of me. Rows and rows and rows of shelving units, at least two stories high and reaching back farther than I could see. The only point of reference I could think of as to the size of the place was a giant indoor football stadium. And every shelf held hundreds, thousands, of items. Random things: pencils, erasers, corkscrews, lightbulbs, coins, rings, pendants, necklaces . . . all sorts of objects.

All sorts of hearts.

"What do we do now?" Will said.

Jack still looked too angry to speak.

"We wander the aisles, hoping our hearts find us," I said.

Cole shook his head. "I'm not sure your heart will be in

here," he said. "For some reason I think that the hearts of transitional people, like you, they're immune to the lockdown."

"Why?"

"Because they're not fully developed. Your heart still belongs to me. Not the Everneath. I think it's still wherever the old Cole hid it."

I rubbed my forehead. "Maybe this is something you could've remembered *before* we came here!"

Jack squinted toward the room we'd just come from. He held up his hand. "Shades are coming."

He ran into the anteroom and pried the door from where it had been embedded in the wall. He hoisted it over his head and carried it back. Just then, several Shades entered the anteroom. Jack grabbed the door and heaved it back into place behind us.

"I'll hold them off," he said. "Go find Cole's heart."

I nodded, and then Cole and I were off. We ran in different directions. All the while, I pictured my compass, and Cole's guitar pick, in my head. I thought of my compass just in case Cole was wrong, and I thought of his pick because I was desperate for him to find it.

We ran up and down the aisles.

Finally I turned a corner and saw a small dark object flying toward me.

It was a pick.

"Cole! Your pick!" I grabbed it out of midair and started

running back the way I thought Cole had gone. I had no time to figure out why it had come to *me* instead of to him.

I turned a final corner and froze. My blood turned cold at the scene in front of me. Cole lay sprawled out on the floor. He wasn't moving. Above him, holding a compass between her fingers, was the queen. Adonia. She'd found us.

THIRTY-THREE

NOW

The Everneath. In the vault of hearts.

"Cole!" I couldn't help saying it. He didn't move.

At the sound of my voice, the queen turned to me. "You," she said. "I remember you. The girl who showed me my soldier. The girl who made me think I could have everything I wanted and then made it disappear. I've been hoping to run into you again."

Cole stirred behind her. And beyond him, down one of the corridors, Will crept forward. Quietly, so the queen wouldn't notice him.

The queen held up the compass. "He told me this belongs to you?" How did she have my compass, and why did Cole's heart come to me and not him?

I thought fast. What had I been thinking about when Cole's pick came to me? I was literally thinking about Cole's heart.

"So tell me, girl who survived the Feed . . . girl who conjured a person out of thin air . . . girl who wants my throne . . .

why shouldn't I snap your heart in two right now?"

Snap my heart in two. What would that mean? Would that mean I would no longer be in this halfway limbo between human and Everliving?

"I don't want your throne," I said. "I never did."

"Yet you destroyed my Shade army, and you broke into my vault of hearts. Quite unusual for a girl who doesn't want the throne."

"Then break my heart. You'd be doing me a favor."

She narrowed her eyes and let up on her death grip on my compass. "If I break your heart, all you'll need to do is feed on your Everliving again three times in the Everneath to get another one." She brought a finger to her cheek. "Instead, I think I'll keep your heart for myself. Until I kill you."

She started toward me.

Cole had worked to a standing position. I flashed him a glimpse of his heart in my hand. Jack showed up next to Will. He looked as if he had been running. Obviously his barricade at the door had given way.

They seemed to be waiting for something.

I backed away from the queen.

"Now!" I screamed.

The three guys rushed toward me, tackling me all at once, and in a split second we were in the air, the queen's angry face spinning away.

We landed on the Surface, on asphalt in the parking lot near the Shop-n-Go. And I kissed the ground.

"See?" Cole said. "All part of the plan."

It was a miracle no one hit him as we made our way to Jack's car.

I experienced only a moment of relief before I realized the queen held my Surface heart. Which meant only *she* could feed me.

Which meant we had to get back to the Everneath before nightfall or my energy would be gone. I was sure the others had realized it too, but they weren't talking.

"Say it," I said.

They all looked at one another questioningly, as if they couldn't imagine what I was referring to.

"Say it," I said again.

"What?" Jack said.

"Don't pretend like you all haven't reached this conclusion," I said.

Jack took one hand off the steering wheel and put his arm around me. "We don't have to think about it now," he said.

"Yes, we do. The queen has my heart. In order to destroy the Everneath, I have to kill the queen. And I have to kill her tonight. Because only she can feed me now that she holds my heart, and I don't think she'll want to feed me."

"Don't think about that," Jack said. "We'll kill her before it comes to that."

Cole grabbed my hand. "Jack and Will, you guys go get explosives ready and then do any research you can about the queen. Nikki and I are going back to the Everneath."

"Why?" Jack and Will said simultaneously.

"Because I've got to train Nikki how to conjure a fuse that will explode the bombs."

After Cole packed a bag—he was very secretive about the contents—he took me to the Shop-n-Go and we went under.

We landed in a place that looked like a clearing in the middle of a forest. "Where are we?" I asked.

Cole shook his head. "I'm not sure. In my head I thought of something remote, away from the five Commons. We're probably somewhere along the Ring of Earth. No-man's-land."

Cole gathered up a bunch of objects: sticks, stones, branches. . . . He put them in a pile on one end of the clearing.

"Go stand over there," he said, pointing to a spot on the other side.

"What are you going to do?" I asked.

He shrugged. "I'm not telling you. But . . . defend yourself."

He wound up and threw a rock at me. My first instinct was to duck, so I did, and the rock went flying overhead.

"Don't duck," Cole said.

"I can't help it."

Cole took a step closer, cocked his arm back, and threw another rock at me. I racked my brain for something to conjure that would help me, but the only object that came to mind was the last thing I'd seen on the Surface. A fountain drink at the Shop-n-Go. And the only thing that appeared out of that image in my head was a straw.

The faint outline of the straw appeared in front of my face, but the rock tore through it as if it were smoke. Again, I dived out of the way.

"Don't move!" Cole commanded.

"I can't help it. Someone throws a rock at you, you're gonna move."

Cole sighed. "I thought that might be the case."

He dropped the backpack that had been slung over his shoulder and unzipped the largest pocket. He pulled out a bundled length of rope. It wasn't very thick, but it looked strong.

"What are you doing with that?" I said.

He didn't answer. He unwound the bundle. I could see that the rope was pliable and not stiff.

"Why are you carrying rope around with you?" I asked skeptically.

"Stop asking me dirty questions," he said with a smirk. I was totally confused until I imagined what someone would do with rope.

"Uh . . . that's not why we're here," I said.

"Don't get your panties in a twist," Cole said. "I don't have that sort of thing in mind."

"Wow," I said.

"What?"

"Nothing. You're starting to sound like the old you."

He held my gaze. "Maybe it's all coming back to me."

For an instant I wondered how much he knew. Had enough of his memory come back to make him realize we wanted different things?

After all, at this very moment he was training me to kill a queen. We were closer to his original goal than ever.

I almost laughed. After everything that had happened, we finally wanted the same thing. I guess it didn't matter if he had his memory back or not. It would only have changed his motives, not his objective.

He walked over to me, the rope clenched in his hands, and I instinctively took a step back.

He rolled his eyes. "Stand still, Nik."

With the deft fingers of someone who at least subconsciously had experience tying up people, he bound my feet together, tight enough that any movement would cause me to fall to the ground.

"Now your hands," Cole said. "Put them behind you."

I shook my head. "No," I said emphatically. "There's no way I'm letting you tie my hands together."

He cocked an eyebrow. "You let me tie your feet, but you draw the line at hands?"

I put my wrists together in front of me. "I won't be able to keep from falling."

"That's the point."

I sighed deeply. Was there any bigger sign of trust than

letting someone tie your hands and feet together?

And I was doing it with the guy who had totally betrayed me just weeks ago.

Cole looked at my face. "I know you don't trust me because of that guy I was before. But I'm not him."

I still hesitated. "But for how long? Your memory's coming back."

He put his hands on my shoulders and leveled his gaze with mine. "Memory or not, I'm not him. If I wanted to hurt you, I could've done it before now."

I closed my eyes, nodded, and put my hands together behind me. I heard his footfalls as he walked around behind me and gently took my hands in his. And then he wrapped the cord around them, tightly.

"Ow," I said. "A little looser?"

He answered by tying it off.

"Now. Again. Conjure a shield. And know that if you try to duck, you'll fall, and it will hurt worse than the rock."

I pressed my lips together and nodded.

He stepped back, but not as far as his original position. It worried me, because now that he was closer, I wouldn't have as much time to react.

I pictured a shield in my head before he even cocked his arm, which I guess was cheating a little, but I'd probably need a shield no matter what kind of fight. He let the rock loose, and I wasn't fast enough. Even worse, I couldn't stop myself from flinching, and I fell to the ground on my side, my hip crunching against the hard ground. I felt my bone grinding against the rocks.

"Ow!" I said.

Cole came over and pulled me up by my bound hands.

"Again," he said.

After each of the next three attempts, I ended in a similar heap against the ground. When I stood up the last time, I felt something liquid run the length of my thigh and down my leg. A trickle of blood appeared at the hem of my jeans.

Cole glanced down at the blood, but only quickly, as if he didn't want me to see that he was concerned. He hoisted me up once more.

"Again, Nik," he said softly.

He walked back. I hadn't felt this frustrated in a very long time. I was bleeding. My hip felt as if it were broken. I couldn't even bring my hand around to wipe the tears that were now falling down my cheeks.

Cole leaned down and picked up a particularly jagged stone.

"Wait," I said, my voice coming out much weaker than I'd meant it to.

Cole acted as though he didn't hear me.

He cocked back his arm.

"Wait," I said louder.

He froze for a split second but then continued with the motion. "The queen's not going to wait."

"Wait!" I screamed.

Just as he was about to release the stone, I squeezed my eyes shut, and when I opened them, a small, white, stick-like object shot across the air from me to him. It hit him in the head. He grabbed his face and turned, doubled over and groaning.

"Cole!" I said. I hopped toward him, trying to free my hands as I went. "Are you okay?"

He straightened up, turned toward me. Impaled in his cheek was a plastic straw.

"Ooh. That looks like it hurts." I took a little bit of triumph in the damage I'd caused.

He frowned at me, and I couldn't help grinning. With a quick movement, he loosened the rope at my wrists and I shook it away. Gently, I raised my hand and grabbed the straw and plucked it out of his cheek. A drop of blood bulged out of the tiny hole the straw left behind.

He rubbed his cheek. "What's with the plastic straw?"

I shrugged. "It was the last thing I saw before we came here." I smiled.

"Don't smile. The queen is going to come at you, and she's going to conjure up a . . . machine gun, and you're going to counter with a plastic straw. You can't kill with a straw."

I tried to frown, but my emotions were upside down, and instead I smiled a little bigger. "I could kill someone with a straw."

"How?"

I bit my lip and squinted one eye. "Secondary infection. It would take a long time but . . ."

Cole's lips twitched, and he pressed them together. "This is serious, Nik. This is your life."

"Okay, maybe I can't kill with a straw, but I can maim." I touched his cheek, wiping off a drop of fresh blood with my thumb. He closed his eyes at the contact, and I immediately took my hand away.

I nodded.

"Now," Cole said. "Let's try to transition from plastic straws . . . to sparks and flames. Will's explosives won't mean much unless you can set them off."

We worked for what felt like hours, but I was reassured knowing they were only Everneath hours.

By the time Cole took me back to the Surface, I had conjured up an ordinary Fourth of July sparkler. Without him even having to throw a rock at me.

Now all we could do was hope that Will had actually built devices that could be lit with a sparkler and that he and Jack had found something in their research that would make Adonia weak.

THIRTY-FOUR

NOW

The Everneath. Ashe's house.

Cole sent Ashe up to the Surface to get Jack and Will, and then we all gathered in Ashe's house.

"We have the explosives," Jack said, leaning back in the chair at Ashe's table. "But we don't know much more about Adonia's life. She was born in 1831. Grew up in rural England near the Cotswolds. Fell in love with Nathanial Hawking, but before they could be married, he went to serve in the war. That's when she met her Everliving."

"Ashe," I filled in. "When Adonia wouldn't return with him, he betrayed her to the queen. But we know now Adonia defeated the queen."

"That's it. Mostly stuff we already knew." Jack sighed. "We saw the queen hours ago. Do you remember anything unusual about her?"

I thought back to our encounter in the vault. "Her image

oscillates between a petite blonde and a tall redhead. She wears a token around her neck."

"I didn't get a good look. What does the token look like?" Jack asked.

I squeezed my eyes shut and focused on the memory. "It's a wreath with two swords crossing it. Like the medal her soldier wore." I opened my eyes and shrugged. "That's all I have."

Jack threw aside the papers. "It's not enough."

I looked down at my wrist. The second shackle was so dark.

Jack looked from me to Cole and back to me again, as if waiting for something. "How was the training?"

"Our best hope are the bombs. They have to work," I said. "We have to hope the blast will be enough, because right now, if I face the queen, I'll lose."

When we left Ashe's house and stepped onto the narrow streets of Ouros, I really noticed how much the place had changed. The city itself looked as if it had aged a century since we'd last seen it. The building right next to us was missing its facade. The entire thing had crumbled to the ground.

Everliving men and women wandered aimlessly, seeming to search for something they had no hope of finding. Some had given up long ago, and sat with backs against walls, staring dejectedly at the ground.

The scene was one of constant movement, but in slow motion—the still-simmering fallout from the lockdown event.

Jack and I looked at each other, and for a moment the

churn of the chaos surrounding us melted away, like a parade going the opposite direction.

"Are you ready for this, Becks?"

I nodded. "Let's blow up the Everneath. Or die trying."

He gave me a faint grin, then pulled me close and kissed me in a long, hard, end-of-the-world kind of way.

Ashe broke us up. "Let's move."

Jack took my hand as Ashe led us through the streets toward the secret chamber that acted as the Shade launching pad to the High Court, the evidence of the effects of the lockdown on display the entire way. If we failed to destroy the Everneath, the place would still have a long ways to go to reach its former glory.

At the very least, we struck it a blow.

But that wouldn't be enough for us to survive.

Once at the chamber, Ashe took our hands and we were in the air just like before, gliding through the sky over the elemental rings of the labyrinth. But this time, as we descended toward the High Court, I noticed strange branches emerging everywhere, from the walls and the ground to the windows and the turrets, twisting and turning, entwining in thick braided knots high up into the air.

As we got closer, I noticed thorns sticking out of the branches. Sharp and jagged, and bigger than any natural thorns.

"Slow down," I said.

"I can't," Ashe said. "It's like autopilot."

We careened through the gigantic briar patch, the sharp thorns ripping through the material of my pants, cutting and tearing at my skin. I cried out in pain.

There was no way to avoid the thorns. They ranged in size from small needles to spikes the size of railroad nails sticking out of the ground, the walls, everywhere.

"The queen must've added this layer of protection since so many of the Shades are abandoning her," Ashe said. He pulled out his sword and began swinging.

Something on my wrist caught my eye.

"Jack!" I said, holding up my wrist. The second shackle was just as dark as the first now. Which meant I would have to Century Feed soon, or I would die. I wondered how dark the line had to be before that happened.

Jack came over and examined my wrist. Then he lifted his eyes to meet mine.

I was overcome with emotion, the pain of thinking of the life we wouldn't get to have, the time we wouldn't get to spend. The pain of the unfulfilled potential was almost incapacitating, and yet I wouldn't trade it for anything in the world. I wouldn't give it up.

"I love you," I said.

"It's not over," he said.

"Over or not. I love you."

"I love you too."

The vault of hearts was completely overrun by briar bushes. They reached inside the red stained-glass door that Jack had smashed in the last time we were there. Past the door, they grew so thick, only something the size of a rat would've been able to get through. It was something we hadn't planned on. Once we passed through the door, we would be stuck.

"Ashe!" Cole shouted.

"I'm on it." He swung like a knight on a mission, like the prince at the end of "Sleeping Beauty." Thorns and branches exploded off the end of his sword, and yet our progress was slow.

We took it inch by inch, shuffling forward. I couldn't help looking at the entryway we'd just come through. When would we be found out?

Ashe swung and swung, slicing through the boughs.

Suddenly, shadows filled the room.

"Shades!" Cole said.

Ashe tossed the sword to Jack, who caught it by the hilt. "I'll hold them for as long as I can," Ashe said, and started swinging his fists.

Now it was me, Jack, Cole, and Will. Jack had Ashe's sword. He swung it wildly again, and we were halfway across the room. I could see the vault door with the ship's wheel through the thick of the branches.

But at the rate we were going, Ashe wouldn't be able to fend off the Shades before we got to it.

I glanced frantically at Will. He closed his eyes, and suddenly energy leaked out of him at an alarming rate. He was making it happen, mentally forcing all the pent-up emotions inside him to spill out. He ran from the room, and every single Shade followed him. Cole looked at me. "I'll help him," he promised, and then he ran out after Will.

Jack swung against the branches, but they were too strong, and the sword broke. We'd gone as far as we could.

"Attach the explosives!" I said.

Jack reached through what was left of the briar patches. The thorns didn't give at all; they simply dug into his skin and tore giant holes in it.

I held his other hand, trying not to imagine the pain he was feeling at that moment.

He winced, but he didn't make a sound.

Blood ran down his arm, falling in large drops off his elbow and splashing onto the branches below him. And yet he stayed, attaching the device just as Will had shown him on the Surface. So much damage had been done while he inserted his arm, and the thorns were facing away from him. They were like a thousand fishhooks. How would he ever pull it out again?

And yet he still worked at the device.

A bead of sweat ran down his forehead, down his cheek. The pain must be excruciating.

"One more turn," he said. I could hear the pain in his breathy voice. "And . . . got it."

The way the device was made, Jack needed to hold the button down while I created the spark to light the fuse, and then we would have twenty seconds to get a safe distance. But now, looking at Jack's arm, I knew it would take longer to get his arm out. Gingerly, I grabbed one of the nearest branches and tried to pull it apart, but it didn't budge.

Jack just shook his head. "There isn't time. Ready?"

My eyes went wide. "We can't do it yet."

"We have to," Jack said. "Get the spark in your head. Ready? Count with me. One . . . two . . . three!"

He pressed the button. I shut my eyes and focused on the spark that Cole and I had worked on, but I couldn't get the image of what we would have to do to free Jack's arm out of my head.

"Becks," Jack said, "you're worrying about me."

I opened my eyes and saw that all I had created was a couple of inches of extra space for Jack's arm.

"Stop worrying about me," he said.

I pressed my lips together. "Never."

He grinned. "Okay. Then stop worrying about my arm. Instead, worry about my life."

That was what I needed to hear. I thought about the spark and instantly heard the click of the fire starting.

"You did it," Jack said. "Quick. Help me." He started to pull out his arm, but even he couldn't bear so much pain.

I shook my head. "I can't."

"Pull me."

Three seconds ticked away. Four.

I grabbed his hand and, bracing my feet against some of

the branches on the ground, I sprang in the opposite direction.

He grunted loudly as his arm came free. The blood poured from the gashes there.

"Run!" he said.

We ran out the doorway and through the corridor and out the entrance. I hoped to put at least a football field of distance between us and the explosion. Jack slammed the door shut behind us and then tackled me to the ground, lying on top of me, shielding me.

The crack of the explosion pounded my eardrums, the aftershocks vibrating through my chest.

I was panting. Jack was breathing hard on top of me.

"We did it," he said. At least I think that was what he said. I couldn't hear him.

We pulled ourselves up to a standing position. My ears rang with a high-pitched tone. I tilted my head and shook it, feeling frustrated by the foreign sensation of being unable to hear.

"Becks?" Jack was saying my name, but I couldn't hear him. *Are you okay?* He mouthed the words.

"I can't hear," I answered. At least I hope I did. I couldn't tell if I was making noise.

But then I realized what was more wrong with the picture than me not being able to hear. The Everneath was still here. It hadn't disappeared.

Something behind me caught Jack's eye. He didn't look at me, but his lips moved. I could see he said one or two words, but I couldn't tell what they were.

"What?" I said.

He glanced at me and tried again, this time enunciating each syllable.

The queen is here.

THIRTY-FIVE

NOW

The Everneath. The High Court.

I turned around, and there she was in all her red-headed glory. But that disguise lasted for only a few moments before she turned into Adonia with the blond hair again. Maybe since we knew who she was, she didn't feel the need to hide.

Her face looked pale and ghostly. She glanced around her, and with a quick snap of her fingers, she conjured a cage around Jack. Then she turned her attention to me. "Why did you do it?" she asked.

"Do what?"

"If you wanted to rule the Everneath, why did you destroy it?"

I shook my head. "I told you. I never wanted to rule the Everneath. I just wanted my life back."

"You wanted *your* life back by destroying *mine*. You wanted your life back by killing thousands of Everlivings."

"I'm not killing them. I gave them their mortality back."

She smiled. A wide, sharp smile that seemed much closer to a sneer. "You don't know what happens, do you? When Everlivings lose both of their hearts?"

What was she talking about? "They lose their immortality."

"So naive." Her eyes narowed, blazing with the anticipation of a fight.

She closed her eyes, and her lids fluttered. I couldn't feel anything, so I thought this would be the perfect time to strike; but when I went to think of some sort of weapon, I suddenly had no control over my thoughts.

Involuntarily, the memory of my mother dying flashed inside my brain. I tried to think of anything else. Jack's face. Tommy. My dad. Even my school. Anything. But I couldn't navigate my own memories. My eyes flew open to find the queen staring at me with her vicious smile.

"Did you know your mother didn't die from the crush of the car that hit her?" The queen said. "At least not directly. She suffocated."

Every instinct was telling me to run away, but I couldn't move. My lungs tightened at her words, and for a moment it felt as if I had been the one crushed by the car. I was trapped and fighting for breath.

I tried to expand my lungs, but it was as if someone were pouring liquid cement down my throat, and my chest was turning to stone.

I squeezed my eyes shut. "Mom," I whispered.

The queen laughed.

I opened my eyes and narrowed them at her. The queen was lying. She couldn't possibly know what had happened.

"My mom didn't suffocate," I said, breathless. "Why would you say that?"

"Yes, she did. But you don't remember. You've blocked it. Let me help you unblock it."

Suddenly, another image appeared in my head. A doctor coming to talk to us in the hallway of the antiseptic hospital wing. He'd said her ribs were crushed, and she died because she couldn't breathe.

"I'm so happy you believe me now," the queen said. "Because I have something special for the girl who made me think Nathanial was still alive."

She closed her eyes, and at that moment a glass wall appeared on every side of me. She'd conjured up a giant glass box. I felt cool liquid at my feet and looked down to find that water was filling the glass. I pounded on the walls and the ceiling, so hard that my knuckles split and blood smeared on the glass. But it didn't crack. I put my hands on one wall and my feet on the opposite one and tried to use the force of opposition to break through. But it didn't work. The water had reached my chest and was rising rapidly.

Within twenty seconds of facing the queen, I was trapped in a box full of water with a locked lid.

As the water crept up my face, I gulped in one last breath of air. My last breath of life. Glimpses of people flashed through my mind. Tommy. My dad. Jules. Jack. I had failed them all.

I could see the queen through the distorted view from underwater and through the glass. I tried to pound on the glass, but it didn't even make a sound. I pressed my lips together, trying to make the seal watertight. If it was Everneath water, I didn't want to drink it and forget I was fighting for my life.

Jack thrashed against the bars of the cage, pushing and pulling. The bars didn't budge.

This was it. I was going to die in the worst possible way, with Jack in sight but just out of reach.

He was always in sight but just out of reach.

Instinctively, I rose to the top of the water, to where there was maybe half an inch of air, but I couldn't orient my face close enough to get a clear breath. I would need a snorkel.

Or a straw! I thought back to my training session with Cole and focused all my energy. A faint white line appeared in the water in front of my face. The longer it floated there, the more it transformed into a solid thing.

My plastic straw. I grabbed it and blew the last of my air through the straw to clear it of water and then held it against the top of the lid and sucked in a giant breath.

I got one more breath in before the queen realized her mistake and filled the rest of the space with water.

But I'd bought myself another twenty seconds.

Twenty seconds to do what?

I could see Jack in the cage. He'd stopped thrashing, and now he just had his hand raised, palm outward toward me. I put my hand on my lips and then laid it flat against the glass pane.

I didn't want to drown. But at any moment I wouldn't be able to fight the urge to suck in a giant lungful of water.

I closed my eyes and thought about my mom. Maybe I would find out exactly what it felt like to be deprived of air, just as she had been. Maybe I would see her soon.

Suddenly I felt a knock on the glass. I saw Cole's face, sick with panic. He held a large club in his hand, and the queen was hunched over behind him.

Cole pointed two fingers at his eyes. *Watch me,* he mouthed.

He pointed to the queen and then used his index finger to draw a heart on the glass. Then he held up a paper with a drawing on it. A wreath with two swords crossing in the middle.

He was describing the shape of the queen's Surface heart, the one I'd seen when I'd faced her before. The one I'd seen when she fought the queen before her. I remembered how when I'd thought of Cole's heart, it had come flying to me.

I was out of time and out of breath. I closed my eyes and pictured the queen's heart.

Suddenly, I heard a tap on the glass. Her heart, a metal version of the wreath symbol, had landed flat against the glass. I focused even more on the heart, and tiny little fracture hairs broke out from the point where the heart made contact. And then came the sound of glass shattering.

Water poured out of the splintered glass box, and I poured out too, the queen's heart in my hand. I'd been strong enough to conjure her actual heart and send it through the glass.

The queen lunged for me, but it was too late. I'd broken her Surface heart. She paused midstride, then fell to the ground in a slump. Her translucent skin became wrinkled before my eyes; her hair turned from bright blond to gray, then to white.

And then she turned to dust and blew away in a soft breeze I didn't even realize was there.

Everything she had conjured—the glass box, the cage, everything—disappeared. And Jack, Cole, and I were left breathing hard through bits of dust that used to be the queen.

THIRTY-SIX

NOW
The Everneath. The vault.

The ground beneath my feet rumbled, causing me to lose my balance. I fell to the dirt as the rumbling turned into swaying. Jack pulled me up. "Run!"

The walls lurched back and forth. Granite-like boulders from the highest wall began to fall to the ground. The Everneath was deteriorating around us, and there was no place we would be safe.

Actually, there was one place.

"Go to the lake!" I screamed. The lake was where the Tunnels were hidden—maybe the Tunnels would be the only place we could find refuge. We ran along the wall until we found a hole large enough for us to squeeze through. I could see the lake up ahead.

"Are you sure?" Jack said.

I forgot he had no idea why we were about to jump into the lake.

"The lake is the entrance to the Tunnels!" I said.

He didn't even hesitate. He just followed me and Cole.

I paused for a split second, remembering the last time I'd jumped into this same lake. I'd held Cole's hand. We'd counted down together and jumped together.

Here we were again. Full circle. And for a split second I looked into Cole's eyes. He stared back at me with the depth of that memory behind his eyes, and then I knew. I knew he was remembering that same moment. He was reliving it, just as I was.

His memory was back.

I didn't have time to dwell on the revelation, or wonder if he was on our side anymore. Besides, the Everneath was in ruins. There was nothing really left to rule. We jumped into the lake just as the nearest wall of the High Court crumbled and fell to the ground.

"Dive," I shouted to Jack as I braced myself for the impact of the water at the end of the long fall.

The impact didn't hurt as much this time, probably because I hadn't done a total belly flop. We swam to shore in the pitch-black and waited.

The rumbling went on forever, as if the ground had swallowed something it didn't like, and its intestines were twisting and turning, trying to rid itself of the object.

Cole flicked on his lighter, illuminating the giant cavern sheltering the lake we'd just jumped into. Rocks and dirt fell to the ground all around us.

A particularly large jolt sent shock waves through the cavern. We heard a giant crack coming from above.

"Nik!" Cole shouted. He dived toward me and tackled me to the ground just as a boulder the size of my bedroom fell from the ceiling.

He'd landed on top of me. I breathed hard, knowing he'd just saved my life. Again. "Thank you."

Jack ripped Cole off me. "We have to get out of here! It's not safe."

Cole grabbed our hands and zapped us back up to the High Court just as the last rumbles faded away.

At least it was supposed to be the High Court. But the entire thing was decimated. The flames of the inner ring of the labyrinth had been doused, leaving a circle of scarred ground behind. As far as I could see, everything had been flattened. There was no labyrinth left.

In the middle of what used to be the High Court stood a pole, with a single flag swaying in the wind. A green flag.

"It's the same green as your eyes," Jack said to me. He raised a hand to touch my cheek, but just before he made contact, his hand became blurry around the edges. I blinked, trying to clear away the film from my eyes, but it wasn't a film. The blurrier his hand became, the more I could see *through* it.

I looked up at his face.

"Jack!" I said. His face was doing the same thing. I could see the landscape behind him through his translucent skin. I reached out for him, but I only touched air. I panicked, grasping and straining to make contact.

"It's okay," Cole said. "I expected that. There's no energy left here to keep humans. He'll be waiting for you back on the Surface."

I released a breath of relief and then shook my head and looked around me.

"Where are the other Everlivings?" I said.

Cole frowned, somehow exhibiting a look of both extreme grief and extreme relief. "We destroyed their hearts. They're probably back on the Surface by now."

"Why is there *anything* left? Shouldn't it all be gone?"

Cole came up beside me. "There are still two hearts left to destroy." He pulled out his guitar pick and my compass. The one he had stolen that night from my bedroom. The one he swore he couldn't find.

A flash of anger rose in my chest. "Where did you—"

"I always had it, Nik. Ever since we went back to look for it at my condo. I found it in a guitar case, and I took it, even though at the time I didn't really understand what I was doing."

"What about the compass that the queen had?"

"That was just another compass I'd found in the vault. Apparently compasses are common objects for hearts to be turned into."

Cole had my heart. He'd had it the entire time. There had been no reason for me to come down and kill the queen, because she never held my compass. It was always in Cole's possession.

"Why?" I said. "Why didn't you tell me?" And then I realized why. My breathing became frantic. My earlier suspicions were right. Cole had regained his memory. "You lied to me. You wanted me to take over the throne. You wanted me to feel like I had to kill the queen."

"No," Cole said. Then the carefully crafted blank facade of his face cracked, and with a deep frown he revealed a rueful expresson. "But for a moment, after my full memory returned, I wondered what I really wanted."

I crumpled to the ground. "Did I just do what you've wanted me to do all along?"

Cole sank to the ground beside me. "My memory started to return right after the Feast. After I saw the band get murdered before my eyes. I didn't get my full memory back, though, until we'd broken into the vault of hearts. When the queen showed up, I grabbed the closest compass I could find. There were literally like twenty compasses to choose from." He looked down. "I also remembered getting tortured by the queen. Remembered when she leaned over me with her hot poker; the token hanging around her neck fell out of her dress. I saw what *her* heart looked like."

"Why didn't you tell me right away?"

He looked up and gave me an impish grin. "Forgive me, Nik. For a weak moment I remembered what I used to want. And I wasn't ready to give it up." He reached toward my hand and closed my fingers around my compass. "But look. Now your heart is in your own hands. And you can do what you want." He paused. "And just so you know your options, you're in charge here now. The Everneath, the little part that's left of the Everneath, will obey your every whim if you want this life. You are the queen."

I looked all around at the rubble and the desolation. There wasn't another Everliving in sight. There were no structures. No labyrinth. No High Court. But even if there had been . . .

"No," I said. "I don't want this."

Cole nodded. "I know. Then are you ready to break your heart?"

"Yes," I whispered. "You know, if I had known how this was all going to end . . ."

He frowned and closed his eyes for a long moment. When he opened them again, I would've sworn they were watering. He blinked and cleared the tears away. "Nik, think about it. You've always known how this was going to end."

He touched my face lightly. I didn't stop him.

It was just me, and Cole, and the tiny patch of land we were on, and each of our hearts in our hands.

He held his pick, ready to snap it in between his forefinger and thumb. I held my compass. It had a cover, like a pocket watch. I bent it backward at the hinges.

"Ready?" I asked.

"Wait," Cole said. He looked me in the eye. "I always knew you'd change my life." He glanced away, briefly, and shook his head at some unknown memory. "You know, a psychic once told me I would have no other Forfeits after you. That you would be my last. At the time, I let myself believe that it was fate that we would end up together, ruling the world. And if it was fate, why fight it? It gave me license to do whatever I needed to do to keep you.

"But even then I knew. Deep down I knew you would be my beginning and my end. My moral consciousness began taking shape the moment I met you. In that way, my own soul began. And then when I fell in love with you, my own heart began."

"Cole, we don't need to talk about this now," I said.

"We do," he said emphatically. Then he took a deep breath. "I mean, we're finally alone. We have nothing tying us together anymore. It might be our only time to say these things."

I hadn't thought about that . . . that this might be the last time I saw him. I was sure he would form a new band on the Surface, but really, there was no reason we would see each other.

But I'd never liked good-byes. "We're not going to say good-bye. We've been through too much for good-byes. Besides, we'll see each other."

He gave me a sad smile. "Still, just humor me. If you have anything you want to say, say it now."

If I had anything I wanted to say. What *did* I want to say to him? He had taken me to the Everneath. Fed on me for a hundred years.

But he would say he had saved me from my own pain. Made

the loss of my mother bearable.

He had betrayed me in the Everneath. Tricked me into feeding on him three times so I would be forced to become an Everliving.

But he would say he was simply giving fate a little push.

"I don't know what I want to say to you," I said. "Maybe, after some time, I'll know. But not now."

He frowned and nodded. "Okay. It's okay."

He lifted his eyes skyward, and was it my imagination or was he blinking back tears again? He let loose a shaky breath. He seemed so disappointed not to know right at this minute. I put my hand on his arm. "I promise I'll tell you one day," I said.

"Okay," he said, bringing his eyes down to meet mine.

I stood and reached my hand toward Cole. He took it and I pulled him up beside me. I held the compass out again. "Ready?"

He closed his eyes. Squeezed them shut. Why was he so scared? It wasn't as if breaking our hearts would literally hurt us. He should know this. Breaking our hearts would make us mortal. Wouldn't it?

He squeezed the pick, bending it.

And then suddenly I knew.

"Cole," I said.

He stopped. I thought about the queen and how she had died when I had broken her heart. She had basically turned into an old lady and then transformed into dust before our eyes. I'd thought she had just died a dramatic death because we had destroyed her world.

But before she had died, she'd said I didn't know what really happened when Everliving hearts were broken. Cole was scared to break his own pick, but he didn't seem as worried about me breaking mine. If he thought it would be painful, he'd be comforting me right now. I knew enough about his love for me to know that.

But he wasn't concerned about me. How was breaking my own heart different from breaking his? And how were *we* different?

Besides the fact that he was about a thousand years older than me.

A thousand years old.

"Cole," I said. I spoke slowly. "What happens when we break our hearts?"

He gave a nervous smile. "You know what happens. We become human."

I sucked in a gasp of air and tried to pry the pick out of his hand, but once I started to fight against him, he closed his fingers around it tightly.

"What are you doing?" he asked, accusation in his eyes.

"Give me your heart, Cole," I said, my voice catching on the word. "Give me your heart. I know what happens. I know why you're scared."

He blinked a long blink. "No, you don't."

"Yes, I do. Breaking your heart returns you to your natural

state. And your natural state is . . ." I gasped as my voice drifted off. I didn't want to finish that sentence.

Cole finished it for me. "Over nine hundred years old." He nodded.

I started shaking. "No. We can't do this." I tried to pry his fingers open, but the stupid Everliving was strong. I dug my fingernails into his skin. He winced, but he didn't budge. "Give me your heart."

He slowly shook his head.

"Give me your heart!" The tears sprang to my eyes, and my lower lip trembled violently.

"Nik, you know we have to finish what we started. And that will only happen when every heart is destroyed. Every. Heart."

The other Everlivings hadn't simply gone to the Surface. They'd grown old and turned to dust.

I was having trouble breathing. "Please. There has to be another way. Our hearts are the only ones left. We're the only Everlivings left. We can just go on. I'll break my own heart. But you . . ."

My hands shook. Cole grabbed them. Held them still. Looked me in the eye. "We see it to the end. We don't stop until it's done."

I bit my lip to keep it from trembling. "Give me your heart," I said.

He tilted his head, leaned forward, watching my eyes the entire time to make sure it was okay, and kissed me lightly on the lips. "You already have it."

I heard a faint snap, and I wondered for a moment if an actual broken heart made a sound.

The lines around Cole's mouth became deeper. The skin of his eyelids sagged a little lower.

"Cole?"

He held my gaze for a moment longer before his knees gave out, and he began to sink to the ground. I went with him, supporting his weight as we sank. I put my arms around him and held him tightly, and then in front of his face, I snapped my compass back, breaking the hinges.

"We do this together," I said.

He nodded. And then his hair started to go lighter, turning white and thinning out; and before either of us could say another word, he collapsed in my arms.

Moments later he was dust. My hands were empty. And I was alone.

THIRTY-SEVEN

NOW
The Everneath.

The moment the last two hearts in the Everneath were broken, the Underworld—what was left of it—began to swirl around me. Darkness around the edges began to encroach on the land. Piece by piece, acre by acre, the Everneath was being swallowed up by the vast nothing surrounding it.

I put my hand against my chest and pressed it there, and as a faint beat began pulsing beneath my skin, I shot up into the sky.

I had my heart. And at the same time, I'd lost it.

Jack and Will were waiting for me at the Shop-n-Go. When I landed on the floor, Jack scooped me up in his arms and held me tight against his chest. Will smiled, sighed, and then walked out of the store to leave us alone.

Jack dipped his head and kissed me, and then he caught the look on my face. In one split second he knew.

"Cole?" he said.

I nodded and collapsed against him. He crushed me close and held me together, rocking me back and forth. "I'm sorry, Becks. I'm so sorry."

Jack and I stayed in each other's arms for a long time after that, days maybe. Each of us had a heart in our chest. Each heart beat for the other. And for the first time in a century, we had a future. Together. Jack and me. No ticking clocks.

I thought of how far we'd come from that moment I'd first Returned to the Surface after the Feed. How the Tunnels were coming for me. How impossible everything had seemed.

I had believed there was no such thing as redemption. I knew now I was wrong. Cole had shown me that. Redemption had not come from grand gestures of dashing bravery. It had not come from successfully completing twelve impossible labors. Instead, redemption transpired from the small, quiet places: in the palm of his hand, in the flick of his fingers that had snapped a guitar pick.

My dad returned home from his futile search in Los Angeles. The level of his anger was exceeded only by his relief that I was still alive. Tommy returned home from my aunt's house, and our family reunion was marred only by the fact that I would be spending the next six months in rehab, per my dad's request.

Six months. I could do anything for six months. As long as I knew that a long, healthy, mortal life was waiting for me on the other end.

A long, healthy, mortal life with Jack.

Jack came over to help me pack for rehab. As he smushed my suitcase shut and zipped it up, he smiled at me. "Do you think rehab will stick this time?"

"I think I'm finally ready to make the commitment." I smiled. "Maybe someday I'll actually try the vices I'm supposedly recovering from."

Jack shrugged. "After everything we've been through, I don't think I'll ever have a desire to artificially mess with my emotions again."

He leaned back on my bed and put his hands behind his head. I fell on top of him and nestled my nooks in his crannies. His heart beat softly against my ear.

"We have a lot to do when you get home," Jack said.

"We have time to do it."

He sighed. "Time." He said the word as if it was something we'd fought for. Something we'd risked our lives for.

Time.

"I love you," I said.

He kissed my head. "I'm Ever Yours."

And I was Ever His.

ACKNOWLEDGMENTS

Thank you . . .

. . . to my extraordinary editor, Kristin Daly Rens. Somehow she manages to take the wadded-up clumps of yarn I throw at her and help me weave them into a beautiful sweater. I can't believe we made it to the end, K!

. . . to the entire team at Balzer + Bray, and HarperCollins, for giving me the most beautiful covers, the best copyedits, the most brilliant feedback, and the most support a girl could ask for. And I asked for a lot. Special thanks to Caroline Sun, Alessandra Balzer, Donna Bray, Emilie Polster, Sara Sargent, Brady the camera guy who made my book trailers, and all of the other brilliant minds at the office! I know I'm leaving people out. But it's the third book, and my brain is kaput.

. . . to my fabulous agent, the incomparable Michael Bourret. I love you, even through our differences, like your fondness for rare meat and my love of violence. You keep me grounded and yet you're always there to give me a lift when I need it. No words.

. . . to the rest of the team at Dystel & Goderich, especially Lauren Abramo. You are the gateway to the world for the Everneath series. I love you, girl!

. . . to the person who helped me with that one scene on that one page (306). Without you, so many things wouldn't exist, including that one page. Okay, maybe that page would be there, but still, it wouldn't be as squishy. . . .

. . . to my loyal, brilliant, extraordinary, miraculous writers' group. Providence led me to you, and I will never be able to repay him. (Or is Providence a her?) Sara Bolton, Kimberly Webb Reid, Emily Wing Smith, and Valynne Maetani Nagamatsu.

. . . to my writing community, local and national, and international—okay, let's just say worldwide—especially those who have literally held the pieces of my brain together, like Cynthia Hand, Jodi Meadows, Tahereh Mafi, Veronica Rossi, and so many others.

. . . to countless friends, neighbors, bloggers, acquaintances . . . hell, even enemies. Thank you. Not sure what I'm thanking the enemies for, but I don't want to leave anyone out. You know who you are! (The friends do. Okay, the enemies probably know who they are too.)

. . . to my family, extended and immediate (Mom, Erin, Dave, Gublers, Johnsons, other Johnsons, Frank and Kathleen, Ellingsons, Otts, Jacksons, Ashtons, Ashton clot . . . etc.) for reading countless bad drafts and for your never-ending support and love.

. . . to Sam, Carter, and Becks. My boys. You have put up with so much. For reals. I mean, the house is never clean, the food is never cooked, in fact, there never really is any food, the clothes are strewn about . . . I forgot where I was going with this. My point must have been buried under piles of laundry. Thank you for welcoming me every time I come home, and acting sad when I leave.

. . . finally, the most important thank-you to you readers. Without you, there'd be a book, but if a book falls in the forest and there's no one there to hear it, does it really go *ker-plunk*?

What I mean to say is, I love you, dear reader. Yes, *you*.

ONLY TRUE LOVE
CAN SURVIVE

Don't miss a second of this breathtaking series
about love, loss, and immortality.

An Imprint of HarperCollinsPublishers

www.epicreads.com